"I'm cracking up. That's what you think, isn't it?"

"I think something weird is going on." Agatha frowned. "You feel trapped in your life, that's it, and this fantasy is like an escape. But you know it's a fantasy, don't you?"

Agatha was clearly distressed and so was Amy. I decided to intervene, hoping I didn't end up making things worse. I shifted to Agatha and contacted. *It's not a fantasy, Agatha. I really have been contacting Amy, as I'm doing with you now.*

Agatha's heart began to pound. Her shoulders rose and her muscles contracted as if she were trying to make herself smaller and shield herself. *There's no danger. It's new and mysterious but not threatening.*

"*You're* doing it!" Agatha looked accusingly at Amy.

"What?"

It's not Amy, I said. *My name is Jenna. I'm contacting you by telepathy. Amy was telling the truth. It's an exciting truth, but it doesn't have to be a frightening one, Agatha. See if you can relax. Take a deep breath.*

"What's the matter?" Amy asked.

Agatha took several deep long breaths. "I heard a voice. It's impossible."

Books by Camarin Grae

Winged Dancer
Paz
Soul Snatcher
The Secret in the Bird
Edgewise
Slick
Stranded

stranded
BY CAMARIN GRAE

The Naiad Press, Inc.
1991

Printed in the United States of America on acid-free paper
First Edition

Edited by Ann Klauda
Cover design by Pat Tong and Bonnie Liss
    (Phoenix Graphics)
Typeset by Sandi Stancil

Library of Congress Cataloging-in-Publication Data

Grae, Camarin.
    Stranded / by Camarin Grae.
        p.   cm.
    ISBN 0-941483-99-1 : $9.95
    I. Title.
PS3557.R125S77   1991
813'.54--dc20   91-25243
                                                                          CIP

Afloat in the void. I could have been drifting for one jetur or a thousand. I have no idea where I am. Most of the time I don't care. The drifting is beautiful and exhilarating. Often Billy is there. We're at the beach. Then we're running in a field of wildflowers. We lie side by side, make love, slowly, lovingly. Sweet smells, moistness, her inside of me. Moving together, my love and I. I look into the oval of her lovely face, touch her soft skin. I am happy and content.

I'd been happy that last morning of our freedom too, the day the Wraunkians came and took us away. Over dinner the night before, Billy and I had spoken of the child we'd soon make, and how it didn't matter which of us was the seed parent and which the birth parent. Out on the porch, she'd stroked my face tenderly with soft hands. "I'm loving you, Jenna," she'd say, and I'd had no doubt that it was true.

Wozar had warned us that we might be stranded in the void forever. Worse fates are possible, she'd said. She could assure us only that we'd arrive at a place called the United States.

I wish I didn't know what had happened. Maybe then the void would be enough. But I knew that there were real worlds out there and that I might never see my Billy again. I couldn't actually cry, but sometimes I felt the tearless, soundless despair of the absolute aloneness that might never end. Then the colors would come again, and the music and images, and I would forget all fear, all pain.

In the middle of a particularly engaging fantasy, a vibrating hum edged into my awareness. This was not a product of my dreamy mind, I knew. It came from out there. I hoped desperately it was the *buzzing* I'd been waiting for. I focused. The tingling buzz got stronger. I knew what to do. Mustering my energy, I pushed my mind into the buzz, straining, willing it with all my might.

There was a whoosh. Rumbling. Then blinding light. Real light from a real sun glimmering on trees and casting shadows on shrubs and tall waving grass. The sounds were real. A bird's call, a breeze whispering among leaves, crickets chirping, water splashing. The splashing, I realized, was from a stream of liquid coming from . . . I couldn't believe it . . . from a penis! Too much. I'll think about that later.

I wanted to dance and shout with joy. I had

made it! I'd arrived! How long it had taken me I do not know, but I had entered a human being and was seeing Earth.

I watched the last drops of liquid fall from the penis.

"Mini-riding," Wozar had told us, "will give you sight and hearing. You will see through the host's eyes the images that enter her optic nerves, hear through her ears the sounds that vibrate her tympanic membranes. But the perception will be yours, the meaning will be made by you."

My host's eyes swept the field in a hundred-eighty-degree arc. I felt slightly nauseated. We were moving.

"It will take time to adjust," Wozar had warned. "Stay with mini-riding until you are comfortable with it."

We went bumpily along a path. I could hear my host's footsteps. We came to a road and a parked vehicle. Its door opened and then we were inside sitting on a red seat. Through the peripheral vision, I could see her hands on the steering wheel. They were large and brown. I felt a gush of loving feelings for her, feelings of tremendous gratitude. The vehicle, a truck, began to move along the road. It was a country road that reminded me of home.

Music came from the radio, clanging string sounds and wailing singing in the strange, alien language that was now mine. English. Just before our departure, Wozar's technicians had zapped the new language and its concepts into our minds, replacing our own Sanilese.

I saw a farm in the distance nestled among large, leafy trees. I wished I could get a better look, but my host kept the eyes fixed on the road. Soon we turned onto a tar-covered street. There were buildings. An alien town in an alien land. And yet the streets and the people had a comfortable familiarity. In fact, the people could have been Alloys except for their clothing. I thought of Billy and of Cass, and hoped desperately that they too had found hosts and were riding and seeing towns and people and that soon we'd be together.

My host stopped the truck and went into a red, one-story building. I was able to see some of the people close up now — actual living beings of a distant planet. I marveled at the sight of them.

We stood in front of a cashier, a counter between her and us. In her surprisingly low voice, my host ordered two *Big Macs* and two *fries*. The cashier filled a sack with little boxes and bags.

Back in the truck, I watched the sights passing and wondered what the food in the sack smelled like. I was afraid to find out, fearing that if I maxi-rode already, I might get overwhelmed.

"On Wraunk," Wozar had said, "we recommend that the newly disembodied wait for several jetur before maxi-riding. It can be very disjointing to feel hands which are yours but not yours move without you willing it, legs that feel like yours taking steps you did not direct, the mouth emitting words you never thought. Take it slowly," she'd said. "Zephkar will have to adjust also."

The thought of Zephkar made me feel weak, and then angry. I didn't want to think of her. Not yet.

The truck stopped at an intersection. My host moved her head close to the rearview mirror and I saw her face. She could have been an Alloy except for the patch of hair growing beneath her nose.

We continued through the town until we came to a peach-colored house built back from the street. My host pulled into the driveway. I wished I could be alone for a while now, to think about what was happening, to look at the trees and sky of Earth and let myself absorb the miracle of my arrival. But now that I had entered a host, I was afraid to propel to the void and risk being stranded.

The house door opened. The person who greeted my host looked exactly like an Alloy. She had sparkling dark eyes and tawny skin. "I'm starved," she said. She took the sack of food and set it on a low table in front of a sofa.

The Earthlings watched TV as they ate, not speaking much. I had time to think. The magnitude of what was happening struck me again and I felt frightened but also enthralled. It seemed so long ago that I had been at home, harvesting the wheat, canning the banta fruit with Billy poking her fingers into the sticky syrup and laughing mischievously. And now I was a disembodied mind on a planet I had never heard of, far outside of our galaxy, riding in the body of an Earthling who urinated through her penis and had hair above her mouth.

I tuned into the television show. There were closeups of angry faces. An argument was taking place and the characters got into cars and drove very rapidly through the streets of some large dirty city. Cars crashed into other cars, rolling over, bursting into flames. What sort of culture do they have here, I wondered, worrying. Wozar had told us so little. "Technologically, they're at about the same level as Allo," she had said. "There is one species of intelligent life form, similar to your own."

Another show came on. There were animals similar to tangors, but which people sat on and rode. Why would they do such a thing? I'd often watched the herds of tangor grazing and running in the fields near my farm. A deep sadness came over me as I thought of the home I would never again see.

It had been dark outside for some time when finally my host, whose name I'd learned was *Bert*, turned off the television, and she and her companion, *Eva*, talked about people and events and places that meant nothing to me. When they went to the bedroom and Bert removed her clothes, I realized with a jolt that her breasts were completely flat. In the bathroom, she urinated again in her odd way, then brushed her teeth. I had a sudden desire to taste the toothpaste. I knew that all I had to do to maxi-ride was to wish it hard enough and it would be. Hoping I was ready, I made the switch.

The minty taste was minor compared to the other sensations that came upon me all at the same moment. I could smell the odors of Bert's body and of the soap on the sink. I felt the tongue in the inside of the mouth, its tip resting against the lower teeth, and I was aware of the feel of the saliva, the taste of cigarette smoke and toothpaste. I could feel that our penis was not retracted, which seemed odd, and I felt a lump of some kind beneath it. Did Bert have a tumor, I wondered. I was aware of various sensations throughout the body, a little growling in the gut, a stuffy nose, slightly achy back muscles. They felt familiar yet they did not feel like my own. I felt the texture of the rug against the bare feet as my host walked us from the bathroom to the bedroom where the other human was brushing her hair.

Bert caressed Eva's neck. The skin was soft and warm against the rather rough skin of Bert's hand. Eva turned her head upward and Bert moved us closer to her. Eva's facial features blurred. Then I felt her lips press against our lips and our tongue being pushed into her open mouth. Our penis was enlarging. It was obvious what my host and Eva were going to do. I felt us breathing heavily as Bert moved us to the bed, our hand around Eva's waist. Bert stretched out next to Eva and slipped our hand beneath Eva's garment and between her legs.

Eva's penis was still retracted and although the heel of our hand pressed her pubis, I could not feel her penis port, only solid bone beneath the skin.

Stranger still, the skin of the pubis had hair covering it. Humans had hair in odd places, I thought, as I felt the fingers probing her moist vagina.

Suddenly I did not want to be there, did not want to be part of this. I considered shifting to the void, but was afraid of getting lost there. Instead, I switched back to mini-riding. I was then aware only of sight and sound. Much of the time Bert's eyes were closed as the lovemaking continued. Although the sounds were sparse I couldn't ignore them — Bert's panting, the little grunts and groans.

Finally they finished. Bert lay face down breathing heavily. Soon she was asleep. Everything was pitch-black.

As I listened to Bert's snores, I wondered if I too would sleep this night. I let myself feel the overwhelming amazement of what I'd experienced since entering. Seeing another planet and its alien beings who were so much like us. Riding in another's body, seeing through her eyes. Just like being unilaterally boosted except that when I was boosted by that first Wraunkian on Allo, it was terrifying — being totally out of control and having no idea why. Now, because I knew what to expect and because I knew what was happening, the fear was minimal and I could experience the mind-boggling thrill of it. But as amazing as it was, more than anything I yearned to return to the life I had before the Wraunkians had taken us.

They'd come on a beautiful spring morning. Billy and I had awakened late and lolled around in bed, chatting and cuddling until we felt guiltily lazy, so finally we got up and dressed. In the middle of breakfast a car pulled up to the house. We both went to the door and watched as two people came up the stairs.

"Good morning," one of them said. "My name is Hylor and this is Lanaru. We want to show you the handcuff trick." She spoke Sanilese oddly, not pronouncing the words quite right. "Watch," she said, and she locked a pair of handcuffs onto Lanaru's wrists.

"What's this about?" I asked, puzzled by the oddness of the scene but also somewhat amused. The pair didn't seem threatening. I wondered if they were magicians, a circus act maybe.

The next thing I knew, Billy was locking handcuffs onto Hylor's wrists and I was holding a weapon and pointing it at Lanaru and Hylor, feeling strange and disoriented. Billy walked towards the visitors' car.

"Get moving." The words came from my mouth.

The shackled pair walked to the car. I followed them, but I was not directing my own movements. It was a terrifying feeling. I climbed into the back seat with Hylor. Billy took the driver's seat and Lanaru sat next to her. I wanted to speak but was unable to. Something was horribly wrong with me. It was as if my body was disconnected from my mind.

Billy started to drive. I sat with my arms folded, staring silently at the road, wanting to look at Billy and talk with her, but unable to. Billy kept driving, not speaking. This is a dream, I thought, of course; this isn't real at all. Who are you people, I wanted to ask, but I sat stonily silent.

Finally, when we had driven about a mile, Billy spoke. The sounds that came from her mouth were complete gibberish. I was even more shocked when I found myself responding with similar gibberish. I felt waves of panic. What was happening to us? I could think the thoughts, but I could not utter the words I wanted to say. Instead, more strange sounds came from my mouth, from lips I did not move, sounds I did not will, though clearly they came from me. I wanted to scream but my mouth remained closed.

We continued driving, my panic escalating as I sat looking out over the landscape, seeing the familiar hills and forests but totally without control over where my eyes focused, when and how I moved, the rhythm of my breathing. Obviously, the same thing was happening to Billy, and despite her apparent calm, I was sure she must be as terrified as I. The other two sat silently, staring into the distance.

Billy drove for miles, finally leaving the green hills of Pendirale and approaching the edges of the Molarat Desert. *Stop, don't go in here,* I wanted to yell. She drove farther and farther, occasionally speaking to me in gibberish, to which my mouth responded in kind. I wanted to scream and cry and run away, but instead I sat calmly, staring at the endless sandy expanse of the harsh desert. At Kunespat, Billy turned off the main road and took a narrow one toward Smarklace.

Something has taken over our bodies, I thought, but that's impossible.

Starklace was as barren and desolate as I'd heard. No one ever went there. No one but the exiles who had no choice. Yet Billy drove past the warning signs and continued on for miles, into the very heart of the Region of the Exiles.

Everyone knew that the only people who lived there were those who wore the marks of an Incorrigible and had been sent by the Highest Tribunal, condemned to live out their lives in the arid wilderness away from the rest of us.

Another hour of silent driving went by. We passed through several oases with exile towns of rough-hewn stone buildings and tents. We came to a huge sandy hill where the road ended.

"Get out, please," my mouth said, in mispronounced Sanilese. I gave Hylor a slight nudge. She got out of the car, as did Lanaru and Billy. We walked for ten minutes through the sand, me in the rear with my weapon. We came to an odd-looking vehicle with huge tires. Everyone climbed aboard.

Billy drove the vehicle for another fifteen or twenty minutes over roadless dunes. Then we rounded a bend and I couldn't believe my eyes. Sitting on the golden sand in the middle of nowhere was a huge, blue-gray, circular object the size of a three- or four-story building. This has to be a dream, I thought.

My legs took me toward the massive craft and, as we approached it, a door opened and a staircase appeared. No, I thought, but I walked up the stairs behind Billy and the two strangers in handcuffs.

We walked down a long corridor and entered a room furnished with soft sofas and white chairs. Without willing it, I sat on one of the chairs. Attached to its arms were metal rings. I fastened one of them around my wrist. One of the spaceship people fastened the other around my other wrist. Billy was locked into the chair next to me. Hylor and Lanaru were standing next to us when suddenly

I felt a dramatic shift. I took some deep breaths. I was me again. In charge of my body again.

"Billy, are you all right?"

"Can you believe this?" she said. "It's a spaceship, Jenna. These aren't Alloys."

"I know." The words came out in a croak.

Hylor said something in her strange language, then she and Lanaru unlocked each other's handcuffs.

"Who *are* you?" I asked.

"You'll find out," Hylor said.

"Aliens," Billy exclaimed. "They're aliens."

A beeping alarm clock woke me. I knew we were still in bed but I couldn't see anything since Bert's eyes were closed.

Aliens, I thought, they're aliens.

Eva moved and the beep stopped. She lay down again. I listened to her quiet breathing, wondering if I dared make the shift. I decided I would. I concentrated, pushed, and then almost instantaneously was looking at the ceiling through new eyes. I had entered my second human being. From Eva's peripheral vision, I saw my former host lying on her back.

The Earthlings got out of bed. While Eva was eating breakfast, I switched to maxi-riding. Again the onslaught of stimuli from the other senses momentarily shocked me. I was aware of the press of the chair against the buttocks; the slightly bitter taste of the hot *coffee* she drank; the heavy, groggy feeling in the head. Her body felt more comfortable than Bert's. There was no mass between her legs, and her penis was retracted — or perhaps she actually didn't have one, I thought, recalling that last night there'd been no sign of it. I thought of my own body and felt a deep mourning. Had Wozar had it buried in the desert, I wondered.

Bert left first, telling Eva she'd see her that night. Then Eva went out to her car. The morning was bright and warm; a breeze grazed the cheek as we drove. It seemed to be summer. The fruit trees at my farm would be due for pruning if it were summer there, I thought, and wondered if anyone was tending them. But that was no longer my concern, I reminded myself. My concern was adapting to my bizarre circumstances, and finding Billy and Cass, and perhaps stopping Zephkar Tesot.

Eva parked the car and entered a shop with purses, belts, wallets, suitcases. They were made of a material I'd never seen on Allo, called *leather*. Eva greeted another human who was dusting shelves. I liked Eva's voice. Higher-pitched and softer than Bert's, it felt better in the throat. She went behind one of the counters and brought out a case of jewelry from a wooden cabinet. I began to feel frustrated as this body that felt like it was my own did things I did not choose. I wanted to scrutinize the other human in the shop, but Eva went to the cash register and began counting out bills.

Soon after Eva pulled up the shade on the door and undid the lock, people began entering the shop. Eva showed them various items. The unusual fabric of the purses and gloves felt very soft, but my wish

16

to have the fingers linger over the textures was repeatedly thwarted. I thought about how it would be when I took over a body, overriding the will of the owner. *Boosting*, this was called. Billy had said she didn't know if she could bring herself to do it, but we all knew we had no choice.

The head had a slight ache. The pain seemed not to bother Eva, but it was bothering me. I considered shifting to another host, one of the customers, but since I'd planned to dip Eva before I left her, I stayed. Despite Wozar's warning, my rapid move to maxi-riding had not been too much to handle. Of course, dipping was a much larger step.

While Eva continued to wait on customers, I thought of how astounded my friends at home would be if they knew what was happening to me. Just then Eva bumped her knee on the edge of a counter and the pain was intense. I immediately switched to mini-riding. The change was a little disconcerting, like suddenly going numb all over. When I returned to maxi-riding, the knee pain was just about gone. I wanted the mouth to smile about how wonderful it was that I'd been able to escape the pain, but of course, Eva controlled the mouth. That got me thinking about dipping and eventually boosting.

With maxi-riding, I was aware of the sensations impinging on Eva's senses, from within and outside of her body, but I was interpreting them myself. I was not aware of any of her thoughts or feelings. If I dipped, I would be. I would tap her conscious mind and have access to the meanings she was attributing to her experience. When dipping, Wozar had told us, we would become aware of whatever was going on within our host's mind at that moment, what memories she was having, what hopes, fears, frustrations, resentments. At the same time, we would retain our own thoughts and feelings.

"You may also mind-tickle," Wozar had told us. Cass had giggled nervously at the word. "Through mind-tickling," Wozar had explained, "you will be able to tap into whatever content of the host's mind you are interested in simply by sending a key word to the host. Despite herself, the host will then associate to that word." Billy had looked frightened as she listened and then her eyes had glazed over. Wozar saw her reaction and had done what she could to reassure Billy. The idea of reading people's minds had frightened me too, but now I was feeling eager to try it. Maybe I'd even go to boosting and then take a pill for the headache.

After Eva's customer left, she sat on a stool and rubbed the temples. I wondered if it was my presence in her mind that was causing the headache. No, I thought, Wozar had said nothing about that. Eva's eyes were directed toward the entrance door, unmoving. I suspected she was not seeing anything, that she was looking within herself. If I wanted to, I could have access to her thoughts.

I watched passersby outside the door, not really attending to them. Finally I gathered my courage and made the move. Slowly, bit by bit I let myself slip more deeply inside Eva's mind. It was like turning on a radio broadcast inside my head, the volume very low at first, then getting louder.

Eva was troubled, full of anxiety and doubt. She and Bert were in the peach-colored house. They were fighting, yelling at each other. Then Bert struck Eva, her face distorted with contempt. In the next image,

Bert was holding her tenderly. I was aware of Eva's feelings — anger, fear, tenderness, love, sadness, uncertainty. She began remembering things from the past, how warm and sweet Bert had been; then the images switched to Bert striking her. Eva was outraged. Then Bert became contrite. She held Bert. Everything seemed all right. But then again Bert was slapping her, calling her vile names, then throwing her across the room. I found it unbelievable and appalling. The images switched back and forth from flare-ups and violence to closeness and tenderness. Eva clearly was tormented and confused.

I felt shocked by what I was witnessing in her mind. Was this true? Had these things happened? What sorts of beings were these Earthlings?

The whole process of dipping into another's mind and simultaneously observing and reacting with my own thoughts and feelings was very disturbing. Wozar had been right. It was too much to handle all at once. I slipped out, back to mini-riding. I thought about what I would do next, how I would get a newspaper and check for ads from Billy and Cass, and if no ad was there, how I'd put one in myself. But I'd have to boost to do it, or maybe contact, and I didn't feel a bit ready for that.

While Eva continued waiting on customers, I thought about the first time I'd seen Zephkar. Billy and I had just finished another interview with Wozar, this one about parenting on Allo, when the door burst open and Zephkar stood there with Toma in front of her, a gun in Toma's back. I recognized Zephkar from the newspaper photos. She was wearing a wig, and the exile tattoo on her forehead was covered with makeup, but she had very distinctive features — a large nose and thin lips set in a perpetual smirk. Like most other Alloys, I had been relieved to learn of her exile to Smarklace.

She made our guards relinquish their weapons. Then she spoke to Wozar, taunting her about how lax the Wraunkian security measures were, how easy it had been for her to slip aboard the ship and stow away. She said she had a trade to make — Toma's life in exchange for Wozar sending her, Zephkar's, mind to a place called Earth. "You won't be able to trick me," she had said. "I've been using your information center. I know the transportment procedures as well as you."

Wozar, generally very calm, had been enraged and frightened. We all knew she was in love with Toma, who was one of the first Alloys the Wraunkians had taken when they'd arrived on Allo. Toma had agreed to remain with the Wraunkians when it was time for them to leave our planet. Wozar told all the captured Alloys that we had a choice — when they were finished with us we could either go with them to Wraunk or be mind-wiped and allowed to remain on Allo. The mind-wiping was a method of destroying recent memories, although there was a risk that more memories than intended could be eliminated by the process.

"I will take over that planet," Zephkar had said, still holding the weapon to Toma's back. She was smiling malevolently. "Earth will be mine." At first, she told us, she had planned to take over Allo, but then when she learned about the Wraunkian's success at interplanetary transportments of disembodied minds, she decided to have even more fun and to go to Earth. "Prepare the decorporator," she told Wozar.

I knew well the power of disembodied minds and was relieved that Zephkar was choosing some alien planet on which to wreak her havoc. Wozar did as Zephkar demanded. Zephkar watched every command Wozar entered into the computer. Then she stepped onto the decorp platform and slipped her head beneath the dome. After making the rest of us back up across the laboratory, she pushed several buttons on the console in front of her. Her body went rigid and then limp.

Wozar raged for a long time after Zephkar's mind was gone. "I want her destroyed," she said as she paced back and forth across the room. The only others in the lab were me, Billy, an Alloy named Cass, who we had become friends with over the twenty-five jetur of our captivity, Toma, and two Wraunkian guards. Suddenly Wozar stopped pacing. She looked at us. "You three will go," she said, indicating me, Billy, and Cass. "You will go to Earth and destroy that monster."

Of course we argued. We even pleaded. But Wozar was adamant and wouldn't be swayed. Though not an evil being, she believed "the rights of others sometimes had to be forfeited for greater needs," as she put it. As the Chief Culture Explorer of the Wraunkian expedition, Wozar's word was law on the spaceship.

Because of her awareness of our morality, Wozar apparently had complete faith that we would follow through on the assignment, assuming we succeeded in entering a *human being*.

Well, I thought, I had succeeded in entering. This is my planet now. I wondered if I would succeed in stopping Zephkar.

Eva approached a new customer. The person was plump with graying hair and deep dark eyes. She reminded me of my seed parent, Neryoim, and I felt immediately drawn to her.

"Yes, these gloves are exactly what I've been looking for," she said. As she was paying Eva for her purchase, I made a snap decision and shifted. I mini-rode at first to cushion my adjustment to a new host. Eva put the gloves into a shiny red and white bag, and my new host put the bag into her purse. As we left the shop, I felt a little pang of sadness knowing I would probably never see Eva again, hoping she would be all right and that Bert would treat her well.

The street was full of humans. There seemed to be three types — those who used makeup, had normal breasts, and wore garments which left their lower legs exposed; those with flat chests, wearing pants, and having quite short hair; and a third type that seemed to be a combination of the first two.

We walked slowly along the street pausing now and then to look into shop windows. My host entered a building, and as she was waiting for the elevator I switched to maxi-riding. I wished I hadn't. She was not well. Breathing was difficult and her joints were painful. We rode the elevator up one floor, then entered an office where a human dressed in white led us to a small cubicle with a padded table. A doctor's office, I surmised. After removing her clothes, my host put on a thin gown and sat on the little stool. The joints were aching and it was very difficult for her to get enough air. I switched back to mini-riding.

The doctor came. She greeted my host, then pulled aside her gown and listened to the chest. I shifted, entering the doctor. I heard the sounds of the patient's heartbeat and hoped that what I was hearing didn't reflect anything defective in the elderly human's heart. The doctor was one of the second type humans, flat-breasted and hairy.

The next patient was waiting in another cubicle. The doctor felt the patient's abdomen, then examined the protruding penis and the mass of tissue beneath it. The mass felt like little balls of something hanging in loose sacks of flesh. Like Bert, I thought, and decided that this extra stuff must be normal anatomy for some of the humans. I wondered what the function was and why the penis apparently was not retractable. I was thinking about this when the doctor looked beneath the sack of flesh and I realized to my horror that there was no vagina. How grotesque! I quickly reminded myself not to do that, that I had to suspend my judgment about these beings and try simply to learn and understand. The people of this planet apparently have more similarities to lower life forms than we do, I thought, trying to remain objective and accepting. Earthlings would probably think we were odd, too, I told myself.

The next patient, a fairly young one, seemed more normal. She had a normal amount of breast tissue and no facial hair, but when my host put a tight rubber glove onto our hand and felt within the patient's vagina, it was obvious that she had no penis, just a patch of hair where the penis should be. I felt shaken, struck again by the fact that I had entered an alien world. Wozar had said the differences were insignificant. But, of course, Wozar had traveled to many worlds and must have seen great variation in life forms. I wondered if Earth people were restricted to being either birth parents or seed parents.

After finishing with her next patient, a breastless one, the doctor went to her office. "That man has every ailment known to man," she said.

"Mister Pritzker?" The nurse laughed. "Maybe next he'll develop some gynecological condition."

"I wouldn't be surprised," the doctor said, chuckling. I didn't get the joke. "How many more today?" she asked.

"Just Missus Silverman, the hypertensive. She's due in a few minutes."

As I had noticed with Bert and Eva, the meanings of some of the Earthlings' words were only partially clear to me. I knew that *minutes*, for example, was a measure of time, but I didn't know exactly how long a minute was. Also the word, *he*, confused me. It was clearly a pronoun, referring to humans, but I was puzzled why sometimes they said *she*, and other times, *he*. I supposed the meanings would emerge in time.

As the doctor talked into a machine, dictating notes about her patients, I switched to mini-riding. Thoughts of Billy came. I hoped she had found some human to enter, and was not still stranded somewhere in the void. Could she have permanated, I wondered. We had said we would, but I wondered if we really could bring ourselves to do it.

The sounds of the doctor's speech intruded on me

from time to time. I thought again about boosting — taking control of her body. There are three levels of boosting, Wozar had told us: boost-blocking, and two forms of open-boost — unilateral and bilateral. When boost-blocking, the host's mind is in the void. She is aware of nothing going on in the real world. When unilaterally boosting, it's as if the host is maxi-riding her own body; in this level, communication between the host and the disembodied mind, or DM, is possible, and the DM can dip and mind-tickle. Bilateral boosting is the same except the host is also able to dip the DM. I doubted that I'd ever use that level.

From time to time, Wozar had said, the host's mind would come back from the void and the DM would suddenly be aware of the host's thoughts. Wozar explained that when that happened, the DM could choose to switch right back to boost-blocking. She added that the Wraunkian mindologists were still working on eliminating the spontaneous switching, but so far had been unsuccessful. "Maybe we DM's need it as a reminder that we are not alone," she'd said. She seemed to be only half-kidding, I'd thought.

The alternative to riding or boosting was to permanate. "It's murder," Billy had said, and Cass and I had agreed. "But if someone is ready to die," Billy had added, "that would be different." I wasn't really sure.

The doctor went to the next patient, called Missus Silverman. She took the patient's blood pressure and listened to her tell a story about someone she referred to as her *daughter*. That was another one of those words. By the context, I

25

assumed *daughter* meant friend or some sort of relative. Missus also talked about her *son-in-law,* another word I didn't understand, and referred to her as *him.* Strange.

Missus Silverman was a human of the first type — breasts, no facial hair, less prominent muscles. I would guess she had no penis. I certainly hoped she wasn't missing her clitorises too. Then I began thinking that if it were a choice between having a non-retractable penis and no penis at all, I might prefer to go without. It certainly must get in the way hanging out all the time with that mass of tissue squished beneath it. It seemed to me, too, that it would make more sense for the penis people to be the ones to wear the lower garments that weren't divided at the legs. I supposed I would figure out the Earthlings' ways eventually.

I stayed three days with Dr. King. *He* meant a *male,* I learned, one of the hairy-faced ones without vaginas, uteri, or ovaries. For reasons I hadn't yet figured out, the males had more status and authority on Earth than the other anatomical type, called *females.* Females didn't have penises and only they could give birth; they also took the major responsibility for raising the young. Males were supposed to have sex only with females, and vice versa. People who broke this rule were disdained by those who didn't. I hadn't figured out the reason for that yet either.

I learned where I was — Walnut Creek, northern California, United States of America, North America.

26

I'd entered my first human, Bert, during the lunar *month* of July, on the eighth time of the earth's axial revolution that month, called *day*, in the *year* 1992. Year, I learned, measured the time it took the earth to make one complete revolution around its sun. I had no idea how long I had waited in the void until Bert came along.

One of the ways I learned so much so quickly was by boosting Dr. King's *wife*, Eleanor. On my second night with the pair, I boost-blocked Eleanor while she slept. It felt odd to control someone else's body, but I was getting used to odd things. While Eleanor's mind drifted in the void, I used her body to creep out of the bed and go to the living room where Ralph had left the newspaper, the *San Francisco Chronicle*. I searched the *Personals* column, but there was nothing for me. That was a tremendous disappointment since Billy and Cass and I had agreed to contact each other by putting ads in the most widely circulated newspaper of each of the ten most populated United States cities. I checked the Kings' almanac and learned that San Francisco was *not* one of the top ten. That elevated my spirits considerably.

I read sections from the Kings' set of encyclopedias, finding answers to many of my questions about Earthlings. When I was exhausted and daylight was about to break, I took Eleanor back to bed, shifted to Ralph, and fell asleep.

Over the next couple of days, I dipped and mind-tickled Ralph and other humans he had contact with. I read through Ralph's eyes whatever he read. I watched TV. At night I read the encyclopedia. I can't say I was particularly liking what I learned about the Earthlings. They seemed unable to get along with each other, and even had *wars,* in which trained fighters from one *country* used weapons against fighters from another, *enemy,* country.

The governments of the different countries had scant regard for the welfare of the *citizens,* often imposing severe restrictions on their freedom. People who objected risked imprisonment, torture, and death. There was rampant poverty in most of the countries, and starvation was not uncommon. If the people succeeded in overthrowing the oppressive leadership of their country, they generally established equally oppressive regimes. Earthlings made Alloy criminals, even the exiles, look altruistic and peaceloving by comparison.

At some points during my education I became so homesick I thought I'd rather be dead than be stuck on this hostile planet. They deserve Zephkar, I'd think, but then I'd think of Billy and get motivated again to continue learning about Earthian culture so I could find her and Cass and do what we had come here to do. Besides, there was another side to the humans. They could be creative, humorous, and even loving and kind.

On the fifth day of my life on earth, I entered one of Ralph's patients, a female named Kathy, and decided to stay with her. From Ralph's office, Kathy left Walnut Creek and drove to a big hilly city that was almost attractive enough to remind me of home.

Kathy lived in a second floor apartment. From her front window we had a beautiful view of a house-lined hill and a hilly park. My new host clearly appreciated beauty; her apartment was decorated with artistic prints and interesting sculptures and vases.

Kathy had weekly meetings with a trained listener called a social worker. The social worker was a female human who seemed more self-assured than the other females I had entered. Her name was Pat Capp.

I enjoyed dipping and mind-tickling Pat. Her thoughts were complex and interesting. She was adept at entering into her *clients'* emotional worlds and helping them explore their feelings and beliefs. The whole time I stayed with Pat, which was four days, she never had a male client. It didn't take me long to figure out why. It had to do with females' or *women's* roles in Earthian society. Some females were trying to change the social structure which kept them in lower positions. The philosophy advocating such changes was called *feminism,* and Pat was a *feminist therapist.* She was delightful. Knowing Pat gave me hope that I would find some Earthlings I'd want to befriend.

Most of Pat's clients felt dissatisfied with themselves. "Low self-esteem," Pat called this. Many were depressed. Some had problems with food, eating great quantities, for example, then inducing vomiting. Some had gotten so distressed that they had actually tried ending their own lives. This was called *suicide.* Of course, it reminded me of *chosen death* on Allo, but on Earth, some people wanted to die even though they didn't have a terminal illness. The emotional pain I witnessed was heartrending and it made me wish I could teach these beings that there are much better ways to live. It seemed like an impossible job, though.

On my fourth day with Pat, she went to an apartment on Fair Oaks Street where she and several other women played musical instruments together. The music was raucous like much of the music I heard on the Earthlings' radios and stereos. At first, I'd found it annoying, but I was getting used to it. There were three other musicians. One, named Amy, had big round brown eyes and short blonde hair that didn't lie flat but stuck out around her head in a very interesting style. I wondered how that would go over on Allo. People were always experimenting with hair styles at home, but this was a new one. I liked Amy's looks. I entered her and dipped and liked her thoughts. Through mind-tickling, I learned that she believed in *spiritual energy,* a concept I couldn't quite grasp, but that had something to do with benevolent feelings and inclinations.

I ended up staying with Amy rather than returning to Pat. Amy might be the one I'll contact, I thought. I was feeling desperate to get hold of a newspaper from one of the ten largest cities. Maybe, through Amy, I'd be able to. I also wanted to have a conversation with someone. It can be lonely being a disembodied mind.

Before trying to contact, I spent a couple days getting to know Amy. I did a lot of mind-tickling. I'd send a word or phrase to her mind and that would cause a string of associations to enter her consciousness. I learned that she worked as a graphic designer, but wasn't happy with her job, believing it restricted her creativity. She was a *lesbian,* which meant she preferred other females rather than males as emotional and physical intimates. She had been involved in numerous feminist causes in the past but had become disillusioned with the slowness of the changes. She'd experienced some discrimination in her career because of being a lesbian. She'd also been hurt in several love relationships. Recently she'd turned her interest to what she called *women's spirituality.* It was this part of her that gave me hope that I'd be able to contact her without frightening her into idiocy.

On my second day in Amy, she met a friend at a restaurant on Valencia Street. Her friend was unusually tall for a female human and walked with an easy, agile gait. Her name was Agatha. Amy was very fond of her, though not in a sexual, romantic way.

The women ordered their food and chatted about different people they knew. Then Agatha asked if Amy had heard about a new cult in a place called Chicago. "There was an article in the paper today," she said. "They claim the second coming is near and that God has sent a messenger to pave the way."

"That's news? Someone's always making a claim like that."

"Yeah, but this one is a little freaky. The messenger speaks through little children, five- and six-year-olds. The kids preach about the messenger and the *New Direction.* They talk like adults. I was talking to my roommate about it. She thinks it's a form of child abuse, to use kids that way. Pumping that crap into their heads and then making them stand up in front of a bunch of gullible people in churches and spew it out. But the freaky part is that the parents claim no one worked with the kids, no one told them what to say. One mother said her little boy only went to Sunday School because she made him and that he never showed any particular interest in religion, then all of a sudden he started preaching about the New Direction and all the sinning that was going on. The mother took the kid to a psychologist."

"Did you read about it in the *National Enquirer*?" Amy asked.

"No, the *Chronicle*."

"Really? So what did the psychologist think?"

"The article didn't say."

"Maybe there's something to it. There *is* more to life than just what you can see and touch, you know." Amy set her jaw defensively, ready for an argument.

But apparently Agatha did not want to argue. "Yeah, I suppose," she said.

After dinner we went to the *Women's Building*, a rundown structure just off Valencia Street, where we ran into my favorite previous host, Pat Capp, the feminist therapist. I was happy to see her again. We watched a *karate* demonstration which I found strangely fascinating, though I was saddened that it was necessary for Earthlings to learn self-defense methods.

After the karate, Amy, Agatha and Pat went to a cafe for coffee. Pat pulled a clipped newspaper article from her pack. "Did you guys see this?" She laid the article on the table. It was from *Time* Magazine.

Chicago Churches Finding New Direction, the headline read.

"Agatha mentioned something about it," Amy said. "Some new religious movement."

"It scares me," Pat said. "They're taking over one church after another in Chicago. I've never seen anything like it. They're trying to start a new political party. They believe that civil laws should be based on the Bible — a literal reading of the Old Testament. God's law, they say."

Amy shrugged. "Harmless kooks."

"Potentially dangerous kooks," Pat said. "They blame secular humanism for everything that's wrong in the world. But what's scary is that apparently they just go into a church one day and the next thing you know the whole congregation joins up."

Amy was becoming interested. She took the article and read it. I read along with her. "I wonder how they do it," she said.

"Possession," Agatha said.

Everybody laughed.

On my third night with Amy, I decided the time had come to make contact. We had just returned from taking her two dogs for a walk and Amy was reading a novel.

Hello, I began, feeling very nervous. *Is anyone receiving? Let it in, someone.*

Amy's mouth fell open. She looked around the room. "Who's there?"

Amy, can you hear me?

"Who is it?"

I could feel her heart pounding. *Yes, you are receiving. This is Jenna. You're very receptive, Amy. You're in the United States, aren't you? In San Francisco.*

Amy gasped. "Uh . . . yes," she muttered.

I'm contacting you from France. Do you understand what's happening?

"No," Amy said. "I don't. I hear your voice, but . . ."

Mental telepathy, Amy. I'm receiving you clearly. Is this your first time with extrasensory perception? You're an excellent receptive.

Amy's mouth was still wide. "You're contacting me by telepathy?"

Yes. From France. I was feeling very excited and frightened myself. It was certainly a new experience to me to be communicating this way.

Amy looked around the room again. "Come on, what's going on? This is a trick. Electronics or something."

It's no trick, Amy. I know it's hard to believe but it's true. I was having trouble believing it myself. *This must be your first time,* I said.

"I hear you inside my head." She stood up and walked around the room, pressing her palms to her temples. "How . . . how do you do it? I mean . . . well, God, it's too much. Wow!"

Very few of us can do it, I said. *Your energy is quite strong.*

Amy was perspiring. "This is fantastic."

Amy, I've contacted you for a reason. I need you to do something for me. It's important. I want you to do me a favor. Sit down, all right? And listen.

34

Amy sat on the sofa.

Good. I need to contact some friends of mine who I was supposed to meet in San Francisco this summer. A lot has happened and I'm not going to be able to come.

"You want me to get in touch with them for you?" Amy was blinking her eyes rapidly, a big smile on her face. "Is this really happening?"

I know. It takes some getting used to. Yes, I need to reach my friends, but I don't know where they are. We agreed to meet in San Francisco sometime this July. We didn't know exactly when or where but agreed to contact each other by newspaper ads. The personals column. I need you to check the ads for me.

"The newspaper?" Amy continued blinking. "Well, sure," she said. "All right. I could do that. What paper? The *Chronicle?*"

No, I said. *It has to be a paper from one of the ten largest cities in the U.S.*

"The *New York Times,*" Amy said. "I know a place in Noe Valley where they sell it. I can go buy it if you want."

All right.

"Now?"

If you would.

Amy hesitated momentarily. "OK," she said. "Wait here and I'll be right back." She grabbed her jacket and ran down the stairs. I continued maxi-riding. She was tremendously excited, wondering if it was really happening, thinking about telling Agatha, wondering if she'd ever meet me in person, and so on and so on. She rode her motorcycle to a large newsstand on Twenty-Third Street, bought the paper, then sped back to the apartment. She was worried that I'd be gone.

"I've got it!" she said the moment she entered the door. "Are you still here?"

I'm here.

She tore the paper open and shuffled through the pages until she came to the personals. "What should I look for?" she asked.

Anything for Jenna, I responded, *or anything with the names Billy or Cass.*

I spotted the ad before she did. *Jenna, Billy: Call 312-508-2631. Cass.* I wanted to jump up and down with joy.

"Here it is." Amy read the ad aloud. "That area code's in Chicago. I used to have an aunt there."

I guess Cass didn't make it to San Francisco either, I said. *Will you call the number? Tell Cass who you are and that I've made contact with you through mental telepathy. Will you do that?*

"Yes, of course. This is fantastic. Cass knows about the telepathy?"

Yes, she knows all about it. I'll tell you what else to say when you get her on the line.

Amy went to the phone and pushed buttons. We both waited anxiously as the phone rang. Then we heard an answering machine. . . . *not able to take your call right now, but if you leave your name and number . . . get back to you soon.*

Tell her this is Jenna, and leave your phone number.

Amy did as I asked. After she hung up, she stared dreamily into space. "I always believed in

ESP," she said. "This is great. It's just absolutely great." She took a deep breath. "So . . . um . . . so you're French. Do you live in Paris?"

No, I live in the country. On a farm.

"Well, tell me about yourself. Um . . . how old are you?"

I decided to choose an age close to Amy's. *Thirty,* I said. *You're thirty-two, right? I sense that you haven't been real happy lately. You're kind of bored with your life, aren't you?*

She can read my mind, Amy thought.

Yes, I can, I said.

Amazing. Absolutely amazing, she thought. "Are you a farmer?"

Yes. I grow fruit trees and different grains.

It must be hard work, Amy thought.

Not really. The machines do the hard part.

"Do you live alone?"

I didn't answer right away, suddenly feeling very sad. *Yes,* I said finally. *Billy was going to move in with me, but then she had to go away. She's my lover and I miss her terribly.*

How about that, she's a lesbian, Amy thought. "Did she go away with someone else, another lover?"

No, I said. *They . . . there was a nasty person. A . . . a wizard. She caused Billy and me to be separated. It's very . . . it's a strange story, Amy.*

What wizard?

The wizard's name is Wozar. She has amazing powers. She came into our lives — mine and Billy's — and she . . . she used us. She took us from our lives in the country and . . . she separated us and

. . . and she did things to our minds. She's the one who gave us the power to communicate like this — through telepathy.

One of Amy's dogs, Isis, came and lay at Amy's feet. *Isis is a beautiful dog,* I said. *You love animals, don't you?*

Amy nodded. She reached down and scratched Isis's ears. "Why did the wizard do things to you?"

To learn about us. She sent Billy and Cass to the United States. Amy, are you doing OK with this? Most people would think they were going crazy if they were contacted like this by . . . by someone so far away. Are you OK?

"I think so. It is scary, I'll admit that, but I don't think I'm crazy. Actually, I think I'm . . ."

Lucky.

"Yes. That's amazing how you read my mind. Weird, though. I couldn't have any secrets from you."

That's upsetting?

"Kind of."

If you want me to end contact, all you have to do is close your eyes and think, Out, Out, Out, *and I'll leave. OK?*

"Yeah, that's cool. And if I want you back?"

Just call my name, Jenna, Jenna, Jenna.

Amy shook her head. I listened to her thoughts and laughed. *No, Amy, you're awake. It's not a dream.*

"No one will believe it."

Probably not.

"You know, if anyone saw me now, they'd think I *am* nuts, that I'm sitting here talking to myself."

You're right. They probably wouldn't believe you.

"So tell me more about this wizard," Amy said. "Where is she from? What powers does she have?"

I'm afraid to tell you, I said. *You'll think it's too weird.*

"It couldn't be weirder than what's happening right now."

Oh, yes it could. I don't want to get you so upset that you close me out. I want us to keep in contact.

Am I in danger? Amy thought.

No, I said, *it's not that. You're in no danger at all. I just think maybe I should go slowly with you. Not tell you everything at once. It's a lot to handle.*

"You're getting me real curious."

I know. But I think it's better if I go away for a while now, and let you digest all this. Later, I'll come back and then I'll tell you more. All right?

"You promise you'll come back."

I promise.

"What if Cass calls?"

I'll know. I'll hear the phone, and I'll come back then.

Fantastic.

I know. I'll be in touch, I said. *I'm glad it's you I reached, Amy,* I added, and then I stopped contacting but continued to dip.

Amy sat motionless on her chair, staring at nothing. I listened to her thoughts for a while, then switched to mini-riding. I had thoughts of my own to listen to. Cass had made it! I couldn't wait to hear from her. But what about Billy, I thought. Why was there no ad from her?

* * * * *

The next morning, Amy staggered out of bed to get the phone. She mumbled a blurry hello.

"This is Cass," the voice said.

"Uh, right, yes." Amy blinked rapidly. "Cass. From Chicago. You got the message."

I was so excited I wanted to scream and cry.

"Yes."

"I'm Amy Klein. Your friend, Jenna, she . . . um, she communicated with me. From France. She's still in France. She reached me by telepathy." Amy squirmed. "Do you know what I'm talking about?"

"Yes. Is she communicating with you now?"

Ask her if she's heard from Billy, I said excitedly.

Amy was startled by my voice. "Yes, Jenna's in contact with me. She wants to know if you've heard from Billy."

"No. Not yet. I'm glad to hear Jenna's all right. Tell her I permanated."

I heard, I said. *Tell her I haven't.*

"She hasn't," Amy said.

"Yes, I realize that. Ask her —

"You can talk to her directly," Amy said. "She can hear you."

"Thanks, Amy. This must be weird for you. I hope we get to meet some day. So, Jenna, how long have you been . . . uh . . ."

Tell her thirteen days, I said, *since July eighth.*

Amy told her. Cass said that she'd made her first entry on April seventeenth, almost three months before I had. "Jenna," she said, "is it possible for you to contact me directly, you know, to boost?"

Tell her, soon, I said to Amy. *Tell her I'll call her soon and we'll have a real talk.*

Amy did what I asked, and then we said goodbye

40

to Cass. "What does *permanate* mean?" Amy asked when she'd hung up.

I didn't respond right away. I was thinking of Billy. I had the sinking feeling that Billy was lost, that I would never hear from her again. *It has to do with the wizard,* I said at last. *I'll tell you about it when I tell you the rest. How are you doing?*

"I'm doing fine," Amy was back in bed, stretching and yawning. "Are you afraid I'll freak out when you tell me more?"

I think you'll handle it, I responded.

I rode with Amy to her job in downtown San Francisco. She spent most of her day hunched over a drawing board. She seemed quite talented, but obviously was bored with the work. I didn't contact her all morning and only dipped from time to time. Mostly I stayed with mini-riding and thought about Billy and Cass and what I should do next. I was immensely relieved that Cass had made it. Hearing her voice, even though it didn't sound a bit like Cass and even though the words were in English, made me realize how terribly lonely I was. Cass and I had grown close on the Wraunkian ship. I'd often wished our friendship could continue after the Wraunkians let us go and we returned to our lives on Allo, but our memories of the ship would have been erased and we would have had no idea the other existed. Now our friendship could continue, I thought — that was the silver lining of our transport.

At lunchtime, Amy went to meet Agatha at a

tiny Vietnamese restaurant near her office. I was struck again by how tall Agatha was. I was finding her more attractive than most Earthlings. That got me thinking about Billy again.

Amy could barely sit still. She was thinking of how to tell Agatha about me and was hardly listening to Agatha's talk about a human named James Lane who was the leader of that new religious group she'd talked about before. James Lane lived in Chicago, she told Amy.

". . . and he claims this Zephkar speaks to him directly and guides what he says and does," Agatha said.

If I were boosting my jaw would have dropped to the table.

"Who's Zephkar?" Amy asked absentmindedly. Her thoughts were still on me.

"The messenger from God," Agatha said. The waiter came and the two women ordered their food. "Zephkar Speaks," Agatha continued. "That's how the media refer to it. They interviewed this James Lane last night on the news. He's started a new political party." Agatha looked at Amy. "You're miles away, aren't you? What's going on?"

Amy twisted and turned on the flimsy wooden chair. "Something happened to me," she said.

Agatha looked concerned. "What, hon? Tell me." I was liking her more and more. I wanted Amy to tell her about me.

"I'm afraid you'll laugh."

"It's funny?"

"No." Amy searched for how to begin. "You know

42

there's been a lot of research on extrasensory perception."

Frowning, Agatha said, "Yeah, some, I guess. So?"

"Even the scientists who study it say there seems to be some evidence for mental telepathy. You know, communicating with each other through thoughts, without speaking." Amy looked Agatha directly in the eye. "I've experienced it," she said.

Agatha smiled. "Oh, really?"

"Someone has been sending her thoughts to me. And she can read my thoughts."

"Is that so? Anyone I know?" Agatha took a sip of her tea.

"No. She's French."

"OO-la-la," Agatha said, then she looked seriously at Amy. "What's this about?"

"I don't exactly know," Amy said. "She contacted me last night. She lives on a farm in France and she's been separated from her lover. She's trying to find her."

"This is a joke, right?" Agatha said.

Amy looked at her friend with a deadpan expression. "I was sitting at home last night and suddenly I heard this voice. It sounded sort of like a radio, but not quite. She said her name was Jenna and she was using mental telepathy to contact me from France. I couldn't believe it at first."

"But now you do." Agatha looked quite worried.

"Absolutely. She had me check the newspaper for a message to her and there was one, and I called the number and talked to her friend, Cass, in Chicago."

"I don't like this," Agatha said. "Come on, Amy, say this is a stupid joke. I don't think it's funny. Either it's a joke or . . ."

"Or I'm cracking up. That's what you think, isn't it?"

"I think something weird is going on." Agatha frowned pensively. "You feel trapped in your life, that's it, and this fantasy is like an escape. But you know it's a fantasy, don't you?"

Agatha was clearly distressed and so was Amy. I decided to intervene, hoping I didn't end up making things worse. I shifted to Agatha and contacted. *It's not a fantasy, Agatha. I really have been contacting Amy, as I'm doing with you now.*

Agatha's heart began to pound. Her shoulders rose and her muscles contracted as if she were trying to make herself smaller and shield herself. *There's no danger. It's new and mysterious but not threatening.*

"*You're* doing it!" Agatha looked accusingly at Amy.

"What?"

It's not Amy, I said. *My name is Jenna. I'm contacting you by telepathy. Amy was telling the truth. It's an exciting truth, but it doesn't have to be a frightening one, Agatha. See if you can relax. Take a deep breath.*

"What's the matter?" Amy asked.

Agatha took several deep long breaths. "I heard a voice."

Amy smiled broadly. "Jenna? She spoke to you?"

"It's impossible."

People used to think airplanes were impossible. It's not impossible, Agatha, just new.

I'm hearing voices. I'm going crazy, Agatha thought.

No, I reassured her. *You're totally sane. So is Amy. This is real. There's nothing wrong with your mind. I'm contacting you because I need some friends here . . . in the United States. I need some help.*

Agatha was breathing noisily through her mouth. "What help?"

"What?" said Amy.

Agatha looked at her. "I'm talking to the ghost."

"Oh."

Say this, Agatha. 'I'm not in danger. I'm not crazy.'

"I'm not in danger. I'm not crazy."

"Right," Amy said. "Isn't it fantastic?"

"I don't know," Agatha said warily.

"She's contacting you from France."

Agatha shook her head.

"Isn't it great?" Amy said enthusiastically. "Don't you feel lucky?"

The important thing to remember is that there's nothing to be afraid of, I said. *You're having an adventure, Agatha.*

"Adventure," Agatha echoed dully.

"Right," Amy said.

This can't be happening, Agatha thought. She looked at Amy. "I can hear the voice as clearly as I hear you. It's amazing."

"I know. Hi, Jenna," Amy said.

Tell her hi from me.

45

"She says hi," Agatha said, and burst out in hysterical laughter.

When she settled down a bit, I said, *It's confusing and scary, but the scary part is just because it's new. Because there really is no danger.*

"Just to my entire understanding of reality," Agatha mumbled.

Yes, I acknowledged, *that's disturbing.*

"What are you two talking about?" Amy wanted to know.

Agatha sat in stunned silence. Her thoughts raced, then they stopped, then raced again.

I'm going to leave you now, Agatha. I won't contact you again unless you want me to. All right?

Agatha nodded. She looked at Amy, and after a few moments said, "Is she gone?"

Amy shrugged.

"She said she was leaving."

"Well, then I guess she left."

Agatha was staring blankly into space.

Amy started talking, telling Agatha everything I had told her, including that there was someone who I called a *wizard* involved in this and that I'd promised to tell her more soon. Neither woman ate much of her lunch.

Amy went back to work and I stayed with her but didn't contact her the rest of the day. From time to time I dipped into her thoughts and feelings. She was doing very well, was in a great mood, in fact. Her thoughts were on me much of the time as she worked on designing a label for onion rings. There was no indication of fear. She felt the sort of excited anticipation people often do when they're about to go on a vacation trip. She was a little worried about

Agatha, though, and during her afternoon coffee break, decided to phone her.

"How're you doing?" Amy asked.

"We didn't have lunch together today, did we?"

Amy chuckled. "It was real."

"I've been thinking about the ramifications," Agatha said. "If the government got into your French friend, I'm sure the CIA would make her an offer she couldn't refuse. Do you see the potential?"

"Super spy," Amy said. "I'm sure Jenna wouldn't be interested."

"She knew what I was thinking, Amy, and what I was feeling! That's frightening. There are multiple potential uses for a power like that. Some of them pretty scary."

"I guess," Amy said, "I mean, it could be if the person were malicious or something, but Jenna wouldn't do any harm."

"We don't know that. We don't know anything about it, really. If everything was so innocent, why didn't Jenna just phone her friend in Chicago once she got the number? Why is she contacting her through you? And what is this business about a wizard? I don't think she's being honest with you, Amy. No matter what she says, I find it extremely frightening. It's creepy. For all we know she's listening to our conversation right now."

"You just have to say, *Out, out, out,* and she'll leave," Amy said.

"So she says. I don't like it. It crosses the line, Amy. Not only does it defy reality as I thought I knew it, but when you think about it, the potential uses of that power are . . . ooh, I hate to think of it."

"I shouldn't have involved you," Amy said.

I was thinking the same thing, but Agatha insisted that she was glad Amy had involved her. "As weird as it is, I have to admit I'm very intrigued."

"She's going to tell me more soon," Amy said, "about the wizard business. Maybe tonight."

"Do you want me with you?"

"No, I don't think so."

"Well, let me know what happens."

Amy agreed to call Agatha that evening whether I contacted her or not. "By midnight at the latest," she said. They hung up and Amy went back to work. She wasn't concentrating on what she was doing and ended up having to do some of the lettering over. She wasn't upset though. She was thinking about tonight and hoping I would come again.

While Amy had her dinner, I shifted into the void. I couldn't stand the sight or smell of what she was preparing — pasta mixed with tuna fish. I knew the fish was some kind of animal flesh. I checked back with her frequently, since time could be so slippery in the void. I made sure I kept my concentration, not letting myself drift too far or I knew I might end up floating for days. On my third check-in, Amy was clearing up the dishes so I stayed. She went to the same chair she'd been sitting in the previous night when I had first contacted her.

"Jenna," she said aloud. *Jenna, Jenna, Jenna,* she thought.

Hello, Amy. What's new?

Her face lit up. "Not much. I've been looking forward to talking with you tonight. Do you feel like talking?"

If you really feel like hearing, I said. *Remember, what I have to say will be a bit shocking.*

"I'm ready," she said determinedly. "Tell me about the wizard."

There's something I have to tell you before that, I said. *About my life before the wizard ever came. But let me ask you something first. Do you know how many planets there are in the universe?*

Amy was surprised at the question. *No one knows that,* she thought. "There are nine in our solar system," she said, "but I don't think anyone knows how many there are in the universe. There could be millions."

Do you think any have life on them?

"I think so, yes." *Why is she asking about this?* she thought.

Do you think there might be some planets somewhere in the universe that have life similar to life on earth, with people similar to human?

"Probably," Amy said. "I've always thought there probably is and that some day we'd find out about them, but —"

I always thought so too, I said, but I never expected to meet anyone from another planet.

"I've often wished I could," Amy said. "What are you trying to tell me?"

The wizard isn't from Earth.

"Oh my God!"

Scary, huh?

"Uh, yes . . . but tell me more."

She's from a planet called Wraunk. Who knows where it is? Light years away from here. The Wraunkians are far more advanced than us, technologically. The wizard came on a space ship. Just like in the movies, I said. I waited, dipping. She seemed to be handling it all right so far, so I continued. *The wizard and the others from Wraunk landed not too far from my farm —*

This is too much, Amy was thinking. *This is getting crazier and crazier.*

Just new, I reminded her. *But the ideas aren't new, are they, Amy? You knew about telepathy. You knew about beings from other planets. You just weren't sure they were real. Now you're learning that they are.*

Amy moved from her chair to the sofa where she had a blanket. She pulled it up over herself. *I hope I'm not going insane,* she was thinking.

You are completely sane, I assured her, *and very lucky. You're a pioneer.*

That's true, she thought.

Shall I go on?

"Yes."

I was at my house with Billy. Two Wraunkians came and took us to their ship. But they took us in a strange way. They entered our minds and took over our bodies. And then we all drove together to their ship. You see, they can . . . the Wraunkians are able to separate their minds from their bodies and then enter other peoples' bodies. They can come and go that way.

Amy was feeling weak.

It's straight out of science fiction, I said lightly, hoping to switch her mood. *Isn't it?*

She rubbed her forehead. "Partly I love it," she said, "but I can't help being scared."

Tell me about the part that loves it, I coaxed.

"People from other planets. Minds entering our bodies and communicating with them. It's great. It's marvelous. I always believed things like that were possible, sort of, but now . . ."

I know. The reality of it is pretty jarring. Should I stop?

"No," Amy said immediately. "Tell me the rest. I want to hear it all. Is there a Wraunkian mind in you now?"

No, I said.

But your mind is in mine, Amy was thinking, and her fear escalated again.

The most important thing is for you to realize that I will not harm you, I said. *You're involved in something very strange, but it's not dangerous. Do you believe me, Amy?*

I don't know, she thought. She had a fantasy of wispy smoke swirling around in her brain and pulling her apart, pulling her soul to pieces until she was no more. "I want to believe you," she said. She was chewing her lip. "So they took you to their ship . . ."

Yes. They had dozens of experiments set up and hundreds of questions to ask us. They treated us well on the ship. They were going to let us go soon. They had come to learn about us, not to harm us. I really believed that. I was sure it was true.

"But then . . . the wizard . . . you said the

51

wizard gave you the power of mental telepathy and that she took Billy away and . . ."

I want to tell you everything. From beginning until now. The beginning for me was not here, Amy. Not on earth. Shall I tell you?

Amy nodded. She was frightened but also very curious and fascinated. I decided to proceed. I told her I was not really from France, but from another planet, called Allo. Her vision grew hazy. I told her a few things about Allo, about how similar our planet is to Earth. I focused on the similarities, figuring I'd save the differences for later. I told her about Wozar and our lives on the ship and then about Zephkar coming. When I told her about the decorporation, she got real queasy again and we had to take a break. But then she wanted to hear the rest. I told her about Zephkar transporting to Earth, and that Billy and Cass and I were sent to stop her. I told her about the void, and about mini- and maxi-riding, about dipping and connecting. I didn't mention permanating or mind-tickling. I was about to explain the different levels of boosting when the phone rang. It was Agatha.

"You didn't call," she said. "It's after midnight. Are you all right?"

"I don't even know if I'm real," Amy answered numbly.

"Oh, shit. What's happening, Amy?"

"It's OK, I'm OK. I've just been hanging out on the other side of the reality line tonight, that's all, and I'm a little stunned. I've been having a long talk with Jenna. Oh, Agatha, do I have some news for you." Amy suddenly stopped. *Should I tell her?* she thought.

I'd take my time, I cautioned. *Give your own mind a chance to settle before you blast hers.*

"Right."

"What?" Agatha said.

"I'm going to tell you all about it, my friend, in due time. Agatha, I'm fine. I'm wonderful. I'm sane and excited and very very glad I'm alive. I'm having a ball tonight. I'll call you tomorrow."

"Are you sure? Do you want me to come over?"

"Not yet," Amy said. "Soon I'll tell you everything."

"This isn't going to go away, is it?" Agatha said. "This is big doings."

"Big doings."

"You're sure everything's all right."

"As sure as I can be." After promising to call Agatha the next day, Amy hung up. "I just hope I don't wake up and find out this was all a dream," she said.

No such luck, I responded, laughing.

She didn't want to stop. She had question after question and we talked long into the night. I told her almost everything, including about mind-tickling, but I didn't yet mention permanating, nor did I tell her about the anatomical differences between Earthlings and Alloys.

Finally we were both too exhausted to go on. Before going to sleep Amy told me that she wanted to help us stop Zephkar. I told her that maybe she could.

* * * * *

As soon as Amy woke up she asked if I was there. *Of course,* I told her.

"My constant companion," she said. "It's almost like you're part of me."

I didn't answer.

"I dreamed about you."

I know. We were flying through the cosmos and then some monster came.

"It was Zephkar," Amy said, pulling the cover up to her neck. "She frightens me."

For good reason.

Amy got out of bed and called in sick at her job. "I wish I never had to go back there," she said. "So, what would you like for breakfast?" She giggled oddly. *Eating for two,* she thought.

Cereal, I said, *or toast. Anything but animal flesh.*

"How about a cheddar cheese omelette?"

I told her I did not consume such items as fowl ova or products made from the milk of domesticated animals. *If you have to eat food like that,* I said, *I'll shift to the void until you're done.*

"Don't you use any animal products at all on Allo?" she asked.

It would be unthinkable, I answered.

We continued the conversation in the shower. "If you only eat plants, then how do you get your protein? Is there enough in plants?"

I told her there was.

"Is it for ethical reasons that you don't eat

meat?" she persisted, "or can't your bodies digest animal protein?"

The idea of consuming animals is repugnant to us, I said.

Amy squirted shampoo onto her palm and rubbed it into her hair. "What about microorganisms?"

We make an exception for them, I answered, *if they happen to be in the air we breathe or grains and fruit we eat, but we don't fry them up and put ketchup on them.*

"I never liked the idea of killing animals to eat them," Amy said, "or to use their fur or whatever. But I'm so used to it. Most Earthlings are. I guess there are some pretty major differences between your world and ours." *I bet she's homesick,* Amy was thinking. She was right about that.

Amy had a bowl of *Mueslix* for breakfast and then some coffee. The cereal was excellent, but I couldn't seem to adjust to the bitter taste of the coffee drink Earthlings were so fond of. I asked Amy about it.

"It contains caffeine," she told me, "a stimulant. Helps you get going in the morning. Do people use drugs on Allo? I mean like mind-altering drugs — alcohol, cocaine, marijuana, heroin, things like that?"

Some Alloys do, I said. *Drugs like that aren't particularly popular.*

"They're legal, though?"

You mean do we have laws forbidding people to consume them? The idea seemed outrageous to me. *No. People are free to use them if they choose.*

Amy told me about the drug abuse problem in

the United States and other countries on Earth, the ruined lives, the network of crime linked to drugs, the futile efforts of governments to curtail their production, sale, and use. I was amazed to hear the extent of the problem.

I don't think excessive drug use would ever catch on on Allo, I said, *but even if it did we wouldn't make it illegal. We try to keep laws at a minimum.*

Amy wanted to know more about Allo. I said I'd be happy to tell her, but that I'd like to give Cass a call first if she didn't mind. *I'd like to boost to do it,* I said.

"Oh."

I didn't blame her for being nervous. My mind being inside of her was bad enough, but the idea of me taking control of her body was more than she wanted to deal with. *We could try a little experiment first,* I said, *so you could get a feel for what it's like. I'll boost you for just a minute or so and then I'll stop. Will you give it a try?*

"What will you do?" she asked. "I mean, with my body?"

I'll take it to the kitchen and drink a glass of water, I said. *And then I'll stop boosting. Are you willing to try it?*

Amy took a deep breath. "OK, but just for a minute."

It took me about half a minute to switch to boosting. As I started to walk toward the kitchen, I could hear her thinking, *Oh, God, this is too weird. It's like dreaming. Sleepwalking. It feels so unreal. I feel like I'm a puppet.*

I got the water, drank it, then returned to the

living room. "So what do you think?" I asked, still boosting.

I think it's chillingly fantastic, she replied.

I switched back to riding.

Amy moved her arms and stared at her hands. "I'm me again." She took a deep breath. "It wasn't so bad." *It would be, though, she thought, if she kept doing it when I didn't want her to.*

I won't, I said. *I'll only boost when you give me permission.*

I hope I can trust her, Amy thought.

I didn't respond to the thought. *Would you like to check out the void?* I asked. *Remember, though, it can be very enticing. I wouldn't want you to get hooked on it.*

"Not yet," Amy said.

All right. Maybe later.

"I know you want to call Cass. If you don't block and send me to the void, then I'll hear the conversation. Is that a problem for you?"

Not really, I said. *I'll use unilateral dip-boosting so you'll be able to contact me. If you need me to stop, just let me know.*

"You want to do it now?"

I'm pretty eager to talk with Cass, I said.

But what if . . . She was imagining herself without control of her body forever, a helpless puppet.

All you have to do is signal, Amy, and I'll switch out of boosting. You can count on me.

Amy nodded. *If she wanted, she could take my body over completely,* she thought. *I really have no power here. I just have to trust her. Should I ask her to leave? To leave me alone? To go use someone else's body?*

If you really want me to do that, I will, Amy. I won't do anything against your will. I'll leave and never come back if you want.

"No, I don't want that."

Or I'll agree never to boost you.

Amy was silent awhile. "No," she said. "You need someone. A body. You need me and I do trust you. Go ahead and call Cass. And . . . well, if you really don't want me to listen, I guess you could send me to the void."

I don't mind if you listen.

"OK," she said. She took two deep breaths. "OK, do it."

One more thing, Amy, before I do. In my conversation with Cass, we'll probably talk about permanating. I think —

"That's right. Cass said she had permanated and you never explained what it means."

I'm going to now. I thought for a moment about how to do it. *It means going from being a DM — a disembodied mind — to being a person,* I said. *When a DM permanates, she's no longer a DM, no longer just a mind. She has a body. She becomes mortal.*

"You can do that? How?"

I guess the best way would be to find a host who's willing.

Amy blinked rapidly. "Oh, you mean . . ."

We can't create a body out of thin air, Amy.

"So that means . . . for a DM to permanate someone has to . . ."

Their mind disappears . . . dies, I guess. Their body remains.

"But their mind is the DM's mind."

Their mind is gone. The DM's mind uses their brain.

"Gosh," Amy said dully.

I'm sure Cass didn't do it to just anyone, I said, knowing how frightening this was to Amy. It was frightening me too.

She seemed to spark up. "Yes, someone with a terminal illness, probably, who was ready to die."

Unfortunately that wouldn't do, I said. *If Cass took such a person's body then Cass would be terminally ill.*

Amy was quiet a moment. "Can you take a body against a person's will?"

A DM could, if she chose to. Amy was thinking the obvious, that I could take *her* body, permanate her. *If I had any intention of doing that, Amy, I never would have made friends with you. But I'd never permanate someone like you. I'll probably never permanate anyone at all.*

I have to trust her. I have to trust her, Amy was thinking. I remained quiet.

"Is there anything else you haven't told me?"

I laughed. *Isn't this enough for now?*

"It's enough forever." She took a deep breath. "All right, you can call Cass now. I'm ready to be boosted. Go ahead."

I was feeling very warmly toward this Earthling. *Ready?*

"Hit it."

The moment I was controlling the body, I went to the phone. Cass answered on the second ring.

"Hi, alien," I said. "Jenna here. I'm boosting my friend, Amy Klein. Unilateral. How're you doing?"

"Oh, Jenna, it's you! I've been afraid to leave my apartment. I didn't want to miss your call. Can you talk freely? Does Amy know . . . you know, about . . ."

"She knows everything. She's not used to being boosted, though, so we might get interrupted. I told her I'd stop if she got too uncomfortable with it."

"I want to say something to her," Cass said. "Amy, you must be quite a person for Jenna to have chosen you to . . . to contact, to tell about us . . . who we are. I hope we get to meet, get to know each other."

Tell her I hope so too, Amy said.

I told her.

"Oh, Jenna," Cass said, "it feels so great to hear your voice, even though it doesn't sound anything like your voice. Some days I still have crying jags, missing Allo. And I've had a lot more time to adjust than you. Are you adjusting?"

"Slowly. Apparently I was in the void for some time."

"I think I was, too, but obviously not as long as you. Were you afraid that you'd always be stuck there?"

"Sometimes," I said. "Mostly I just drifted and enjoyed it."

"I kept remembering things from the past. Actually it was more like re-living them. And new things happened too. I had so many wonderful experiences. I knew they were all fantasies but they seemed so real."

"I know. It's very different from dreaming, so vivid. Were you tempted to stay there?"

"Yes. When I sensed the buzzing I had to force myself to respond to it."

"And you arrived in Chicago then?"

"No, I've only been here a few weeks. I arrived in a place called New York City. It's a huge city, Jenna, jammed with people. Chicago's almost as bad. I figured I must have been in the void for a fairly long time, maybe even a year."

"How do you figure that?" I asked.

"Because Zephkar had already gotten a good start before I got here, even though she left Allo only a few jetur before us."

"You're right," I said.

"I was stranded on the roof of a skyscraper. That's why it took me so long to enter. Great place to land, huh? My first host was an architect, a male human. Do you know about the two se—"

"Lucky for you he came up there," I interrupted. I wanted to keep Cass away from the subject of our anatomical differences. I hadn't said anything to Amy about that yet and I didn't want to get into it now.

"I never did find out why he did," Cass said. "I was in a daze at first, Jenna, trying to believe yet not believe that this bizarre nightmare was real — that I was beginning my new life in a disembodied mind on a planet that no one had ever even heard of."

"Nightmare is right," I said. "I felt the same."

"I kept wondering if you and Billy might be nearby. I'd look at different Earthlings and wonder if they were your hosts. Did you land in San Francisco?"

"A place close to it," I said. "In a field. I'll tell you all about it, Cass, but you go on. So you entered the architect . . ."

"Yes. I mini-rode for a long time before I got the courage to switch. When I finally did try maxi-riding, it was terrible. I felt dizzy and disoriented. How unnatural, I remember thinking. How absurdly grotesque — parasitically merging with a total stranger, an alien being yet. Sensing the creature's every itch and twinge. I hated it. But at least the Earth people didn't look too weird. That helped. You know, Jenna, even though Wozar had told us they looked like us, I was worried. I was afraid they'd look alien and strange."

"Yeah, that would have made it even harder."

"I was very relieved. Of course there are differences."

"How long did you stay with the architect?" I said quickly.

"Two days. From him I shifted to a female friend of his, an interior decorator. I had several other hosts after that and then this attorney named Jeffrey Worthingham. It was through him that I met the woman I ended up permanating. Jeffrey was the prosecutor at her trial. He was the first human I boosted. I liked boosting a lot better than riding."

"Right," I said. "It's more like being a real person."

"Exactly. I rarely boosted Jeffrey when he was awake though. A couple of times I did."

"Did it freak him out?"

"He thought he was having blackouts, *fuzz outs,* he called them. He worried that he might have a brain tumor. I didn't like doing it to him but I had to check the newspaper ads. I knew if you or Billy had made it, the *New York Times* would definitely be one of the papers you'd use."

"How frustrating it must have been for you, Cass, finding nothing in the paper from either of us."

"I was afraid I'd always be alone. That might have been why I started obsessing about permanating. The need to have my own body, my own identity, became overwhelming. Remaining a disembodied mind definitely was not for me. I knew that from the start."

"I'm still adjusting to being one," I said, "still not fully believing any of this is real."

"You don't sound stressed out, though."

"I am, but to tell the truth, I'm also fascinated by it, being able to jump around to different hosts and . . ."

"I guess you're more adventuresome than I am."

"I don't know," I said. "Maybe. Or maybe I'm still in the daze phase. So what happened then, Cass? How did you come to permanate?"

"That came later. I remained a DM for almost two months. I kept putting ads in all the papers, the ten largest cities as we agreed — New York, Los Angeles, Chicago, Houston, Philadelphia, Detroit, San Diego, Dallas, San Antonio, Phoenix, and Baltimore. I looked up the information and I memorized it. I used the charge cards of my different hosts to pay for the ads."

"That was smart."

"Deviously so," Cass said. "I'm becoming like an Earthling — oops, sorry, Amy."

Tell her it's OK.

"I know many of you Earthlings are honest," Cass added.

I'm not offended, Amy said.

"Amy's not offended," I told Cass. *You doing OK?* I asked Amy.

I'm doing great, she said.

"During my stay with Jeffrey, I learned a lot about Earth," Cass said. "Some of it wasn't so pleasant."

"To say the least."

To say the least, Amy agreed.

"For example," Cass continued, "they have so many laws. And so many lawbreakers. Jeffrey's job was to get as many lawbreakers imprisoned as he could. They don't have Self-Awareness Programs or Re-evaluation Centers for the people found guilty of crimes. They lock them up in prisons. Earthlings are such aggressive, violent creatures, Jenna."

"I guess Zephkar chose the right planet," I said.

"Maybe so. She's in Chicago, you know. That's why I came here. She's telling the Earthlings she was sent by their deity. We sure have our work cut out for us. But I don't want to talk about Zephkar right now. Tell me how it's been for you so far. Who were your different hosts and what's been happening? Then I'll tell you more about me."

Cass suggested we hang up and she call me back so Amy wouldn't be stuck with the phone charges. While I was waiting for the phone to ring, I checked with Amy again. She gave me the go-ahead on continuing the conversation.

I told Cass about my experiences since entering Bert in that field outside of Walnut Creek. I censored many of my reactions since Amy was listening, but I made a point of mentioning that I found lesbians to be the most tolerable of the Earthlings so far. Cass had met some lesbians, too, and agreed wholeheartedly.

"I suppose you've discovered that Earthlings eat the flesh of lower animals," Cass mentioned at one point.

"Shh-hh," I said, "Amy eats it."

Let her say what she wants, Jenna, Amy interjected. *I don't mind, really.*

"Once I discovered that's what they were eating, I always switched to mini-riding whenever my hosts ate. Their mealtimes made me feel sick anyway."

"I suppose Earthlings would have trouble with some of the things about us," I said. I said it mostly for Amy's sake. "So what else happened with you? You entered that attorney, Jeffrey, and then what?"

"It's a long story."

"I want to hear it. Is the phone bill going to create a problem for you?"

If it is, I can take care of it, Amy offered.

"Not at all," Cass said. "I'm wealthy, Jenna. I mean, extremely wealthy. The person I permanated was rich. She was also a mutant, an ogre, a truly malignant creature. I hesitate to mention her name since Amy might have heard of her."

"I think it's OK," I said. "I'm asking Amy to trust me; I think we better do the same with her."

"All right," Cass said. "Her name was Veronica Bloom. She murdered a man."

I have heard of her, Amy said. *I read about the trial. She was acquitted.*

"Amy says she was acquitted."

"Mistakenly," Cass said. "She was guilty. The woman was absolutely ruthless, Jenna. No sense of morality whatsoever. She did whatever served her own purposes with no regard for how it affected anybody else. That's how she lived her life."

"Then I guess you made a good choice," I said.

"That's what I keep telling myself. She truly was worse than the worst exiles. Entirely lacking in empathy and compassion. She felt completely justified for having killed the man — Rodney Cartwright was his name; he was her business competitor — because he was apparently trying to edge her out of the cosmetic industry. Murdering Rodney wasn't Veronica's only crime by far, but it was the only one the legal people had any evidence about."

"She sounds abhorrent."

"A vile mutant," Cass said. "I shifted into her during the trial, and mind-tickled. She committed the murder, all right. I was tempted to boost her and confess. Maybe I should have. Anyway, after the trial, she and her lover, a male named Samson, flew to some sunny island for a celebration vacation, and I went with them.

"The more I got to know Veronica Bloom, the more I'd think about taking over her body and bringing an end to her evil mind. I knew I wasn't going to remain a DM for long and I doubted I'd find a better candidate to permanate than this one. It took me a long time to actually do it, though. It wasn't the wish to be immortal that stopped me, Jenna. I don't know about you, but I couldn't cope with the idea of an eternity of borrowed bodies with no identity of my own. What kept me from doing it sooner was the idea of destroying another being's existence, even someone as despicable as Veronica Bloom. So I kept postponing it, giving her chances to redeem herself and save her life."

"But obviously, she blew it," I said. "How did you try to salvage her?"

"I started with messages like, *It was wrong of me to kill him* and *I must confess.*

"As if you were her conscience," I said.

"She freaked, but I kept at it. *I've been vile and rotten,* I said, *but it's not too late. I can make amends.* She was at the beach while I was doing this part. She ran and got her boyfriend and told him they were going back to New York. In her suite while she was packing her things, I started again. *There's no running away,* I said, *I must face myself.* She was near panic by then. She turned the radio on so loud the walls were shaking."

"Trying to drown you out."

"But of course she couldn't. On the plane back to New York, I did some more, then more yet when we got her to her condominium. She made an appointment with a psychiatrist. *My life of evil must end,* I said in the taxi on the way to the doctor.

" 'Stress of the trial,' the psychiatrist said after listening to Veronica's story. He told her she was having auditory hallucinations because of the pressure she'd been under. Then he asked if she was aware of any conscious feelings of guilt? Veronica snapped at him for that, said it was ridiculous.

"The psychiatrist gave her a prescription. *Pills cannot take away the truth,* I said. It had reached the point where she'd slap her hands over her ears whenever I'd contact her. *I must make amends for the harm I've done. No more hurting people,* I said. *No more evil.* The pills put her to sleep but the moment she began to regain consciousness, I'd start again. *I must stop using people. I must change the way I am.* I was relentless, Jenna."

"Hoping to pressure her into changing," I said.

"But maybe also hoping it wouldn't work."

"So you could feel justified . . ."

"Yes, in wiping her mind completely out of existence. If she'd showed any signs of changing, I probably wouldn't have done it."

"I guess it's impossible to implant a conscience into someone," I said.

"She never had one warm or caring thought the entire time I was with her. She brought pain to everyone she had contact with. I knew I was going to do it — permanate, but I was scared, Jenna, really scared."

I could imagine what it must have been like for Cass, knowing she was about to take someone's life. "I'm sure you were," I said.

"I mind-tickled her to get information about her finances. I practiced writing her signature. I learned as many details about her as I could. And then there was no reason to postpone it any longer. It was a sunny afternoon. She was alone in her condo. First, I boost-blocked, sending her mind to the void. She'd have a pleasant exit at least. Then I went and stood in the center of her living room and looked out the window at Central Park. I closed my eyes. I took in deep, deep breaths."

I could hear Cass's breathing in the phone.

"I started the chant."

She meant the Wraunkian chant that Wozar had taught us. Sometimes I dreamed the strange words.

"*Maynek. Waloo,*" Cass intoned. "*Soneyhora, maynek. Maynek. Waloo. Soneyhora, maynek.* I said the sounds over and over, until finally I began to feel the vibrations. They got stronger. Then I began to shake. I was down on the floor. I might have been convulsing. I lost consciousness."

There was a long pause. Finally Cass spoke again. "When I woke up, I was alone."

Cass was silent. I didn't know what to say. Finally I said, "If anyone deserved to go it was Veronica Bloom. You know that, Cass."

"Yes. I just . . . I don't know. No matter how I justify it, it was still killing."

"True, but —"

"And I despised her, Jenna. What I did was partly a crime of passion."

"Let it go, Cass," I said.

"I'm trying to. After I did it . . . afterwards for several days, I just . . . I was immobilized. I told people I was sick with the flu, and I just stayed in the condo. I went over it and over it. I suppose it will never be completely resolved for me, but I was able to get myself moving. I got rid of all Veronica's old friends — acquaintances, I should say, including Sampson. You'll love how I did it."

Life had come back into her voice. "Tell me," I said.

"I got religion. I started going to this Pentecostal church in New York. It's a sect of the main religion here — Christianity."

"The one Zephkar's infiltrating."

"Yes," Cass replied. "I went to one of the churches and pretended to become a convert. The religion is quite primitive, Jenna. They believe in a God who's supposed to have created everything that exists. I suppose that would include Allo. Centuries ago He sent his son, Jesus Christ, to prepare the people for the Kingdom of God. Something like that. I don't really understand it very well, but I got baptized, became an official member."

Cass had several reasons for doing this, she told me: Being a Christian convert provided a believable explanation for Veronica Bloom's sudden personality change, and for her breaking off from Veronica's acquaintances. Also, she thought, it might help her get to Zephkar.

"I took Jesus into my heart," Cass said. "That's how they refer to it. Jesus is supposed to be their savior; I'll explain more about that later. So after becoming a *born-again* Christian, I took care of some financial matters and then I moved to Chicago. As I mentioned, I have a lot of money. *We* do, I should say. What's mine is yours, Jenna . . . and Billy's, of course. I sold Veronica's business before I came here. That was a little over a month ago, early June. I've been following Zephkar's career ever since."

Through James Lane, Cass had learned, Zephkar would make various predictions that would then *miraculously* come true. More and more people were being convinced that Zephkar was sent by their God. There was also speculation that Zephkar might try to become president of the United States.

"This is where you need to be," Cass said, "in Chicago. If you want to help stop her, that is."

"Of course I do," I said. "That's what we're on Earth for."

"Or we could just let the Earthlings cope with her as best they can."

"To tell the truth, that had crossed my mind," I said. "It's not *our* planet. It's not our responsibility. But it is our planet now."

"Yes, and we're the only ones that know what trouble it's in."

"It's up to us."

"That's how I look at it. So what do you think, Jenna? Can you get here?"

"One way or another, I will," I assured her. "I'll talk it over with Amy. If she's not willing, I'll find some other way. I'll get there as soon as I can, Cass."

Before we hung up, Cass told me she was going to send some money, a check made out to Amy Klein. After agreeing to talk again the next night we said goodbye.

"Do you want your body back?" I asked Amy.

That would be nice.

I switched to maxi-riding. Amy gave a big sigh. *How are you doing?* I asked.

"I don't know if I could ever adjust to being boosted," she said. "It's the strangest feeling. But you adjusted, didn't you? I mean whenever you're maxi-riding, it's as if I'm boosting you, isn't it?"

Exactly. Yes, I am used to it, more or less. It no longer feels so strange, I said. *It's just another way of being.*

"I can understand Cass wanting her own body, though. I hope she gets over her guilt. I agree with you, Jenna, if anyone deserved to go, that scumbag did. Maybe we can find a psychopath for you to permanate too."

I'm not looking, I said.

"It really is amazing what you DM's can do. I haven't stopped being amazed since you first said hello to me and told me you were a French farmer. What a trip!"

So you don't need a break from me? You don't want me to shift to someone else and amaze her?

"Don't you dare leave me." She laughed. "You light up my life, Jenna Hurilam from the planet Allo."

I chuckled. *I like your spirit, Earthling.*

"And I like you, Spirit. I like Cass, too, even though she's a mere mortal now."

You and she are the only friends I have on Earth, I said. *Besides Billy, wherever she is.*

"We'll find her."

I hoped desperately that Amy was right. *So, what about Chicago?* I said. *Want to go?*

"I thought you might ask. What would you do if you were me?" she said.

I'd do it, I said. *But, of course, you have to decide for yourself. I can't predict what will happen, Amy, but if you stick with me I guarantee you it won't be dull.*

Amy laughed. "Agatha thinks I'm too adventurous, mainly because I go scrambling on my motorcycle sometimes. God, wait until I tell her about this. How long will you stay in Chicago?"

Depends on how long it takes us to stop Zephkar. You heard what Cass said. Using James Lane's body,

Zephkar apparently intends to become president of your country.

"That's scary," Amy said. "She probably boosts James Lane all the time, don't you think? Probably never lets him control his own body."

Probably, I said.

"Zephkar would never permanate, though, I bet. She'd lose her powers. In a way I'm surprised that Cass did. She gave up a lot."

To gain what she needed, I said.

"But you don't feel the way she did? Needing to have your own body, your own identity?"

I feel it, I said, *but not strongly enough to permanate.*

"Maybe because you haven't been a DM very long yet."

Maybe. You know, Amy, if I were you and had a friend who happened to be a disembodied mind, and if I were thinking about sticking with her, going to Chicago with her and such, then I'd want some rules.

"What do you mean?"

Well, if I were you, I wouldn't want some DM dipping into my thoughts and feelings whenever she damn pleased. I'd want some privacy.

"Yeah, what about that?"

And I'd want it understood that there's to be no boosting without my permission.

"We already agreed to that."

Those are the rules I'd want — no permanating, of course; no boosting or dipping without permission; and I'd also insist that the DM let me know whenever she's in me.

"You're in me all the time."

I don't have to be, I said. *You know I can shift to anyone you get within six feet of. And I can cruise the void too, whenever I want.*

"All right," she said. "I'll agree to the rules. Are you dipping now?"

No.

"Would you agree never to dip me?"

If that's what you want.

"I'd rather tell you myself what I want you to know about me, or let you figure it out the ordinary way. I think dipping gives you an unfair advantage."

All right. No dipping.

Amy nodded. "I figured you'd agree. I feel like I'm really getting to know you, Jenna. Like how you think and what your values are, what your personality's like. I have a fantasy of what you looked like. Were you tall?"

Not as tall as Agatha.

"Well, what *did* you look like?"

Like an Earthling, I said. *No antenna sticking out of my head. No pointed ears or scaly skin.*

"I know, but specifically. What color was your hair? Were you thin, heavy, or what? Were you pretty? What were your eyes like?"

I should have brought a picture.

"Tell me."

I was a little bit taller than you, I said. *My skin was darker than yours. The three races of Allo blended together centuries ago. Most of us are brown-skinned. None of us is as light as you. I was about two shades darker. My hair was straight and very dark, almost black. I wore it medium-long, about to my shoulders. My eyes were greenish-blue,* large, but not quite as large as yours. I was moderately pretty. My mouth was my best feature because my lips were shaped nicely and very full. Billy told me that.

"It's amazing that you come from a planet that's so far away and yet Alloys look so much like people on Earth. Aren't your bodies different from ours at all?"

For some reason, I still didn't want to spell out the anatomical differences to Amy. *Not really,* I said. *That's why Zephkar chose Earth. Because of the similarities. I guess there are thousands of inhabited planets. Maybe millions. The Wraunkians were great explorers. They've never been to Earth but they've sent probes. They know the basics about you and your cultures. You're rated sixteen on a one-hundred-point scale.*

"That doesn't sound too impressive," Amy said. "But I'm not surprised. We've made a mess of our planet."

From what I'd learned so far, I wasn't about to argue with her. *Well, you've got your good points, too,* I said.

"What rating did they give Allo?"

Sixty-two. They base it on a lot of factors, including technological sophistication. We weren't too high there and that pulled our rating down. Like Earth, we just recently entered the computer age.

"But you're more advanced than us in other ways."

We're less aggressive. Actually, that might be the main difference.

"And you don't eat meat."

That's right. When I was being hosted by your

friend, Pat Capp, we watched a TV show about animals hunting and killing other animals for food. Predation, I believe you call it. It made me sick and I had to shift to the void until it was over.

"You mean there are no predators and prey on Allo?"

That's right.

"Well, then how are the animal populations kept down? Isn't your planet overrun with creatures?"

No, I said. *The birth rate of animals here apparently far exceeds that on Allo. Fewer young are born on Allo, but they survive. The environment isn't hostile.*

"I'm getting the idea you're not overly impressed with our world," Amy said. "Are things really that much better on Allo?"

I still have a lot to learn about your world, Amy. Do you feel like I'm attacking you?

"Not really. I guess I feel a little ashamed."

You didn't create it, I said.

"I don't mean about the predation. I mean things that it's possible to do something about. Social things. I used to be an activist. Do you know what that means?"

That you were actively involved in trying to make changes for the better. Protesting injustices. Speaking out, marching, writing letters. Things like that, am I right?

"How'd you learn so much so fast?"

From your mind, for one. From Pat's. From reading. I boosted my other hosts at night while they slept. I raided their libraries.

"Do you boost me when I'm asleep?"

Hey, we've got our rules, remember. It's different

with you. You're the only one I contacted, the only one who knows I exist.

"Maybe you don't exist," Amy said. "Maybe I'm psychotic and this is all a delusion."

Delusion, huh? Mine or yours?

"Maybe there's really only one of us. Multiple personalities."

And who's Cass, a hallucination?

Amy's thoughts obviously had moved elsewhere. "What about my job, Jenna?" she said.

What? Oh, you mean if you go to Chicago. I don't know.

"I could take some vacation time. I do have some coming. You need me to go so you'll have a host, right?"

That's one reason, I said.

Amy was silent for awhile. "You know me inside and out, don't you? Because you've dipped me and mind-tickled. When you were telling me about the things DM's can do, you said something about . . . like mutual dipping, something like that, where you can dip your host's thoughts and she can dip yours."

That's right. Bilateral dip-boosting.

"Well, I'd like to try it."

Hm-mm, I said. *Is it because then you can know for sure? Whether you can trust me?* Amy didn't answer. I didn't dip. *All right,* I said. *In fact it's an excellent idea, Amy. I should have thought of it myself. When I switch, you ask me questions, any questions you want.*

"Wait, don't do it yet. You'll be in control of my body, right? And it'll be like when you boosted before only I'll be able to hear your thoughts, right? And know what you're feeling."

That's right. It won't seem that different from what you've already experienced.

"Except that I'll be able to read your thoughts and feelings. If I don't like it, you'll stop, OK?"

Absolutely.

Amy finally gave me the go-ahead and I switched to boosting, then to bilateral dip-boosting. She was a bit startled at first, being able to read my thoughts and feelings. We spent a couple of minutes getting her used to it, then she began asking questions, starting with the big one. *Have you been telling me the truth all along?*

Yes, I said. *I have.*

She was satisfied that my thoughts and feelings weren't contradicting my answer. *Am I in any danger?* she asked next.

Not from me, I said. *I have no intention of causing you any harm, ever.*

This is fantastic. You're hoping I believe you. You want me to stay with you because you think I'm . . . because you like me a lot. If I don't, you'll find somebody else, but you'd really like me to stay. I can hear the thoughts, Jenna. You're feeling very warmly toward me right now. Now you're thinking of Billy. You're feeling sad.

So are you, I said.

Yes, for you. You miss her so much. I can see the images. You're picturing the two of you together. I can barely see you, but I see Billy clearly. She's very attractive. Kind of thin and . . . oh, wait. Wait, Jenna, stop. I'm not feeling well. I feel dizzy. I've had enough. Get me out of here!

I switched to maxi-riding.

"Don't dip," she said. "Don't read my thoughts."

I won't, I responded. *I haven't forgotten our agreement.*

Amy paced the room. I couldn't figure out what had happened. It was the first time I'd bilaterally dip-boosted, but Wozar hadn't said anything about the host getting sick from it. *Do you want to lie down?* I asked.

"Maybe," Amy said, "and . . . I need to be alone for a while, Jenna. You could . . . would you mind going to the void?"

I didn't like the idea but I didn't feel right arguing. *OK,* I said. *In the john, though, all right? Then when you're ready for me again, come back there. I'll sense the buzzing and I'll re-enter.*

Amy went immediately to the bathroom. *See you later,* I said.

"I'll be back for you," Amy said.

I wish she hadn't said that. Until she did, I wasn't really worried about her leaving me stranded. Hoping for the best, I shifted into the void.

I had a wonderful time in the void, but the moment I sensed the buzzing, I re-entered and immediately contacted. *I'm here,* I said.

Amy walked through the hallway into the living room and sat on her easy chair. The dogs came and settled at her feet. From the clock atop the TV set, I saw that I'd been in the void for three hours.

"Go ahead," she said. "Tell me about it. I'm ready to hear."

Hear what? I asked.

"The truth. Billy has a penis. I saw it. But you

told me she was a woman. I thought you were lesbians. She also has breasts."

Ah, so that's it, I thought. I should have known. She'd dipped me when I was thinking of being with Billy. Of course. Though I hadn't realized my fantasies had been so explicit.

Amy's arms were folded across her chest. "Well?" she said.

Well, I echoed. *There's no such thing as women and men on Allo, Amy,* I began. *And no such thing as dykes or faggots or hets. There's only one type, one sex as you'd say here.*

"You're kidding!" She unfolded her arms.

Freaky, huh?

She shook her head back and forth disgustedly. "Grotesque."

That's the word I used, when I found out about you people.

"So everyone on Allo has breasts and a penis. That's what you're telling me?"

Yes.

"What else? What other differences?"

Does it really matter, Amy? Allo's awfully far away; so are our bodies, mine and Cass's and Billy's.

"I want to know."

All right, I said. *Another difference is that the penises are retractable. When we're not using them for having sex we keep them inside our bodies. There's an opening in the pubic bone called the penis port.*

Amy grimaced. "Go on."

We don't use our penises to urinate. That's done through a tiny opening just in front of the anus. Our anuses are located the same place yours are. We have no testes. We produce sperm in sacs within our bodies and, during sex, we eject them through the penis, in semen. Do you want to hear more?

"I might as well."

We have two clitorises, one where you have yours, and one inside the vagina, near the cervix. We have ovaries, just like you, all of us do. We can all be both seed parents and birth parents, fathers and mothers. We don't have facial hair or pubic hair.

"That's it?"

I think so. Those are the differences I know about. There could be others inside our bodies. It seems bizarre to you, I know. I guess that's why I didn't tell you sooner.

A deep frown formed on Amy's forehead. Then she said, "When I got that flash of Billy's body, it made me realize how different you really are. It made everything just sort of crash in on me. It's hard to describe. Grotesque. That's the word that keeps coming to my mind. Like, that's not how bodies are meant to be. Freakish."

Right. That's how I felt, especially about the non-retractable penises with those blobby balls under them. What an annoyance that must be.

"Right," Amy said, chuckling. "You see, I thought . . . I guess I thought you were just like . . . like us, you know, regular . . . normal." Suddenly she put her hands over her face, shaking her head. "I'm sorry, Jenna. That's ridiculous, isn't it? The way your body was, that's normal on Allo. I realize that. But . . . well, it takes some getting used to, that's all."

It certainly does, I said.

"It must have been quite a shock for you."

One of the first things I saw on Earth was urine coming out of a penis. I found it quite gross.

"I find that gross, too," Amy said.

I laughed. *I think you're adjusting. Just be careful when you read my mind from now on. I am an alien, you know.*

"Sometimes *I* feel like an alien on this planet," Amy said. "You know, I think partly I was upset because I thought you'd lied to me. That you led me to believe you were a lesbian so I'd go along with you. So I'd cooperate."

I just didn't want to overload you, I said.

"I realize that now." She was quiet a moment, pensive. "Two clitorises. Wow! It never crossed my mind that there might be a better arrangement of our sexual anatomy."

Oh? You think ours is better?

Amy shrugged. "I don't know. I'd have to try it. Penises have never been my favorite organs. I'll tell you one thing though, you Alloys found the perfect way to avoid sexism." She was chuckling.

I laughed with her.

"I think of you as a woman," she said. "You seem like a woman."

I'm an Alloy, I said. *But I think you're right. Most of us are less like Earthling men and more like Earthling women — women like you, at least, and Pat and Agatha.*

"Lesbians, you mean."

Yes, I guess. I don't know though, there might be some heterosexual women who are like you. Are there?

"A few." She got pensive again. Then she said,

"Hey, Jenna, is there any chance at all that I could ever get to go to Allo?"

Sorry, pal. If there were a way to get there, I'd be on the first flight, believe me.

Amy pouted. "You hate it here."

Do I have to respond to that?

Amy shook her head. "Couldn't the Wraunkians bring you back if they wanted to?"

Earth isn't on their itinerary. I guess they don't find you a very interesting planet. And they certainly don't think I and the other Alloys they sent here are worth retrieving.

"Are they bad guys? The Wraunkians?"

Semi, I said. *They're knowledge-gatherers, not conquerors, though. They don't attack the planets they explore. As far as I know they don't have wars like your people do. So, what's bad guys? Depends on your standards. They do some bad things, like capturing me and Billy, like sending us here. I wouldn't say they're a hundred points on an "ethically-evolved" scale.*

"What was it like having a penis?"

I laughed. *Give me a break, Amy. What's it like having a tongue? I mean, that's a weird question, you know?*

"Yeah, I guess so. How does it feel for you when you're maxi-riding me, or any woman? Do you miss the penis? Or when a man is your host? Does being flat-chested feel odd? You don't have to answer. Of course it does."

Of course it does.

"In some ways I envy you, and in some ways I don't at all."

In some ways, being a disembodied mind who can enter other beings and who can live forever is fantastically marvelous. In some ways, it's the pits.

"I think it's more fantastic than pitty."

Oh yeah? Would you change places with me if you could?

"Umm-m . . . no."

I rest my case. How far is Chicago from here?

Amy was putting on her running shoes. "A couple thousand miles. About four hours by plane. I'm going to go for a run, do you want to come along?"

Sure, I said. *I could use the exercise.* Amy laughed at that.

Before we left, she called Agatha and they made plans to meet at a restaurant for dinner. Both dogs came with us on the run. I was beginning to understand why humans kept them as pets. They were very enjoyable companions. I suspected, though, that if the dogs had a choice they would have preferred remaining wild. When we got to a big hilly park, Amy stopped and sat on a bench.

"When I meet Agatha tonight," she said, "I want to tell her everything. You have to help me, OK? I don't think she's going to take it calmly. So I'll prepare her and then I'll ask her if it's OK for you to boost. Go easy on her. Boost with blocking first, and when she gets used to that, switch to bilateral dip-boosting. Once she reads your thoughts, she'll know you're not an Earthling. Try not to think about naked Alloy bodies, though."

Despite some feelings of uneasiness about another Earthling knowing about me, I agreed to Amy's plan.

After the run, she took us on her motorcycle down to the Bay. She parked the bike, and then walked along the water while we talked. We each had a million questions to ask the other. I still had a great deal to learn about Earth, and Amy was insatiably curious about Allo. She told me about Earthian history, the political structures in the different countries, the tensions and battles between the sexes, classes, races, religions, and nations of her world.

The contrasts between her planet and mine were becoming more and more highlighted. I didn't want to brag, but it was obvious that the people of Allo had developed a much more liveable culture.

We have three continents, I told her, *and the people who evolved on each of them differed in minor ways from each other. I guess you'd say there were three races. But as soon as they began crossing the oceans and finding each other, the merging began. That was many thousands of years ago. The three groups intermixed. We have no pure races anymore and not that much variation in physical type. Skin and eye color, hair texture, size, and certain facial features vary, but there are no extremes.*

Amy laughed. "You don't have any sexism because you only have one sex. You don't have racism because you intermarried and ended up with only one race. I don't think Earth can learn much from Allo. You didn't have the same problems to deal with as we do."

That's true about sexism, I said, *but I suppose our three races could have attacked and tried to* conquer each other rather than welcoming each other. If that had happened, we could have ended up with racial antagonisms too.

"That's true," Amy said. "So why didn't that happen, I wonder?"

She was sitting on a wooden bench by the harbor. From the corner of her eye, I could see that the people on the next bench were staring at her. *Those people think you're talking to yourself,* I said.

Amy looked at them, a man with a bushy mustache, and a woman with long, wild hair. "I suppose I could just think what I want to say," she whispered. "But you'd have to dip then, wouldn't you?"

No, I said. *I can contact without dipping. That means you and I can communicate via our thoughts, but I will only have access to the words you're consciously sending me.*

"I see," she whispered. *Can you hear me now?*

Yes.

There was a pause. "Did you get that?" she said aloud.

What? No, I didn't receive anything.

"I was imagining myself on that sailboat out there, picturing how the wind would feel and the movement of the boat. You didn't see it?"

No.

"But you would have if you'd been dipping."

Yes.

That's neat.

Piece of cake, I said.

OK, so I'll just think what I want to say to you. We were talking about the three races on Allo, that they merged rather than staying separate. So why was that? Why didn't they fight instead of joining together?

To me that seems much more natural, I responded. *Isn't the better question, why are you folks so hostile and aggressive?*

Amy agreed it was. "Maybe it has to do with predation," she said. She was speaking out loud again. "Maybe because a lot of the animals on Earth had to kill to survive, and since humans evolved from them, we inherited that kind of aggressiveness. Yes, I bet that's it. It all started with meat-eating." She was excited and talking loudly. The couple on the next bench looked at her pityingly. "What could be more aggressive than that?" Amy continued. "Predation set the stage. Then, having two sexes was the next step. While the women were dealing with the children and gathering plants and cooking, the men were out hunting. Killing. They killed animals and they killed each other. They became warriors. We never got over it."

I thought it was an interesting theory.

Amy was shaking her head. *You mean there's never been a war on Allo at all, in all its history?*

I never heard of the idea until I got here, I said. *There's very little violence of any kind on Allo. The few people who do commit acts of violence enter Self-Awareness Programs or are sent for treatment at Re-evaluation Centers. If they won't change, they end up as exiles.*

"Like Zephkar. Was he a violent criminal?"

He? I said.

Oh right, she, I mean. Actually, though, I do think of Zephkar as male.

Because she seems more like Earthian males than

*females, I bet. I think you're right. Yes, he was
violent. He used a weapon similar to your pistols.
Rather than working and earning his own way, he
would force people to give him money by threatening
to hurt them, or he'd just go into their homes and
take what he wanted. He was aberrant in other ways
too. He found people who were weaker than he to be
his cohorts and his lovers. He dominated them.
Sometimes she even struck them with her fists. She
. . . he rather, is a real mutant. He did something
else too. I know it happens here a lot. He forcibly
had sex with other people.*

Amy sighed. "Yes, that certainly does happen
here. So Zephkar was a thief and a rapist. And so
they sent him into exile?"

*Yes, violent people who aren't responsive to the
programs we have are designated Incorrigibles, and
have to appear before the Highest Tribunal for their
trial. It happens about ten or twelve times every year.
I figured out that one of our years is about a year
and a half of your time, by the way. Which would
mean I'm thirty-three years old, Earth time. Anyway,
that's what happened to Zephkar. The Highest
Tribunal sent him to Smarklace. Before he went, he
received the mark of the exile — a two-inch wide
strip of hair is removed, starting at the center of the
forehead and going back over the whole head. They
do it surgically, removing the roots so the hair will
never grow back. The exiles also get a tattoo on their
left cheek, a diamond shape with the first letter of
our word "exile."*

"So everyone will know they're exiles. So they
can't go back and live among the regular people."

Yes. There's never more than a thousand of them

living at any one time on the whole planet. Once in a while an exile covers up the markings and sneaks back into society. The exiles are considered total social outcasts, dangerous mutants who no one is very likely to shelter or assist. If an exile who has sneaked back to society commits another violent crime, we resort to imprisonment. It's happened four times in my lifetime. As far as I know, Zephkar is the only exile who managed to leave the planet.

"Sending people into exile wouldn't work here," Amy said.

Maybe not, I responded. She was looking out over the water and I realized the sun was getting quite low. *What time are you supposed to meet Agatha?* I asked.

Amy looked at her watch. "Shit, we're late." She jumped up from the bench and ran to her bike. She tore up and down the hills, winding through traffic rather recklessly, I thought. We were thirty-five minutes late getting to the Full Moon Cafe. Agatha said she'd been worried. "I thought maybe you'd packed up and gone to France."

Amy smiled. "I don't know anyone in France," she said. "Agatha, after we eat, let's go to my place. I think that's where we should be when I tell you."

Agatha kept saying, "It can't be," even after I'd bilaterally boosted and she read my thoughts and had no choice but to believe. "How can a machine remove somebody's mind from their body?" She was trembling.

I was boosting Amy at that point. "I have no

idea," I said. "I guess you'd have to ask a Wraunkian about that."

Agatha rolled her beer can across her forehead. "So are you alive or not?" Her uneasiness seemed to be making her a little hostile.

"Yes and no," I said. "Depending on your definition. Cass certainly is."

"But she has a new body. Whose are you going to take?"

"Probably no one's," I said, although I wasn't sure that was true. "I don't think I'll ever permanate."

"How many people are on your planet?"

"Close to a billion."

"And it's the same size as Earth?"

"That's what Wozar told us."

"And you have one government, you say. A world government that governs all the people."

"That's right, and local councils."

"No wars, no violence, no rape, no prostitution, no drug abuse. Sounds like a fucking utopia."

"We have some problems," I said, "but nothing compared to yours. Allo's not a bad place to live."

My sadness must have shown because Agatha reached over and took my hand. "You're homesick, aren't you?" Her sudden tenderness and sensitivity moved me and tears came to my eyes. "Tell me more about your partner," she said gently.

I talked of how Billy and I had met, how our life on Allo had been — our friends and families, our work, Billy's and my relationship. I told her we'd been planning to make a baby soon.

"And then Wozar got you. You must hate the bastard."

"I hate it that I'll never see my home again." I felt tears coming, but pushed them away. "There are aspects of being a DM that are pretty fascinating though," I said.

The talk continued for several hours. Agatha ended up spending the night at Amy's, sleeping on the sofabed. She was still asleep the next morning when Amy left for work, me riding her.

I dipped and mind-tickled Amy's co-workers while Amy worked on a logo for a new fast food restaurant. In the late afternoon, I entered her boss, Greg Oswald, who had a private office next to the main work area. I'd been in him about ten minutes when he lay down on his sofa and fell asleep. That was a lucky break for me. I'd seen a *Newsweek* magazine on his desk and wished he'd read it. Now I could boost and read it myself.

I almost wish I hadn't. It was disheartening to read about the fighting and the killing taking place on Earth, and the poverty, the corruption and political oppression, the racism and sexism. Then I came to an article about James Lane. "The return to God's law is inevitable," he was quoted as saying.

I put the magazine aside and went back to the sofa to wait for Amy. We'd agreed that at quitting time she'd go around saying good night to each of her co-workers until she found me.

There was a knock on the office door. "Come in," I called.

Amy entered. "Mr. Oswald?"

"No, I'm Ms. Hurilam," I said. "Come closer, my dear." Amy moved into range and I shifted. *I'm here,* I said. Greg Oswald opened his eyes.

"Are you feeling all right, Mr. Oswald?" Amy

91

said. "I noticed you were still here and wondered . . ."

He rubbed his eyes. "What time is it?"

"A little after five. Everyone's gone. I'm on my way out now."

He rubbed his eyes, shaking his head, looking very puzzled. "That's the longest nap I ever took," he said. "What fantastic dreams I had."

The next day a check for two thousand dollars arrived from Cass. Amy used the occasion to tell me she'd made her decision. She would go to Chicago with me. I'd been fairly sure she would. I was surprised, though, when Agatha said she wanted to go also.

"I can't pass this up," she said. "And maybe I can help you stop Zephkar."

I told her we needed all the help we could get.

On the flight to Chicago, I shifted among the passengers, up and down the rows, dipping and mind-tickling them. Each new body I entered felt different from the one before. I wasn't surprised that there were differences, but I'd never suspected that the physical world actually looked and sounded different to different people. Amy, for example, saw colors more vividly than Agatha, while Agatha's hearing was more acute, especially for the higher pitched sounds. I felt comfortable in both their bodies, but more powerful in Agatha's.

Sometimes I wondered if there was still a *me*. I

supposed there was, that the essence of my identity resided in my mind, but not having a body to call my own had certainly left a major hole in my sense of self. There were times when I deeply felt the loss of my body. I guess I was in mourning. I was eager to find out more about how Cass was adjusting to having a new body of her own.

At the airport I spotted a woman in a Susan B. Anthony T-shirt. I was boosting Amy for the reunion. "Cass?" I said.

"Jenna?"

Cass had been an attractive person on Allo, but now she was absolutely beautiful. We wrapped our arms around each other and held on tightly.

I continued boosting Amy for part of the ride to Cass's apartment, then shifted into Agatha so Amy could meet Cass. Cass had changed her name legally, she told us, from Veronica Bloom to the English version of her own, Cass Apeldum.

"I like the sounds," Amy said, "like apple dumplin'."

Chicago was dirty, crowded, unbearably hot, and there wasn't a hill in sight. After fifteen minutes of the place, I was already homesick for San Francisco. Cass lived in a section called Lincoln Park which wasn't too bad. Her apartment was beautifully decorated; it resembled homes on Allo. There were four bedrooms, so Agatha and Amy each got her own. I didn't need one.

We sat in the spacious living room to talk. I was unilateral-boosting Agatha. Cass brought us cold drinks.

"Have you been getting to know any of the people here?" Amy asked.

"A few. I met some women at a place called the Mountain Moving Coffeehouse. They're lesbians, like you and Agatha. I tell them I came to Chicago because I wasn't making it as a singer in New York. How do you like my new voice?" Cass asked me.

"I like it," I said. "I liked your old one too."

"This one is great for singing. I actually do want to sing. It was a secret ambition of mine on Allo but I didn't have the voice for it. I've been thinking of asking some musicians if they want to form a group."

"I play drums," Amy said. "I'm part of a band at home."

Cass looked delighted. "Two of the women I met are musicians — a guitarist and a bass player. We should get together while you're here and see how we sound."

"I'd love to," Amy said, "but my drums are two thousand miles away."

"We'll buy some," Cass said. She smiled at both of us, showing flawless teeth.

As Cass and Amy talked some more about the possibility of making music together, I listened quietly, noticing how comfortable they seemed with each other. When Cass went to get us a snack, Amy went with her.

I think Amy's attracted to Cass, I said to Agatha.

It sure seems that way. We could hear the two of them laughing in the kitchen. *It's the first time in a long time she's shown any romantic interest in anyone.*

As we nibbled our cookies and scones, Amy had eyes only for Cass. "Jenna said you used to work in a bicycle factory," she said. "Was it office work or did you make the bikes?"

"Both," Cass said. "On Allo we rotate responsibilities at our jobs. That's not true here, is it? I'd think it would get pretty boring doing the same thing day after day."

"It sure does," Amy concurred. "I guess some people like the security of it though. Did you like the work?"

"Most of the time. I came up with a new idea for the gear mechanism, a way to improve the speed of shifting the gears. We were just beginning to produce the new version when the Wraunkians came for me." She bit her lip.

We were all quiet for a while. "Did you leave someone behind?" Amy finally asked. "Someone special?"

"My soul partner died several years ago," Cass said sadly. "Of course, I left others behind — both of my parents, a lot of good friends." Her eyes were teary. "I guess it could have been worse. At least we still exist, eh, Jenna?"

I nodded. Neither of us had mentioned Billy yet.

Cass seemed to know what I was thinking. "We'll hear from Billy," she said. She seemed so certain. I wished I could be.

The conversation shifted to Zephkar. "I've been trying to come up with some plan to stop him," Cass said. She, too, had begun referring to Zephkar as a *he.*

"If we could only get him to permanate," Amy said. "Otherwise, he's indestructible, right?"

"That's right," I said, "but he'd never permanate. The only way to get rid of him is trick him into going somewhere where we can leave him stranded. In the middle of the desert, maybe, or a jungle, or an ocean."

"Where no people are," Amy said. "Where there'd be no body for him to enter. If we could get him into a plane flying over the sea, then push him out, that would do it. Or a rocket ship to outer space."

"Something like that," I said.

"He was on the local news last night," Cass said. "James Lane, that is. He said the Mayor of Chicago will soon see the truth. At the end of the show, the anchorman said, 'Remember, ladies and gentlemen, Zephkar speaks.' And the guy wasn't smiling."

"All Zephkar has to do is boost enough of the right people and he'll own this world," I said.

"No doubt about it," Cass responded, "this planet's in big trouble."

So what are we going to do? Agatha wanted to know.

I wished I had an answer for her.

Later that afternoon we went for a walk along Lake Michigan which was just a couple of blocks from Cass's apartment. I was in Agatha, maxi-riding. Occasionally, she'd invite me to boost so I could join in the conversation.

Neither Amy nor Agatha had yet experienced the

void. Every time the topic came up, they had some reason to postpone giving it a try. I decided that very soon I wanted to broach the subject again.

That evening we turned on the ten o'clock news to see if there was anything more about Zephkar or the so-called *New Direction*. We got more than we expected. The Mayor of Chicago announced his full support for the Theocratic Party. James Lane was at his side.

James was an attractive-looking human who appeared to be in his early forties, Earth years. He spoke very self-confidently. "God is the only sovereign," he said, "the source of all law. We've lost sight of this in America, but now we're beginning to do something about it. We will do what must be done. Purge our country of its rampant idolatrous practices. Drug abuse, crime, the spread of AIDS — all of these social ills are evidence of God's displeasure with our civil government. That government must be changed. The first step is the Theocratic Party, as the mayor has said. Many other leaders have begun to see the light."

He gave a list of people — presidents of universities, religious leaders, some congresspeople, corporation executives. "Now we must enlist the support of you, the public," he said, looking directly into the camera. He told the audience they should watch his show, *Zephkar Speaking*, so they would learn how they could help.

A reporter asked if he hoped to turn the government of the United States into a theocracy.

"Exactly," James answered. "That's what the Lord wants."

"Well, sir, not everyone agrees with that," the reporter said. "Edmund Bernard, for example, recently —"

"The Lord is not pleased with devil-driven secular humanists such as he," James interrupted. "Some misdirected civil libertarians are redeemable," he continued, "but not Mr. Edmund Bernard. Bernard has a hardened heart, a closed mind which can't be moved by truth. Yet deep inside, Bernard does know the truth. It is from that depth that he will find the wisdom and courage to eliminate himself as an opposer of New Direction. This is what God declares. And so it shall be with others whose hearts are hardened."

"Shit," Amy murmured, "I bet he's going to kill Bernard."

We all sat in stunned silence. Finally Cass spoke. "We have to come up with something soon."

"If we could get him into a cave," Amy said. "And then seal off the entrance with dynamite."

Everyone was silent again.

I wanted to speak, but had agreed to stay in maxi-riding. A little later, when Cass took Amy to the back porch to show her her bicycle, I said to Agatha, *I'm feeling frustrated. I need to work out a better arrangement.*

"What do you mean?"

I need to boost-block. Maybe I should find somebody like Cass did —

"And permanate her?"

I'm not talking about permanating. Just boost-blocking. I want the sense of having a body of my own, and some privacy at the same time. Maybe I could find somebody who no one would miss and use her body for a while. I have to do something. With you and Amy, I feel like an intruder sometimes, sometimes like a beggar.

"I'm sorry, Jenna. I imagine it must be rough for you."

Cass and Amy returned. "What's wrong with Jenna?" Amy asked.

"She wants to snatch a body," Agatha replied. "I think she wishes she'd never made any agreements with us."

That's not true, I said angrily.

"She wants to find some stranger and use her body for a while, boost-blocking."

"Why don't one of you volunteer to try the void?" Cass suggested. "It's a beautiful experience."

Amy and Agatha looked at each other.

"Why are you so scared of it?" Cass asked.

Amy looked uncomfortable. "I keep thinking I could get stuck there," she said.

"That wouldn't happen," Cass assured her. "You can agree on a time limit and when the time's up, Jenna will bring you back. And I guarantee you'll enjoy the void. It's like drifting in a kind of semi-dream state. Very, very pleasant. There's no sense of time at all. An hour can seem like a minute, or vice versa. You get beautiful images. But you can focus, too, if you want, and think about things. Everything gets real clear. I had some great insights while I was in the void. Your life seems to fall into perspective. There's a sense of wisdom that comes and a feeling of tremendous well-being."

"Sounds like you miss it," Amy said. "Why don't you let Jenna send you to the void."

"I've been planning to at some point," Cass said.

"It'd be OK with me, Jenna, if you want to do it now for a while."

I'd been hoping Cass would volunteer. Of course I jumped at the chance. She was sitting about eight feet from Agatha. *Tell her she has to come a little closer,* I said.

Before Agatha could say anything, Cass came and stood in front of us. I shifted, then contacted her. *Hi, there, pal. Nice body, feels good.*

Thanks. I like it myself, Cass said. *Go ahead, Jenna.* She checked her watch. *Take as long as you want, just make sure I'm back in time for breakfast tomorrow.*

Have a nice trip, I said. It took me half a minute to switch to boosting. Then I went immediately into blocking. "Ah," I said. "I feel almost like my own person."

"But she'll come back from time to time, won't she?" Amy asked. "The spontaneous switch to unilateral boosting?"

"That only happens every couple of days at most," I said. "And if it does, as soon as Cass's thoughts and feelings start coming into my mind, I can just concentrate and block her out again. At least that's what Wozar told us. It's never happened to me yet."

"You haven't done much boost-blocking yet."

"True," I said. I stretched various muscles, and blinked my eyes, getting used to the body.

"Jenna," Agatha said, "when a DM is in the void, are you suspended in the air, or do you fall to the ground, or what?"

"When we propel out of a host and into the void,

we attach to an oxygen molecule," I said. "Then we slowly float toward some object, usually the floor or the ground. When we get within a foot or so of some inanimate object — a stone, a floor, cloth, anything that isn't living — we get pulled to it and attach to it. Then we just stay there."

"Unless a human comes within six feet of you," Amy said.

"Then we can choose to enter the human," I said.

"You said *propel*," Agatha said. "What do you mean? When you leave a body do you shoot out into the air?"

"Yes. We shoot out six feet, then adhere to some oxygen, then to an inanimate object."

"You can't go through things, like walls."

"No."

"So a DM could be locked in a box," Agatha said.

"Yes," I answered.

"So if we could get James Lane to go into a big box or a chamber of some kind, and lock him in, then Zephkar would be imprisoned."

I nodded. "We just have to figure out how to get him into a box, then how to transport the box where we can dump it and it'll never be found."

"When you're boost-blocking," Amy said, "the host's mind isn't left behind if you go somewhere with her body, is it?"

"Her mind always remains with her body," I said.

"So there's no chance of Cass getting stranded."

"None at all. Wherever I go, she goes. Her mind never leaves her own body."

"Well, then, how about this?" Amy said. "Why don't you enter James Lane, you know, when

101

Zephkar is in him. Boost him and climb into a coffin. Then propel yourself out of him and we'll slam the door and he'll be trapped."

I shook my head. "Only one DM can be in a host at a time," I said. "If Zephkar's in James, I wouldn't be able to enter."

"Oh," Amy said, looking disappointed.

"What about drugging James Lane into unconsciousness when Zephkar's in him?" Agatha said. "Would that put Zephkar to sleep too?"

"Nope. The drug would not affect Zephkar. He could still use James' body." It was Agatha's turn to look disappointed. "It's going to be quite a challenge to strand him," I said.

"I wonder what Cass is experiencing right now," Amy said.

"We'll ask her when I bring her back. Are you worried about her?"

"Not really. I guess you two know what you're doing."

"More or less," I responded, smiling.

"If I were a DM," Amy said pensively, "I think I'd end up permanating. I'd find someone who's physically healthy but who's suicidal."

"Or how about a newborn?" Agatha offered.

"I've considered that," I said. "But can you imagine if at age two months or so, I slipped and said, 'Hey, Mom, the water's boiling over'?" Agatha laughed. "Of course, I suppose I could tell the mother who I am, from the beginning. Maybe find someone who's planning to have an abortion, and get her to give birth to me. I've played with the idea, but I've rejected it."

"Couldn't deal with the diapers, huh?" Agatha said.

"Not only that. It's the whole idea of being trapped for years in a child's body." I shook my head. "No thanks."

"But how about what I said," Amy interjected, "permanating someone who wants to die? Someone who's deeply depressed and feels totally hopeless but who's afraid to take her own life."

"Maybe," I said.

"You'd be doing her a favor," Amy persisted.

I looked at her. "Would you kill such a person? Even if you knew you could get away with it?"

"I don't know. If she'd had years and years of therapy and had tried different anti-depressant medications and nothing helped, and if she begged me to do it, then . . . I don't know . . . maybe I would."

"How about someone with a terminal brain tumor," Agatha suggested.

"Then I'd have the tumor."

"I was afraid of that." Agatha shook her head. "Well there's that other alternative you mentioned, borrowing bodies from strangers. You could find someone on the street, a junkie maybe, and boost-block her. Send her for a wonderful sojourn in the void for a year or so, then bring her back and find someone else."

I took a sip of Cass's 7-Up. "Something like that might be my best option," I said. "I don't think I'd want to use drug addicts though. From what I've heard, I doubt that they're physically healthy."

"True," Amy said. "Who could you use then? It

should probably be someone whose life wouldn't be too terribly disrupted if she skipped a year of it." She frowned pensively. "How about a prisoner?" She immediately shook her head. "No, that wouldn't work. First you'd have to escape from prison. And the cops would be looking for you."

"How about some macho creep male?" Agatha suggested.

"Oh, no, not a male," Amy moaned. "You wouldn't want to be a male, would you, Jenna?"

I laughed. "I've only known there were such things as males and females for less than a month," I said. I caught Amy's frown. "Though from the start I preferred females. The first male I entered beat up his female lover. And from what I learned since, males tend to be more violent and insensitive than females."

"True," Amy said, "but there are plenty of nasty females around. Cass found one. You could do what she did. Go to the criminal court building and sit in on some trials and when somebody gets off who shouldn't have, then you can enter and boost-block for a while."

"Right," Agatha said, "only not a junkie, and not anyone with a boyfriend."

"She shouldn't have kids," Amy said.

"Or a job," Agatha added. "Or family or friends who would get worried if she disappeared."

I smiled. "Eventually, I'll find a good solution," I said. "In the meantime, boost-blocking Cass like this is helping a lot. I think I'm going to go take a long, private bath now."

* * * * *

I didn't retrieve Cass from the void until the following morning. I wanted the full night to myself. It was after nine when I awoke and switched to unilateral boosting. "Welcome back," I said.

What year is it? Cass murmured hazily.

You had a good time, I assume.

Fantastic. How did you do?

I found your new body quite satisfactory, I said with mock formality. *Want it back?*

She said that she did and I switched to maxi-riding. Cass stretched and yawned. "Oh, Jenna, I'm so glad you're here. Damn, I've been lonely. And Amy and Agatha seem like terrific humans. You chose well."

You find Amy especially terrific if I'm not mistaken.

She's delightful. Cass looked at her watch. "Oh good," she said aloud, "the paper's here by now. Let's go take a look."

Agatha and Amy were in the kitchen stuffing themselves on grainy toast and strawberry jam. Cass got the paper and quickly turned to the correct page. I read as eagerly as she. We found the ad from Cass but there was nothing from Billy.

"Not yet," Cass said optimistically.

I felt like crying.

"Is that you, Cass?" Amy asked.

"Yes, I had a wonderful time."

"You really did?" Amy looked at her skeptically. "Did you get impatient to come back?"

"Not at all." Cass got a bowl out of the refrigerator and put it in the microwave oven. "I assume today is Wednesday. As far as I could tell,

105

though, I was only gone for a few minutes . . . or maybe ten years," she said, laughing.

"Did you sleep?" Agatha asked.

"I don't know. But I sure feel refreshed. I feel great. How about you two? Were your beds all right?"

Their conversation continued and I continued thinking about Billy. Breakfasts with Billy had always been particularly fun times. She was ridiculously cheerful in the morning and I could never resist her high spirits. It's all gone, I thought gloomily, our world, Billy. *Is there an evening paper too?* I asked Cass.

Yes. I always look at both of them.

Agatha was reading something in the newspaper. "What was the name of that guy?" she asked, "the one James Lane said would eliminate himself."

"Edmund Bernard," Amy said.

"Look at this."

Amy leaned over and read the headline aloud. "Political Activist, Educator, Takes His Own Life: Edmund Bernard Dead at Age Forty-Seven."

"Do you think Zephkar killed him?" Amy asked Cass.

"That'd be my guess," Cass said, reading the article over Agatha's shoulder.

"How do you think he did it?"

"It says Bernard used a pistol," Cass said. "So Zephkar probably entered the poor guy, boosted, and shot him."

Agatha grimaced. "Wouldn't Zephkar feel the pain of the bullet?"

"I doubt it," Cass said. "He could shift to the

void the instant he pulled the trigger. Then he probably just waited in the void until someone found the body — the guy's daughter, it says here. Zephkar probably entered her, then maybe a cop, then who knows who else until he finally boosted someone and went back to wherever he'd left James Lane."

Amy whistled through her teeth. "A DM can get away with anything," she said. She took a couple of deep breaths. "Jenna, are you there?"

Tell her "Boo"! I said.

Cass laughed. "She's here, Amy. You want to talk to her?"

"Good morning, Jenna," Amy said.

"Jenna," Agatha announced. "I'm ready to try the void. Sometime today. Later in the afternoon maybe, after I've seen a little of Chicago."

I'm ready when she is. Cass told her what I'd said.

Cass continued reading about Bernard. Before he died, he'd had a long talk with his daughter, the article said. He told her he realized his whole life had been misdirected. He felt he'd betrayed God, and that he'd done so much harm that there was no way to make amends. His daughter thought he was having a breakdown. She wanted to call a doctor but he refused. Then at eleven-fifteen p.m., the daughter heard the shot.

"Zephkar could get rid of anyone he wants that way," Amy said. "You know, I was thinking . . . since a mind has electrical energy in it, do you think there's any chance of killing Zephkar by electrocution?"

Cass shook her head. "A DM is absolutely indestructible. It will go on forever no matter what happens to it."

"Forever and ever," Amy intoned.

Later that morning, our group went for a walk up Clark Street to look at the shops and people. I was maxi-riding Agatha. The city was hot and congested, but I was finding it rather interesting. The contrasts with Allo were more striking here than in San Francisco. The people seemed more somber and there was less emphasis on beauty than there was in San Francisco. *On Allo everyone is an artist of some kind,* I told Agatha. *We don't work long hours like you do here. Everyone has a lot of free time and we all pursue some form of art — painting, dance, music, writing, sculpture, pottery, acting — something. That part of life is as vital to us as making money seems to be here.*

Agatha tried to get me to tell her more, but I lapsed into silence. I was feeling very homesick again.

We were inside a little shop full of decorative vases and ceramic masks and wind chimes when a woman came up to Cass. "Hey, they let just about anybody in here," the woman said.

"Hello, Cindy," Cass said warmly.

Cindy was dressed in loose-fitting pants and tight tank top. She had very black hair, smooth tan skin, and facial features that reminded me of Billy.

Cass introduced her to Amy and Agatha, then Cass and Cindy chatted for a while. Before they parted they said they'd see each other at the coffeehouse Saturday night. Cindy seemed very excited to be talking to Cass. She also seemed quite flirtatious.

After lunch, Agatha told me I could boost-block her. Amy shook Agatha's hand and told her, "Bon voyage." For the full thirty seconds it took me to switch to boost-blocking, Amy stared at Agatha with her mouth open. I found that amusing.

I kept Agatha in the void for half an hour. As soon as I brought her back, I shifted to Cass. Agatha was glowing.

"Wow!" she said. She sighed deeply. "Oh my God!" She shook her head, then held it between her palms and shook it some more. She sighed again. She looked at her watch. "Is it still Wednesday?"

"Yes," Amy said. "You were gone half an hour."

"Wow!"

"So tell me how it was," Amy prodded.

"The colors," Agatha said. "I have never seen such beautiful, magnificent colors. Bright and then muted, then flashes like fireworks. And the shapes. Beautiful works of art. They were drifting by me and I was drifting among them. And there was music. It surrounded me and then it felt like I *was* the music. Then the music got soft and I saw . . . I pictured Jacquie. She was . . . it was so vivid. And everything became so clear. The confusion disappeared. I understood . . . it was the first time I really understood what had gone wrong between Jacquie and me. I feel so free." She looked at Cass. "Is Jenna in you?"

"Yes," Cass said.

"Thanks, Jenna," Agatha said, looking at Cass.

109

She laughed. "That was worth about six months of psychotherapy." She laughed some more. "You didn't tell us it was that good."

Amy couldn't sit still. She was wiggling on the edge of her chair.

"I want to do it again," Agatha said. "Later this evening maybe."

Tell her it could be habit-forming, I told Cass.

Cass was about to do so when Amy said, "I'd like to try."

"Now?" Cass asked.

Amy nodded eagerly. "If you want to, Jenna."

I wanted to. I made the shift, then contacted her. *How long a trip do you want?*

Check back with me in half an hour, she said, *and if it's as great as you guys say, then you can send me back for more.*

I switched to boost-blocking. It felt pleasant to be back in Amy. Her body was lean with well-toned muscles. I got the urge to go for a run so I went to Amy's room and put on her running shoes and shorts. I told Cass and Agatha I'd be back in an hour or so. I was looking forward to some time alone.

I jogged over to Fullerton Avenue, then east to the lake where there was a running path along the shore. It was close to six o'clock and not nearly as hot as it had been earlier in the day. Lots of Earthlings were out running and biking and walking their dogs and children and sitting along the beaches. I ran south, passing different beach areas, and finally stopping on a bench to take a break. It was at that point that I shifted to unilateral boosting and contacted Amy.

Is this real? she asked. *Are we at the beach? Or is this a fantasy?*

It's real, I said.

Yeah, I can tell now. I was with my mother, Jenna. It was so vivid. We were sitting at her kitchen table. It seemed like she was actually alive and it was really happening. I told her how much I loved her and talked about all the different ways that she and I are so much alike and how much I value that now. I used to hate it sometimes, when I was a teenager, but I told her that changed. I want to go back, Jenna, if it's OK with you. She and I were just starting to pack up a picnic lunch. We're going to Golden Gate Park.

I'll bring you back in by dinner time.

Whenever, Amy said.

Enjoy the picnic. I switched to boost-blocking.

I stayed on the bench a while longer, watching people, fascinated by the two sexes and by the contrasts among skin colors. The differences stood out much more at the beach. I wondered if Alloys would be plagued by sexism if we had two sexes, or by racism if our different races hadn't blended over the generations.

Thinking of Allo reminded me of another sharp contrast. Before going to the restaurant for lunch today, we'd driven through a neighborhood where many of the buildings had boarded up windows. There was hardly any grass or trees and the cars parked on the trash-littered streets were old and banged up, some with cardboard windows, some burnt out hulls. The people looked nearly as bad as the property. Unkempt and downtrodden. There was no such thing as a slum on Allo. There was no poverty. The very idea was obscene; we had plenty for everyone so, of course, no one went without. Amy had told me that Earth had plenty for everyone, but that corrupt, oppressive governments and greedy corporations kept things from being equitably distributed among the Earth's inhabitants. Many people starved to death on this planet, she told me, even though there's more than enough food for everyone.

I thought about what Zephkar was doing on Earth — using his abilities as a DM to meet his mutant needs for power over others. I wondered if there was any chance he could be persuaded to boost influential people into making Earth a better place rather than a worse one. I laughed to myself. Dreamer, I thought. I got to my feet then and started running west through Lincoln Park. I wanted to find a drugstore and buy a newspaper.

Over the next few days, Amy and Agatha competed for opportunities to go to the void. Cass wanted her turns too, so we did it by rotation. I ended up spending almost as much time having a body to myself as not. I was enjoying it, and so were they. Amy started calling me *Jenag* when I was boosting Agatha and *JenCass* when I was boosting Cass. The others picked it up too. Part of me didn't like it, but it did seem to make sense, so I didn't protest.

On Friday night, Cass and Amy had a date.

Agatha was encouraging their budding romance and I was happy for both of them too. I spent most of Friday evening reading while Agatha drifted happily. She did take a break to phone a couple of friends in San Francisco.

Agatha was a writer. She sold articles to magazines and made just about enough money to survive. She also taught writing courses from time to time. I'd read some of her work and I thought it was quite good. There was a feminist slant to most of what she wrote. I had learned a fair amount about feminism since meeting Amy and Agatha, realizing why it had come to be, how much it was needed, and how far Earthian culture had to go towards any semblance of full equity for females.

That was discouraging enough, but before going to bed that night, Agatha and I watched *Zephkar Speaking* on TV. I really felt disheartened as James Lane spoke of the help he needed from the faithful in order to turn the laws of the United States back to God's laws. "We must capture the nation for Christ," he said. "Till Heaven and Earth shall pass, one jot or one tittle shall in no wise pass from the law." Then he enticed his listeners with the promise of rewards to come. "You, the believers, will inherit the wealth of the non-believers. The wicked shall lay up and heap up treasures for the righteous."

Listening to him made me sick to my stomach. Agatha said she felt the same.

He's got to be stopped, she said.

I couldn't have agreed more.

* * * * *

The next night, we went to Mountain Moving Coffeehouse to hear some music and meet some more lesbians. I was riding Agatha. Cass's friend, Cindy, came up to us the moment we'd paid our "donations" and entered the church basement. She gave Cass a big hug. Amy didn't look too pleased about that.

Seeing Cindy reminded me of Billy again — the dark dancing eyes, the narrow nose and high cheekbones. And the way she talked to Cass also reminded me of Billy, when Billy was in one of her seductive moods.

". . . and do a little dancing. I bet you dance real well," Cindy was saying.

I tuned her out. It was too painful to listen. She had a playful, charming way about her and it was impossible for me to observe her without thinking of my lost love. I thought about my trip to the library earlier in the day. I'd checked the ads in the newspapers of the ten largest cities. Nothing from Billy. Since finding out that seventy percent of the Earth's surface was covered with water, I'd begun to worry that Billy might have landed in an ocean somewhere, or maybe in the middle of Lake Michigan. I was tempted to go into the void to get away from these thoughts, but then the entertainment started again at the coffeehouse and I got distracted.

A young woman with short hair sang love songs about women and angry songs about oppression. She had the audience sing along on some of the choruses. I can't say I wasn't moved.

During the break Agatha talked with someone named Gracie Hernandez whom Cass had introduced her to. She was the guitar player Cass had told us about, a tall, sensuous woman with green eyes and a slight overbite. Gracie's biggest dream was to move to San Francisco, she told Agatha. I could understand why. "But I'm stuck here for now," she said. "Besides, I hear it's real expensive to live there."

I could get her thousands of dollars with no trouble at all, I thought. Millions, if I wanted. I started to get off on the fantasy, but Agatha interrupted. *Do you want to boost?* she asked.

No, I said. *It'd be too confusing. People would think you have two different personalities.*

I don't care, Agatha said. *Tell them I'm multi-faceted.*

I told her I was doing fine just riding. She started talking to an older, denim-dressed woman and seemed to forget about me. I went back to thinking of ways I could get money, all the money I'd ever want. I came up with a dozen ways, but my favorite was boost-blocking big time crooks and taking it from them.

After the coffeehouse, we went to a bar called *Venice Dance.* Agatha insisted that I boost. I asked if she wanted to ride or float in the void, and I wasn't surprised by her answer. As soon as we settled ourselves around a tiny table, I switched to boost-blocking. Cass's friend, Cindy, was with us, and so was Gracie, the guitarist. Amy asked Cass to dance and I alternated between watching them do the strange dancing of this planet and watching Cindy watch them, with a bit of a pout on her face.

"Are those two involved?" she asked me. "Cass and her skinny friend?"

"Involved?" I said. "You mean —"

"Are they lovers?"

"Not that I know of," I said.

"Have you known Cass long?" She had to lean close to my ear because, for some reason, they played the music so loud we could barely hear each other.

"No," I said. "We only met recently. She's new here, you know."

"Yeah, from New York. It's weird though, she doesn't seem to know that much about New York. Have you ever noticed that sometimes when you talk about the commonest things with her, like TV shows from last year or movies or something, she acts like she never heard of them."

"No, I hadn't noticed," I said.

"She's so beautiful," Cindy said. "Look at the way she moves. God, I'm going to cream my jeans." She got up and left.

The dance had ended and Amy and Cass were heading back to the table. Cindy cut Cass off and apparently asked her to dance because the two of them went back to the dance floor.

Amy sat on the stool Cindy had been using. "That Cindy's kind of pushy, don't you think, Agatha?"

"Agatha's in dreamland," I whispered.

"Oh." Amy smiled. "Me, too, in a way. I think I'm falling in love." She said it so only I could hear. "Shhh-h," she added

Gracie leaned toward us. "So, Amy, I hear you're a drummer. Cass was saying something about our getting together for a jam."

"Right," Amy said. "I'd have to get some drums though."

"No problem," Gracie said. "I have a set you can use. They're in my brother's garage. We can use the garage to jam sometime if you want."

"That'd be great. I'm not sure how long I'm going to be in Chicago, though. I'm just here on vacation."

"Right, I hear you're from that quaint hilly place that's going to end up under the Pacific one of these days."

"Don't believe those nasty rumors," Amy said.

"This planet is unstable," I said. "I wonder if the Earth is trying to tell us something."

"Don't go mystical on us, Jenag," Amy said.

"Jenag? Is that your nickname?" Gracie said to me.

I chuckled and glanced at Amy. "One of them," I said.

"Private joke, eh?" Gracie said, shrugging. "Anyway, maybe you should consider moving here. After all, San Francisco not only has earthquakes but it's full of queers, too."

"Eat your heart out," Amy responded, grinning.

"I left it in San Francisco." Gracie chuckled. "Seriously, I hope we get together for a jam before you go."

We sat silently for a while watching the dancers. Then Amy leaned toward Gracie. "What do you think of that James Lane?" she asked.

Gracie looked repulsed. "He's a maniac. He ought to be locked up."

"Exiled," I said.

"You know there's a countermovement getting started," Gracie continued. "A lot of different groups are joining together — Common Cause Caucus, People United for Church-State Separation, the Civil

Liberties Coalition, and a bunch of other groups. Have you heard about it?"

"No," Amy said, "but I'm glad it's happening."

"There's something uncanny about James Lane, how he gets people to convert, convinces them that an angel lives inside of him. My theory is that he uses hypnosis. My lover thinks he slips people some kind of drug."

"I think he enters their minds and takes over," I said.

"Yeah, exactly," Gracie said. "The latest thing I heard is that he's going to try to change the Constitution."

Cass and Cindy came back to the table.

Amy was quiet for a moment, sipping her drink. "What do you think of ESP?" she suddenly asked Cindy.

"ESP? I don't think of it at all. Why do you ask?"

"I believe in it," Gracie said.

"How about extraterrestrials?" Amy asked.

Gracie laughed. "Sure, I believe in them too. Goddesses from the Coral Dawn."

Amy looked at me. "I've been playing with an idea."

"I can guess what it is," I responded.

"Cindy doesn't seem interested," she said into my ear, "but Gracie does. Let's invite her over."

"OK with me," I said, "but we don't want to rush it. We better get to know her a little better before we tell her anything. We don't want her to flip out, and we sure as hell don't want her to blab about it. The last thing we need is Zephkar to suspect there are other DM's around."

"I know. We'll be cool."

Although she was talking to me, Amy's eyes were on Cass. The next thing I knew, the two of them went off to the dance floor again. I guess Amy and Cindy were going to take turns, I thought. This could get complicated.

Agatha spent more and more time in the void. Since that meant I had her body for long stretches at a time, I decided to buy some possessions of my own, clothes and toiletries and such. My taste was somewhat different from Agatha's: she liked cotton and denim, which I did also, but I sometimes preferred silk and rayon, and I liked to wear jewelry, which Agatha didn't. I bought a silver and turquoise slip-on bracelet and a silver ring with an opal. After that, when I was controlling Agatha's body, I always wore the jewelry; when she was in control, she took the bracelet and ring off and put them in a pocket.

I began acquiring some books, mostly non-fiction, since I was still in the midst of my crash course on Earth and Earthlings, although Agatha did convince me to get a couple of lesbian novels. I bought a boom box, too, and a small television set. Cass had insisted that I was not to hesitate to buy whatever I wanted, reminding me again of how rich we were.

I took over Cass's third bedroom. When I was in my room among my own possessions, boost-blocking, I felt almost like a real person. Agatha's body had become completely comfortable to me. I even found it hard to remember how my own body had felt. I experienced two spontaneous shifts to unilateral boosting. The first time, I was in my bedroom reading when suddenly my mind was filled with images and sounds that clearly came from within, but which were not my own. I was aware of Agatha skiing down a mountainside, glistening white snow everywhere. I switched back to boost-blocking. The second time the spontaneous shift happened, I was in the middle of a conversation with Cass. Again I quickly shifted to boost-blocking. The spontaneous shifts were a bit annoying, mainly because they were such concrete reminders that this was not my body.

Our group still hadn't come up with any realistic ideas about how to stop Zephkar. So far the most we had agreed on was that Cass should get to know James Lane and that I would ride her when she was with him so Zephkar couldn't enter her and read her thoughts. Through Cass's relationship with James, we would come up with a way to get rid of Zephkar. Just how, we hadn't yet figured out.

We kept up on the new developments in Zephkar's quest for power. James Lane had a coterie of high-powered followers, we learned, called the Divine Disciples of Zephkar. They were busy recruiting others into New Direction. We also learned that petitions calling for a constitutional convention were being circulated in all the states. In yesterday's newspaper, I read that New Direction owned a huge complex in the Virgin Islands. I wondered if Zephkar planned to have his headquarters there. There was also more speculation about James Lane running for president.

Cass, Agatha, Amy, and I certainly were not the only ones worried about Zephkar. Groups in opposition to New Direction were mobilizing. Unfortunately, these organizations would barely begin their work when the leaders would suddenly have a change of heart, declaring themselves newly born and then moving into the New Direction fold with others Zephkar had obviously dipped and contacted and boosted.

There were several women's organizations in Chicago developing strategies to fight New Direction. Cass's friend, Cindy Keating — the one who reminded me of Billy — was involved with one of them, and so was Gracie Hernandez, the guitar player. I wondered when Zephkar would get to them.

We were becoming friends with Gracie. Cass and Amy had gone to a jam session in Gracie's brother's garage, and she had come over to the apartment a few times. I was growing quite fond of her. She was a physical therapist at a local hospital, and her lover, Doris, was a physician at the same hospital. Doris was a quiet woman who seemed solid and level-headed. I liked her, too.

I wasn't sure how I felt about Cindy Keating. She had come to the apartment once and the atmosphere had been a little tense. A couple of days after that, Cindy and Cass had met for dinner and Cass hadn't gotten home until very late. I think I wanted Cindy to stay away and let things develop between Cass and Amy. That's clearly what Amy wanted. I could certainly understand the Earthling's attractions to Cass. If my heart wasn't already taken, I probably would have pursued her too.

*   *   *   *   *

On a Sunday evening a few weeks after we'd arrived in Chicago, Cass, Amy and Agatha were at the dining room table finishing a meal. I was riding Agatha.

Amy had already called her boss, Greg Oswald, and gotten an extension of her vacation. Now she was thinking of asking for another. "I'll borrow on next year's vacation," she said.

"Why don't you just quit," Agatha said. "You know you hate that job anyway."

"I agree," Cass said. "I told you money is no problem. It seems unnecessary to hold on to a job you don't like."

Amy shook her head. "I couldn't let you support me, Cass. That's out of the question."

"I'll support you for the next six months," Cass persisted, "or until we stop Zephkar and you find a new job, whichever comes first."

"Is she serious?" Amy said to Agatha.

"Of course I am," Cass said. "We need you to help us save the world. You can't go back to San Francisco yet."

"What if we can't stop him?" Amy said. "You seem so sure that we'll find a way."

"We will," Cass said. "It may take a while, though. We need you to stay here and help."

Amy thought a moment. "All right," she said, "I'll quit my job and stay here if you give serious consideration to moving to San Francisco when Zephkar is safely stranded. Deal?"

Cass laughed. "Deal," she said.

Soon after that, Cass and Amy announced that

they were flying to San Francisco for a few days so Amy could get her dogs and pick up some things from her apartment.

They left on Monday. That night, Agatha and I did some plotting. We figured that if Cass was really going to meet and befriend Zephjame — we'd started referring to Zephkar-boosting-James as *Zephjame* — then we'd have to know more about his life, how he spent his time, his habits, et cetera. We decided I would do some spying and lay the groundwork for the next steps.

We knew James owned a house on Astor Street, not too far from Cass's apartment. The next afternoon Agatha and I decided to take a hike. It was a pleasant walk despite the heat and I stayed with maxi-riding most of the time. When we were within a half block of the house, I shifted to a passerby, going immediately to boost-blocking. Agatha gave me the clipboard and letter we'd prepared, then she left to go wait for me at a nearby coffee shop.

My host was a prosperous-looking, elderly woman whose body felt very weary and used. I walked up to the eight-foot black iron gate at the entrance to the walkway of James Lane's house. I rang the bell.

A male voice came through the intercom. "Who is it, please?"

"I have a letter for Mr. Lane," I said in my host's thin voice.

The front door opened and a man looked me over. I held out the envelope. He came down to the gate. "Who are you?" he wanted to know. He was a pale, soft-looking man in his mid-thirties.

"Delivery lady," I replied. "Sign here, please." I slipped my clipboard through the grates of the gate, and as he was signing, I shifted into him.

"What's this?" the old woman said. She stared at the clipboard in her hand. "Who are you?"

The man handed her a dollar bill. She stared at it, her mouth hanging open. The man went back into the house, through an oak-floored hallway to the first room on the right, a parlor furnished with soft, pale-hued sofas and chairs, oak tables, and brass lamps. The decor was obviously the work of an Alloy, I thought. Even Alloy mutants had taste.

On a contour divan facing a huge window with a view of a lush garden, James Lane sat watching TV with the Bible in his lap. I figured Zephkar was probably boosting him. To make sure, when my host got near enough to James, I tried to shift. I was unable to.

"Letter for you, James," my host said, placing the envelope on the table next to the divan.

Zephjame examined the envelope. *James Lane* was written on it in calligraphy. Zephjame opened it. *Dear Mr. Lane, I feel drawn to you,* Agatha had written in beautiful script. *We must meet. Godspeed your work.* It was signed, *Veronica Bloom.*

"An old lady brought the letter," my host said. "Said she was a delivery lady. Is it from anyone we know?"

"Just another follower," Zephjame said. "Veronica Bloom."

"You don't say?" I felt his eyebrows lift. "So it's true. I'd heard she'd converted."

"You know her?" Zephjame said.

"You don't? She's the Bloom of Bloom

124

Enterprises. Cosmetics. She was charged with murdering a business rival. Got acquitted. A real beauty. Gorgeous. But I hear she's toned down her sex life considerably, says she's celibate. She sold her cosmetic business and left New York. Claimed she'd found a higher purpose than wealth and feminine beauty, that she was going in a 'new direction.' I laughed at the time." The man looked into Zephjame's eyes. "That was before you and I had met, before I knew there truly was a New Direction."

"Gorgeous, eh? How old?"

"Oh, early thirties, I'd say. She used to be a bitch on wheels."

Zephjame nodded. He put the letter back into the envelope and tossed it onto the table. Then he stretched and yawned. "Cancel today's meeting, Freddie, we're going on the boat. Call a few people — Alexandra and Louise. Try David Stokes, Gary, and maybe five or six others, including a couple of female Testees. Have them meet us at the yacht club in an hour."

I had told Agatha to wait until four and if I wasn't at the coffee shop by then, to leave. It looked like I wouldn't be there. It looked like I was going sailing.

The boat was a huge, beautiful yacht with deep cushioned chairs, a bar, and rows of rooms below. Zephjame's cabin had a double bed and its own bath with shower.

Apparently all the people Freddie had called

dropped whatever they were doing for the chance of going for a boat ride with James Lane. Ten of them showed up, six women and four men.

Freddie was the only one who didn't seem completely awed by Zephjame, though he, too, treated him with great respect. I hoped Zephkar wouldn't try to enter Freddie. If he did I'd have to quickly shift into somebody else to make room for him, or else propel to the void.

By mind-tickling Freddie, I learned that he was a true believer. He saw James Lane as chosen by God to be the vessel for Zephkar and to bring on the New Direction. He believed Zephkar to be an angel. Of course he'd believe this, I thought. It isn't hard for DM's to get our hosts to believe anything we want.

I had intended to stay with Freddie the whole time, but I got curious about the other passengers. They were also believers. Apparently Zephkar had entered most of them at one point or another and won their hearts and minds. The only exception was a woman named Francine who was one of the *Testees*. She didn't seem to fit among this crowd of sycophants. When I dipped and mind-tickled her, I learned she was as calm and self-assured inside as on the surface. She was curious and a bit skeptical about James Lane. She wanted to find out if there really was anything supernatural going on or if New Direction was just a scam.

The other Testee was a young blonde woman named Maribelle. When I dipped her I learned that she was thrilled to be here with James Lane, but nervous about how the day would go. She hoped she'd make it to St. Thomas. I had no idea what that meant, and couldn't figure it out from her thoughts. I could have pursued it by mind-tickling her but I was involved in listening to the conversation.

New Direction, Incorporated, I learned, owned the yacht we were on. They used it for business meetings as well as for pleasure. Today obviously was for pleasure. The corporation also owned a great deal of other property.

Zephjame had chosen a good day for a boat ride — the sky was clear, the air cooled by a light breeze, the water just mildly choppy even as we went farther and farther out into the lake.

The group sat around on the deck for the first hour or so, chatting about the America's Cup, baseball, scuba diving, the stock market, and a number of other topics I found mildly interesting. Then Zephjame suggested they play poker. Six of them moved to the round table, five men and Francine. I was in Freddie. I definitely was finding Francine the most intriguing and attractive of the women present. She was brown-skinned, probably in her late twenties, with very large, deep brown eyes and large breasts. She seemed to enjoy the card game, but not as much as Zephjame did. We had similar games on Allo and I suspected it had not taken Zephkar long to learn the Earthian version. I wondered if Zephkar was shifting around among the players and looking at their hands.

"I love the water," Zephjame said at one point, "and hate the desert."

I could understand why. I'm sure his years in exile in the Molarat Desert had been extremely unpleasant. He talked about his love of scuba diving.

"I'd like to try it some day," Gary said.

"You'll get a chance in a couple of months," Zephjame said, "at St. Thomas."

"You'll get a chance for more than swimming with the fishes there," David said, chuckling.

At last Zephjame called the poker game to an end. He had won six hundred dollars. Snacks and more drinks were served.

"Have you ever heard of a Veronica Bloom?" Zephjame asked the group.

Great, I thought. He's curious about her.

Most of the people said they had and for the next fifteen minutes the conversation centered around her. Gary thought her conversion was a miracle and assumed Zephkar had visited her.

"She was a ruthless viper," he said, "and then she changed — made restitution to enemies she had wronged, got out of the cosmetic business. She started going to churches rather than nightclubs and casinos. A real one-eighty."

Zephjame listened with obvious interest. When it seemed no one had any new information to offer, he turned to Maribelle and suggested they go below. Maribelle was sitting next to Freddie and I shifted into her as she was rising to follow Zephjame. When they went into Zephjame's cabin, I wondered if it had been such a good idea to come along.

They were sitting opposite each other on easy chairs. "Zephkar will speak with you now," Zephjame said.

"I'm ready," Maribelle answered breathlessly.

"You know how it works," Zephjame continued. "The angel Zephkar is going to leave me and enter you. He will speak with you and check the purity of your heart."

"Yes," she said. "I hope I do okay." Pure or not, her heart was pounding.

"I'm sure you'll do fine, my dear. Just relax."

"Yes, Mr. Lane."

"Call me James," he said.

I considered shifting to the void, but decided this was as good a time as any to find out how Zephkar would react when he was unable to enter someone. I stayed where I was. I watched Zephjame concentrate, trying to enter.

"Odd," he said.

"What is it?" Maribelle asked timidly. "Is something wrong?"

Zephjame scrutinized her. "Do you use any drugs?" he asked.

"Oh, no, Mr. Lane. I mean, just aspirin now and then, and . . . the pill."

"Do you have any . . . oh, any unusual abilities or experiences? Do you consider yourself psychic, for example?'

"No, I can't say that I do."

"Have you ever had any brain surgery?"

"No."

"Experienced hallucinations?"

Maribelle shook her head.

"Hmm . . . He continued scrutinizing her. "Tell me about yourself, Maribelle, everything you can think of."

"Are you . . . is Zephkar . . ."

"Zephkar is still in me," Zephjame said. "There's some blockage. I'm not sure what to make of it.

Maybe if you tell me about your life, I'll figure it out."

"All right, but . . . well, I'm not sure how to begin . . . what you want."

"You were born in Chicago?"

"No," Maribelle said. "In North Platte, Nebraska."

"Go on."

She spoke about her childhood, the trips to her grandparents' farm, her dislike of piano lessons, her mother's periods of depression. Then she mentioned her twin sister, Lucille.

"Ah, you're a twin. Identical?"

Zephkar obviously had done his homework. I'd only learned about twins a few days ago. There was no such thing among people on Allo.

"Yes," Maribelle said. "Lucille got married four years ago. They live in Omaha. Her husband's an engineer. They have a two-year-old boy and —"

"Do you and she see much of each other?"

"Not as much as we'd like. We're still very close though. We get together two or three times a year."

"Do the two of you ever . . . do you communicate with each other in other than the ordinary ways?"

Maribelle wrinkled her brow. "Well, sort of," she said, "I mean, there are times when we each seem to know just what the other's thinking. Is that what you mean?"

"Could be," Zephjame said. "Identical twins," he murmured, rubbing his chin contemplatively. "Interesting." He stood and unbuttoned his shirt. "It seems Zephkar prefers not to enter you," he said, "perhaps because you are one of two. It makes no difference, though. We'll proceed nonetheless."

Maribelle took off her thin, short-sleeved top. By

then, James had his shoes off. I had no wish even to mini-ride during this, but I was afraid to shift to the void on the off-chance of being left in the cabin. Maribelle removed her delicate little bra and then her skirt.

I tuned out as much as I could of the sounds and sights, trying to think of other things. I thought about the first woman I had ever entered, Eva, and wondered how she was doing. I remembered the first night with her and Bert, and their lovemaking. I thought of Cass and Amy and wondered if Cass would like San Francisco as much as I did. By the time Zephjame and Maribelle were finally finished, I was very ready to be out of the cabin and shift back into Freddie. But Zephjame apparently had other plans. He pushed a button on the wall. A minute later there was a knock at the door.

"Send the other Testee," Zephjame called. He got out of bed and put on his pants.

I switched back to maxi-riding and dipped Maribelle. She had no more idea than I what James had in mind but she was feeling eager and ready for whatever was expected of her. She kept thinking about St. Thomas.

Francine arrived a few minutes later. She seemed only slightly nervous when Zephjame told her that Zephkar would commune with her. Zephjame was fully dressed then. As he had with Maribelle, he explained to Francine that the angel Zephkar would enter her. They were sitting opposite each other on the chairs. Maribelle stayed on the bed, watching the pair. Zephjame looked at Francine intensely. Suddenly her eyes widened.

"Yes, yes, I hear you," she said, looking into

131

space, clearly stunned and excited, ignoring James now, who sat silently on the chair next to the bed.

Maribelle watched with fascination.

"To be part of it," Francine said, "in whatever way I can . . . yes, I would like to help . . . quite amazing . . . I've never been a devout believer but now . . ." She stared straight ahead as she responded to whatever Zephkar was telling and asking her. "Yes, I've heard of it — the heavenly preview, a *taste of heaven*, they say . . . I would, very much . . . no, I trust you. I have no fear."

As the conversation between Francine and Zephkar continued, I took the opportunity to shift into James. I dipped, tuning into his present thoughts and feelings. He was the picture of serene joy. I mind-tickled him and learned that he was absolutely convinced that Zephkar was the Lord's emissary. James was deeply honored to be chosen as the vehicle for this omnipotent divine spirit, delighted to be allowed so much time in the heavenly preview. That referred to the void, I assumed. There wasn't a malevolent thought in the guy's head. You're a true lamb, James, I thought. That hadn't always been the case, though, I learned, via more mind-tickling.

My life over the last five years, I said, and James automatically began to associate. He'd been a conniving, self-serving lawyer, I learned, although never accused of anything illegal. He'd been quite contemptuous of other ethnic and racial groups and condescending toward women. Not great, I thought, but not grounds for murdering him. *Sacrificing,* I thought, that's a better word, but it didn't change the reality of what we were planning to do.

I shifted back to Maribelle, just in time as it turned out, because a moment later, James got up and left the room. Zephkar had shifted to him briefly, I surmised, and told him to go.

Francine looked at Maribelle with half-lidded eyes. Obviously Zephkar was now boosting. He pulled the sheet down to Maribelle's ankles, exposing the whole length of her naked body.

"I am Zephkar of God and I am going to ravish your perfect body," Zephfran said. He smiled lustfully and fluttered his fingers over Maribelle's breasts. Then, his lips slightly parted, Zephfran leaned over and kissed Maribelle deeply on the mouth.

I was shocked by my own reaction, and wondered if Maribelle felt as aroused as I.

"Ah, yes, this will be quite delightful," Zephfran said. He ran his fingers over Maribelle's jaw. "Go now and bathe yourself so you are pure and fresh for me."

Maribelle got up immediately and went to the shower. As the water poured over her body, I thought about Francine. I was finding her very attractive — sexually attractive. I pictured making love with her and I liked the picture. But she's in the void, I reminded myself. That is not Francine out there waiting for us. As soon as Maribelle had toweled herself dry and was returning to the bedroom, I switched to mini-riding, wishing there was some safe way to get completely out of there.

"Mm-mm," Zephfran said, stroking Maribelle's

shoulders. I could see but not feel the caress. "Very soft. Very lovely skin." He put a finger under Maribelle's chin and raised her head until their eyes met. "Do you enjoy making love with women?" he asked.

"I don't know," Maribelle said softly. "I've never done it."

"You need to be tested."

"Yes."

"For purity."

"Whatever is needed."

"Do you want to be with me?"

"Yes," Maribelle said, and she went to Zephfran's arms. I couldn't feel the embrace, but I couldn't' help imagining what it felt like.

Then they were lying side by side on the bed. Maribelle's eyes were closed so all I was aware of was the sound of their breathing. It grew more and more heavy. From time to time, Maribelle opened her eyes and I could see the glistening brownish skin of Francine's lovely face. Her bare shoulder. Her bare breast. Then the nipple. Maribelle must have taken it into her mouth. I can't explain exactly what happened next, or how it happened, but suddenly I could feel the nipple hardening beneath my lips as I sucked and pulled the supple tip into my mouth.

A moment later, I was gasping for air. Francine's fingers were inside me. Then suddenly — I don't have any memory of doing the switch — but suddenly I realized that I was not only feeling the sensations and having the internal reactions, but I was controlling the movements of Maribelle's body. I made the hand move downward to Francine's crotch. It was my hand. It was my mouth following my hand and my tongue dipping into the warm moistness of this beautiful Earthling, caressing her clitoris, sucking. Her thighs clasped my head. I continued sucking, aware that my own crotch was getting wetter and wetter. I kept licking and stroking her until finally she moaned in a growly, pleasure-soaked way as she rose to her shuddering climax.

There was a moment of inactivity, then Francine's fingers were inside me again, stroking my clitoris, her warm sweet mouth pressed deeply to mine, the tongue fluttering in my mouth. Rising. My back arching, my vagina contracting in great spasms, my fantastic peak, my first on Earth, my first ever with an Earthling, my first orgasm as a DM.

And my lover was Zephkar.

I felt sick.

I was shaking.

"What is it, dear?"

I switched out of boosting.

"Are you all right?" Zephfran asked.

Maribelle blinked her eyes rapidly. "My God . . . the colors, the music! It . . . it was breathtaking . . . heavenly."

"Ah, so you liked it."

An hour later, I was riding Gary as he left the yacht club and caught a cab. I shifted to the cabby as he was dropping Gary off, switched to boost-blocking, drove to a phone booth and called Agatha. Then I drove the cab back to where we'd left Gary and waited for Agatha to arrive.

She parked in front of us and came to the cab. "Jenna?" she said hesitantly.

"Hi, Agatha," I responded in my male voice. "Here I come."

The moment I shifted, the cab driver jerked his head and mumbled something about having dozed off. "Need a cab?" he asked Agatha.

"No thanks," she said.

I told Agatha I was exhausted, that I had learned a lot, but wasn't up to talking about it yet. *I wanted to drift awhile,* I said. When we got home, she went to her bedroom and sat on the bed. I shifted to the void and floated happily to the glorious music, far far away, to other lands and other times, for what might have been centuries.

First thing the next morning I asked Agatha to check the papers for word from Billy. As usual there was none. Over breakfast, I told Agatha about the boat trip, not mentioning the part about boosting Maribelle when Zephfran was making love with her. I still felt very weird about that, ashamed I guess. I told Agatha James Lane was completely duped by Zephkar, as expected. *He thinks Zephkar was sent by God to prepare the earth for the second coming,* I said. *He's ecstatic to be a part of it. Of course, he spends most of his time in the void. He thinks he was chosen by Zephkar because of his strength of character; I think it was because he's handsome and well-hung.*

Agatha laughed. "Also possibly because his law background makes him acceptable presidential material," she said. "That, and the fact that he's never been in politics, and that he has no wife to get in Zephkar's way. So is James Lane an evil psychopath like Veronica Bloom was?"

No, I said. *He's no gem, but he can't compare to Veronica.*

"Too bad. I was hoping he'd turn out to be a total slime. That would make sacrificing him a little easier."

Nothing's going to make it easy, I said.

"I know."

But we have to do it, I said. *There's simply no getting around the fact that someone has to die for Zephkar to be stopped.*

"And James Lane seems the most likely candidate."

It might be by drowning, I said. *Zephkar loves the water. Do you know where St. Thomas is?*

"One of the Virgin Islands," Agatha said. "South of Florida. Why?"

New Direction owns some property there. Zephjame invited Francine and Maribelle to go there with him in October. To be initiated.

"Hmm-m," Agatha said. "Maybe you and Cass should go, too. Go boating with Zephjame and when you get a chance, kill James somehow and then dump him and Zephkar overboard."

I didn't respond. I was thinking about Allo, about Billy and I taking a drive along the Turchiv River and marveling at the fall colors — oranges, yellows, deep reds, brilliant greens.

The phone rang. It was Gracie Hernandez calling to see if Agatha was free for dinner that night. Doris was working late again, she said. Agatha

137

accepted the invitation. When she hung up, she flipped a coin for the body and I won.

"Every time I lose, I win," Agatha said, chuckling. She truly was hooked on the void. I wondered if I should be concerned about that.

When it was time to get ready, I boost-blocked and slipped on the silver ring and bracelet. I also changed clothes, putting on black cotton pants and the turquoise-green blouse I'd gotten at Marshal Fields. Agatha's not a bad-looking woman, I thought, combing my hair at the mirror.

I met Gracie at a restaurant called *Baker's Square*. Our conversation moved rather quickly from small talk to a discussion of Gracie's relationship with Doris, which Gracie clearly needed to talk about. Their love for each other was solid, she said, but Doris worked long hours and was frequently preoccupied or exhausted when they were together. Gracie was frustrated. Doris was in the second year of a three year residency in anesthesiology, Gracie told me. "We haven't had a vacation together in over three years."

While I commiserated with her, I thought of the contrasts with Allo. People often became very involved in their work on Allo, especially those in the professions, and they were often quite dedicated, but they never became obsessed by it. The training for different professions could be rigorous, and yet the demands never left the trainees too busy to do anything else. I wondered why Earthlings did things so differently.

"I get so bored," Gracie was saying. "Maybe I should have an affair."

I looked askance at her.

"Or find a hobby," she said, ignoring my look, "something to put my excess energy into."

That gave me an idea. Actually, it had been Amy's idea originally. I'd tell Gracie about me. I'd tell her about Allo and Wozar and Zephkar. That would be a great distraction for her. Better than a hobby, and maybe as good as a love affair.

"Remember that first night we met, when we were at *Venice Dance* and Amy asked you if you believed in ESP?"

Gracie nodded.

"I've got an ESP story that will knock your socks off."

She chuckled. "OK, start knocking."

"Not here," I said. "Let's go to my place." My lemon pie arrived. "In the meantime," I said, digging into the pie — it was a huge slice — "tell me more about yourself. Are you scared of ghosts? Would you freak out if a spaceship landed in your back yard and the ET's invited you aboard?"

Gracie laughed. "I think you're in your Jenag personality tonight."

I smiled. "You're right," I said. "So you might as well call me Jenag. Tell me, Gracie, what would you do if the spacemen came?"

"Men?"

"Spacewomen."

"Do they want to hurt me?"

"Nope. They just want you to get to know them and be their friend."

"I'd like that."

"Even if they had no bodies, if they were disembodied minds who contacted you from inside your own head?"

Gracie laughed. "Are you writing a science fiction novel?"

"Agatha's the writer, not me."

Gracie looked at me oddly. "Do you have multiple personalities, by any chance?"

"Something like that," I said, offering her a bite of pie, "but not exactly."

She rejected the pie. "You're a strange one."

I nodded my confirmation.

"But I'll tell you one thing," Gracie added, "I'm not feeling bummed out any more."

"We're just getting started," I said. "I'll have you euphoric by the end of the evening."

"Well, don't go too far."

"Farther than you've ever been," I said. "Are you up for it?"

"I'm ready for whatever you've got to say," Gracie said, picking up the check. "Let's go, I want my socks knocked off."

As we were leaving, I noticed that she wasn't wearing any socks. I wondered if that was a bad sign.

On the drive to Cass's, I contacted Agatha and told her what I had in mind. *Good luck,* she said. *Let me know if you need my help.*

I'm sure I will. Expect to surface and be face-to-face with a very amazed Gracie at some point, with me riding her.

I'll do my part.

What's your read on her? I asked. *Think she'll be OK with it?*

Hard to say, Agatha responded, *but I'm in favor of your giving her a try. If you end up telling her everything, we might have another comrade to help us deal with Zephkar.*

And I might have another body to use, I said.

Hmm-mm, Agatha responded, *I don't know if I want another competitor.*

Junkie, I said.

"Where are you?" Gracie asked. "You look like you're in the ozone somewhere."

"Just having a chat with Agatha," I said.

Gracie didn't seem to like that.

I laughed, thinking maybe I'd better watch what I said. "I am not now nor have I ever been crazy," I said. I turned onto Wellington and pulled into Cass's driveway. "Are you worried?"

"To be honest, I am, a little."

"It'll get worse," I said. "What I have to tell you is a lot more mystifying than insanity. Want to forget about it?" I pushed the button and the garage door opened.

Gracie stared at the dashboard. "Maybe so," she said.

"Cold feet," I said. "That's because you don't wear socks." She didn't smile. "So, shall I drive you home then?"

"No," Gracie said. "I want to stay."

Gracie handled it better than either Agatha or Amy had. She turned out to be a very adventuresome woman. She handled it a lot better than I had on Allo, that's for sure. Of course, I was introducing her to the ideas a bit more sensitively than the Wraunkians had with me and Billy. After explaining the basics and responding to her initial skepticism, I entered her and contacted. That really excited her.

"You're in my mind!"

In a sense. I'm making direct contact with your mind, yes.

Can you hear my thoughts?

Loud and clear.

"Well, welcome to the twilight zone, Gracie," she murmured to herself.

At several points during the evening, I suggested we stop and let her digest for a day or two. Gracie insisted we go on. She wanted to hear everything. I had told her most of the essentials already. I added a few more things about Wozar and Allo and Zephkar, then I let Agatha tell her about the void, and about her own adjustment to learning about DM's.

"I feel like I've been born again," Gracie said at one point.

"Don't get vulgar," I responded.

Gracie laughed and then she passed out. She actually fainted. I guess she hadn't handled it as well as I'd thought. I put her head between her knees and fanned her and waited for her to come to.

"What happened?" She was blinking and looking very stunned.

"Your socks got knocked off," I said. "I think part of you is having a lot of trouble with this. Lie down for a while."

She lay back on the sofa and I brought her a pillow.

"I think I told you too much too fast."

"I'm OK," she said. "I'm just not sure I'm real, that's all."

"Oh boy."

"Am I in the void?"

"No, but you might be in a state of shock."

"I want to go to the void."

"Not yet." She really was adventuresome, I thought.

✻

It was close to two in the morning when I finally drove Gracie home and said good night. Her apartment building had a large courtyard. I waited in the car, intending to leave as soon as she got inside the inner door of the lobby. She was halfway down the courtyard when a couple of men appeared from nowhere and started after her. They got to the door just as Gracie did.

I jumped out of the car and ran through the courtyard. The lobby was empty when I got there. I rang Gracie's bell. As I waited, I switched to unilateral boosting. *Trouble*, I told Agatha. *A couple of men followed Gracie into her building.*

Shit.

There was no response to the doorbell. I kept ringing.

Try the other bells, Agatha suggested.

I rang all the bells on the panel. Finally someone buzzed me in. As I ran up the stairs to the third floor, I told Agatha, *Don't worry, I won't let you get hurt.*

I'm not worried about me, she responded.

At apartment 303 I knocked loudly. No response.

143

"If you don't open this door, I'm going to call the police," I said.

The door opened and a man grabbed hold of my wrist, pulled me inside, and closed and locked the door again. He had a knife.

Gracie was seated on the sofa, crying. Doris was on the floor; she was wearing a T-shirt and nothing else. Her torn underpants were next to her. There was a smear of blood on her mouth. A man was standing over her, his belt unbuckled and his zipper down.

"Hey, Joe, we got another one," the man holding my wrist announced. He pushed me toward the sofa. "Sit there and wait your turn," he ordered.

I shifted into him.

"You scuzball bastards," Agatha hissed.

"Keep your mouth shut, cunt," my host said. He eyed her up and down. "God, you're a big one. You're gonna be fun."

During the thirty seconds it took me to shift to boosting, the one called Joe got his pants down and was kneeling over Doris.

I stayed in unilateral boosting, not taking the time to block. I went to Joe and pulled him off of Doris. "We're getting out of here," I said.

"The hell you say." Joe shoved me away.

"I mean it. We're leaving. Come on." I tossed the knife to Agatha.

Joe looked at me incredulously. "You're fucking crazy, man."

Holding the knife threateningly, Agatha stared menacingly at Joe. I strode to the door in my muscular male body. "Come on," I said again.

Joe got up and zipped his pants. "Man, you flipped out," he sputtered.

I gestured for him to go out the door. I started after him, then turned back and poked my head into the apartment. "I'll be gone awhile," I whispered to Agatha. "The car keys are in your pocket. I'll see you at home."

I headed down the stairs after Joe, shifting to boost-blocking as I did.

"What in the fuck is the matter with you, asshole?" Joe said when I caught up with him. "We had it made up there." He gave me an angry punch on the arm. As we walked he kept yelling at me, but I didn't respond. When we were several blocks away, I shifted to maxi-riding.

My host stopped in his tracks. "Son-of-a-mother-fucking-bitch." He stood with his mouth agape, blinking his eyes. "Man, that was too weird. Man, something happened to me."

"You're goddamn right something happened, dickhead."

Joe resumed walking. My host caught up with him.

"I wasn't doing it," he said. "I knew what I was doing but I wasn't doing it, you know what I mean? And then everything got — man, like tripping — no, better, like . . . oh, man what a fuckin' high. Shee-it, it was fantastic. Then, suddenly I'm here with you walking down the fuckin' street. What happened, man?"

"You tell me, Calvin. I think you gone psychotic."

"Yeah, maybe. Hey, maybe I did. Maybe it was that crack I done."

I stayed with the two would-be rapists for the next hour, shifting from one to the other and dipping and mind-tickling each of them. The experience was repulsive. These were not nice people. Both had raped women in the past; both had robbed and beaten people. Both had spent time in jail. They should be exiled, I thought.

They went to a sleazy bar and stayed until three-thirty, then went their separate ways. I stayed with Joe who was the nastier of the two. He took a bus and we ended up in his messy two-room apartment on Argyle Street. He dropped onto the unmade bed and was asleep in two minutes. I maxi-rode, thinking about what had happened, thinking about what mutants this man and his friend were. Finally I too slept.

Joe awoke at noon. He changed his clothes and walked to a nearby restaurant. I shifted to a customer who was about to leave, boosted him, then went to a phone booth and called Agatha. She arrived fifteen minutes later.

How are Doris and Gracie doing, I asked, as soon as I'd entered her.

"They're OK," Agatha said. "Shaken, of course, but I stayed with them until they calmed down. We drank tea."

Those mutants aren't going to get away with this, I said.

"Doris couldn't understand what made them stop, why the big one suddenly backed off."

What did you tell her?

"Nothing," Agatha said. "I was tempted, but I thought she'd had enough stress for one night. I said maybe he got in touch with a thread of decency in himself."

Not a chance, I said. *The guy's a real scumbag, Agatha, through and through.*

"How come you stayed with them?"

To find out about them. Like I said, they're not going to get away with this. Those two can't be allowed to stay on the streets. Agatha was quiet. I was tempted to dip, but did not. *What are you thinking?* I asked.

"About what a mess this world is in," she responded.

She seemed real discouraged. I could understand why. *It's a mix,* I said, *from what I can pick up. You don't think it's hopeless, do you?*

Agatha pulled into Cass's driveway. "No," she said. "Just a serious mess."

On Friday afternoon, Cass and Amy returned from San Francisco with Isis and Persephone. The two dogs had a great time sniffing around the apartment, then they settled into corners and fell asleep.

Cass and Amy seemed very happy together. I was glad for them but it made my longing for Billy even stronger. There were times when I couldn't get her out of my mind, and more and more frequently I found myself shifting to the void and drifting.

Agatha and I told Cass and Amy how busy we'd been in their absence. Cass approved of our having given James the Veronica Bloom note. She also thought the idea of Veronica getting herself invited to St. Thomas, then stranding Zephkar while out on his yacht, had potential. "I think it's the best possibility we've come up with so far," she said.

"You think you could really do it?" I asked. I was unilateral-boosting Agatha. "Kill James Lane?"

Amy and I watched Cass.

Each time we talked about the need to kill someone in order to save this world from Zephkar, we seemed to get a little more accepting of it.

Cass nodded slowly. "I think I could," she said.

"His host doesn't have to be James Lane," I said.

"You have someone else in mind?" Amy scrutinized me. "Who? One of those women from the boat — Maribelle or Francine? Some *Testee* whose body Zephkar would be using to have sex in? How would that be any better than James?"

"I was thinking of Joe Benninger," I said.

That son of a bitch, Agatha hissed.

"Who's that?" Amy asked.

"One of the mutants who tried to rape Doris and Gracie."

"That would be better than James Lane," Cass said definitively. "But how could we ever get Zephkar to enter this Benninger?"

"I have some thoughts about that," I replied.

"I bet I know," Amy said to me. "You could boost Joe Benninger and get him invited onto Zephkar's boat." Persephone came into the room and pushed her snout under Amy's hand. Amy rubbed her affectionately. "I don't see why you couldn't just use the boat here rather than going all the way to St. Thomas, though," she said. "Then when you're on the boat, you get Zephkar to shift into Joe somehow

148

and then you shoot him and push him overboard. Is that what you're thinking?"

I shook my head. "This plan doesn't involve water," I said. "Lake or ocean. I think it would be too difficult to pull that one off — too many witnesses around. My idea requires a deep hole. We push Joe into the hole while Zephkar's in him."

"Then kill Joe and bury him and Zephkar," Amy said. "And Zephkar would be stranded."

I nodded.

Amy shook her head. "This is so weird, talking about killing people like this."

Tell her all of this is weird, Agatha said.

I told her.

"It sounds good in theory, Jenna. But how do we make it happen?" Cass asked. "Have you thought it through?"

"Some. But I need your help," I answered, and that was the beginning of a very long discussion.

The plan involved using Calvin Magriel, the other rapist, as well as Joe Benninger. It also required a doctor and that meant bringing Doris in. I was fairly sure she'd cooperate, once she saw what the stakes were. We also needed a deserted place in the country for the grave.

"I know the perfect place," Cass said. "Cindy's sister has a cottage in Wisconsin. It's in a fairly isolated spot on the edge of a woods. The nearest neighbor's half a mile away."

"I bet she tried to get you to go there with her," Amy said.

That was the first overt sign of jealousy I'd seen in Amy.

"Now I'll accept the invitation," Cass said. "The cottage is about an hour and a half from here. I think it would be perfect for our needs."

"That means we'll have to tell Cindy too," I said.

"I think she'd be a good one to have involved," Cass responded.

Amy didn't look too happy about that.

The next night we had Gracie and Doris over for dinner. Gracie hadn't yet mentioned to Doris that I happened to be a disembodied mind and that Cass and I were from another planet. At my request, Gracie had agreed that if and when Doris were let in, Gracie and I would tell her together.

Doris did not handle it well at all. I think her scientific training interfered. She scoffed at first, and derided us. I do, however, have very powerful ways of convincing people, and ultimately, when forced to choose between seeing herself as psychotic or accepting that what we were telling her was true, Doris chose the latter.

"And it was you who stopped the rape," she said.

"Yes," I answered.

She stared silently at me. There were tears in her eyes.

Cindy's reactions were quite different from Doris's when, the following night, we told her about Allo and the Wraunkians and disembodied minds. She loved it. At first she thought we were playing some kind of practical joke on her, but after I entered and contacted, and dipped, and even boosted her briefly, she was convinced and immediately delighted.

"This is great," she said. She had a hundred questions about our lives on Allo, most of them directed to Cass. It seemed she found Cass even more attractive now, knowing she was an extraterrestrial.

We gave our new recruits several days to get used to the news, then invited all three of them over and told them our plan for eliminating Zephkar.

"My sister and brother-in-law won't be using the cottage any more this year," Cindy said. "There's a private road that goes through the woods on their property. About a quarter mile in, a turnoff leads to a dead end. There's a clearing there. That's where we should dig the hole."

Doris wasn't nearly as enthusiastic. "I despise that creep, Joe Benninger, more than any being on Earth," she said through clenched teeth, "but what you're talking about is murder. I cannot condone killing him."

"Did you read the front page today?" Gracie asked. "Another opponent of New Direction killed himself. That's murder, hon. And not the first one Zephkar's committed."

"So that gives us the right to murder in return?"

The debate went on for a while, between Doris and Gracie. The rest of us kept out of it. I was unilaterally boosting Amy. While Doris and Gracie went through the same arguments Amy and I and Cass and Agatha had been over and over, Amy and

I had a private discussion about Doris and whether it had been a mistake bringing her in.

Finally Doris said, "All right, so someone has to die, but why do *we* have to do it? Why do we have to handle this all by ourselves? Why don't we bring some experts in on it — the police, the FBI maybe, or the army? Maybe they could get someone to volunteer to be sacrificed."

A kamikaze, Amy said giggling.

"You must be kidding," Agatha said. "That's the last thing we'd want to do."

"Why? I don't agree." Doris pushed her glasses up angrily.

"The government people wouldn't want to destroy Zephkar," Agatha argued. "They'd want to use him. And they'd probably end up finding out who Cass is. They'd squeeze that information out of one of us. Then Cass would have no peace. It'd be a circus. And they might even end up prosecuting her for killing Veronica Bloom."

"That's right," I said. "Or worse."

"You people are paranoid," Doris responded. She folded her arms and looked away. Then she looked at Cass. "You don't know how things work here," she said. "This is America."

"Oh, give me a break," Cindy muttered.

"We'll tell the press," Doris persisted. "They can warn the country about Zephkar and what he's trying to do. We'll expose him. Who would join his Theocratic Party then? Who would vote to change the Constitution? They certainly wouldn't elect him president. If the truth were known, Zephkar would be ruined."

"He'd just come up with another plan," I said

patiently. "Doris, I don't think you realize the power a DM has. Zephkar could cause total chaos if he wanted. Think about it. So far things are going his way, so he's being orderly, working toward a nice peaceful takeover of this world. Which gives us the opportunity to stop him. He doesn't know he isn't the only DM here. If he were exposed and if people started opposing him, he could do anything. He can kill people with total impunity, you know. He can do whatever he wants."

"All the more reason to get the experts involved," Doris countered. "Isn't it pretty presumptuous to think we're the best ones to handle this? And isn't it pretty paranoid to think the FBI or State Department or whoever wouldn't be able to figure out that the only reasonable thing to do is eliminate Zephkar, not try to use him?"

"OK, Doris," Agatha said. "Maybe you're right. Maybe they would realize that for the sake of this planet Zephkar has to be eliminated. And maybe they could do a better job of it than we could. They'd eliminate Zephkar, but then they'd use Jenna."

Doris shook her head. "I need an aspirin."

"Do you know what I mean?" Agatha said.

"How would they use Jenna? No, I don't know what you mean," Doris said angrily. "Jenna wouldn't let them. She wouldn't cooperate."

"Not voluntarily," Agatha said. "She'd be blackmailed. She'd be forced to do whatever they want. And you'd be part of it. All of us would. We'd all become hostages. You, me, Gracie, Cass, Amy, Cindy — the dogs too, maybe. And anyone else they thought Jenna cared about."

"I don't believe this." Doris rubbed her temples. Gracie got two aspirins from her pack and handed them to Doris.

"You would when it started happening," Agatha said. "They'd send Jenna to Libya maybe, to boost Khadafy and have him kill himself. Or to Iraq or the Soviet Union. That could be one way they'd use her, as the perfect assassin."

"They wouldn't even have to know she exists," Doris said. "We won't tell anyone about her."

"Oh right," Agatha said, "and how do we convince them there's such a thing as DM's then? They'd think we're more paranoid than you do."

"That's true, they would have to know about Jenna," Doris conceded.

"Of course. And I'm sure they'd have no trouble thinking of ways to make her do whatever they wanted."

"I can't imagine how," Doris said stubbornly.

"They'd threaten to do something to one of us if she refused — cut off Cass's little finger, for example. How many fingers do you think it would take for Jenna to start following their orders?"

"That's barbaric," Doris said.

"Exactly," Agatha responded.

"Do you all agree with what Agatha's saying?" Doris looked from face to face. The rest of us met her eyes, no one saying a word. "I suppose it *is* possible," Doris said at last.

"How's your headache, hon?" Gracie asked.

"This is scary," Doris said.

Cindy nodded. "Do you wish they'd never told you?"

"Do you?" Doris asked her.

"Hell no," Cindy replied.

"Me neither." Doris adjusted her glasses again. "If we did decide to go ahead with your plan, the drugs would be no problem. I could keep those degenerates sedated for as long as you want."

Cass reached over and patted Doris's back. "Great, Doc. Welcome aboard."

Let me drive, Amy said.

I switched to maxi-riding. The moment she was controlling her body, Amy said, "We already checked the ads for trucks. There are a few that look promising. And Jenna's planning to hang out with Joe and Calvin to learn their habits so we can pull off the kidnappings."

"Too bad there aren't two Zephkars so we'd have an excuse to get rid of both those rapists," Gracie said. "Oops." She covered her mouth.

"Have any of you thought about what might happen if anything goes wrong?" Doris asked.

"Think positively, Doctor Doris," Cass said lightly. "Would anyone like a bite to eat? Amy baked some banana bread today."

We talked of other things then, but I'm sure that in the back of everyone's mind was the plan. And the fear. I was certainly shaken by the picture Agatha had painted about what could happen if the government learned about us. Out of the corner of Amy's eye, I kept looking at Cass's little finger.

"I miss my body," I told Cass. "I miss Billy. I want to be on a planet where I belong. I hate it here!"

"I know," Cass said. "I hate it too sometimes."

"I'm not sure I have the energy to go on with this, Cass."

"You have it. I had crashes too. In New York, I even thought about going to a hospital and permanating someone who was about to die."

I sighed. "Do you think we can have lives here?"

"I think we can," Cass answered. "I know it's especially hard for you."

"I can't get Billy out of my mind."

Cass squeezed my hand. "I still believe you and Billy will be together again," she said, "but even if that doesn't happen, Jenna, I know you'll make it. You *will* make a life here, just like I will."

I tried to believe her.

Over the next week, I was distracted from my sorrows by my involvement in the preparations for Pit Flop, which was the name Cindy had given our plan. She referred to our group as ZET, the Zephkar Elimination Team.

Amy and Cass found the perfect vehicle, a roomy white truck with the driver's section separate from the back. They bought it in Indiana with cash and didn't use their real names. They got license plates from an abandoned burnt out car on the west side of Chicago. We fixed up the truck to suit our purposes, installing shelves along one wall, a bench on the floor, and a cabinet in the corner. As a final touch, we installed carpeting.

Amy and Cass got the handcuffs, Agatha was in charge of the costumes, Doris got the drugs. Cindy and Gracie bought a van, again going a good distance from Chicago to make the purchase, and again using cash and an assumed name. Cindy got the guns.

For my part, I spent several days spying on Joe Benninger, Calvin Magriel, and then later on, on Zephkar. Agatha helped by supplying her body when I needed it. Spending time with Joe and Calvin only made me more convinced that we'd chosen the right people. Had they been Alloys, there's no doubt they'd have been exiled by the time they were twenty years old. I will admit that I felt some pity for them too, not only because of Joe's fate, but because of the narrow meanness of their present lives, and the misery of their childhoods. By mind-tickling him, I learned that Calvin, especially, had had it rough as a kid. His father was a gruff, angry man, obviously incapable of fulfilling a parenting role, or of feeling love for his son. On Allo, the few people like that at least had sense enough never to have children. Of course, contraception was a lot more complicated on Earth, I reminded myself. On Allo, a pill a month did the job.

At Zephjame's house, I rode his assistant, Freddie, and listened and observed as Zephjame strategized with his inner circle, converted New Direction opponents who were brought to him, had sex with various Testees. One evening, I went along to a mass meeting and watched as Zephkar shifted among the crowd, entering, contacting, boosting, staying just long enough with each person to make a complete believer of him or her.

I wondered if James Lane realized he didn't have a life anymore. Zephkar almost always used James' body, only occasionally making brief shifts into someone else. Luckily for me, he never tried to enter Freddie while I was riding him.

One of the most useful things I learned while spying on Zephkar was what an avid movie fan he was. He had a large-screen TV, and a huge library of video tapes. Thursday evenings were totally reserved for viewing films. Even Freddie would leave on Thursdays after serving Zephkar his dinner.

On Saturday, all the ZET members — Cass, Amy, Agatha, Cindy, Gracie, Doris, and I — drove to Wisconsin to dig the hole. We'd made pages of diagrams before we settled on the final design for the pit. It would be ten feet deep and L-shaped. Each leg of the L would be four feet wide and five feet long.

The site for the pit was a quarter mile from the cottage, on property also owned by Cindy's sister. Vehicles could get there only by using an overgrown dirt road. The only disadvantage of the location was the tree-house Cindy had noticed several hundred yards from the pit. No kids came around while we were digging and we hoped they'd stay away until the pit flop was complete.

We all wore the thickest gloves we could find for the digging but everyone got blisters anyway. I rotated among all the women and none of them was ever disappointed when it was her turn to be boosted. When the pit was finally dug, we put chicken wire over it and covered the wire with twigs, leaves, and a thin layer of soil. Then we laid sheets of plywood over it in case some trespassing hunter or hiker came by.

On Monday night, Amy took me to the Astor Street house so I could be there for Zephjame's meeting with a Disciple named Andrew Corrigan. Andrew was the president of the Veterans of Foreign Wars. I shifted into him as soon as he got out of the cab.

Only about twenty percent of the members of his organization were converted, he told Zephjame. He asked James to come to the group's national convention in December and do his magic. Zephjame agreed to go. When Andrew was about to leave, I switched to boost-blocking.

"One more thing," I said, trying to imitate Andrew's mannerisms and style of speech. "I have a nephew, name of Carl Fairbanks. He lives in Detroit but he's coming through Chicago in a few days — stopover, then he's flying on to California. The kid's got this idea, sir, about getting people to back the constitutional amendments. I think it's a good one. So he wants to run it by you. He's got a questionnaire he uses."

"Have him see one of the Apostles," Zephjame said impatiently.

"The thing is," I said, "the kid's been dying to meet you, Mr. Lane. I told him maybe I could set it up. He's the steward of his union, you see. He's been working his rear off to help New Direction. Ten minutes, max. Probably less than that is all he'd need. Five minutes would do."

159

"What union?"

"United Auto Workers," I said.

Zephjame nodded brusquely. "All right. Set up a time with Freddie."

Freddie got his notebook.

"Carl's arriving Thursday evening at five," I said, "and flying out again at midnight. So I was thinking maybe you could give him a few minutes on Thursday night."

Zephjame scowled.

"Mr. Lane isn't free on Thursday nights," Freddie said.

"Oh, I see," I responded, disappointedly.

"He can have ten minutes," Zephjame said. "Tell him to be here at seven o'clock sharp."

"Thank you, Mr. Lane," I said, shaking Zephjame's hand firmly. "Carl will be thrilled."

I went around the corner to the coffeeshop where Amy was waiting. We hailed a cab for the VFW president, then I shifted. Andrew shook his head, his mouth working, his eyes saucers.

"You want a cab, mister?" the cabby said. A shaky Andrew Corrigan got into the taxi.

I was totally unprepared for the news Cass had for us when we got home. "Billy's coming!" she shouted, before we were even in the door.

Barely aware of what I was doing, I switched to boosting. My heart was pounding. I couldn't speak.

"She's on her way now," Cass exclaimed. "Her

plane should be landing any minute. She was at a place called Iowa City. Stranded all this time. She just entered her first Earthling a week ago."

I stumbled my way into the living room and collapsed on the sofa. I was crying and laughing at the same time. "She made it!" I could hear my pulse pounding in my ears.

"Today was the first chance she had to check the papers," Cass said excitedly. "We talked only a few minutes because she wanted to call the airline right away. Then she called me back and said she'd be arriving at nine-thirty tonight. I waited here to tell you. Cindy's on her way to the airport to pick her up."

"Is she all right?" My voice was hoarse.

"She sounded fine. She . . . she permanated, Jenamy."

I sat without speaking or moving, thinking about seeing Billy, about her having a different body, wondering how she would look, how it would be for us. Then I was aware of Amy contacting me.

This is wonderful, Jenna. I'm so happy for you.

I feel . . . I'm stunned, I said. *I . . . Amy, are you upset that I boosted without asking? I didn't mean to, but I . . ."*

It's all right, Jen, I understand. God, you must be so thrilled.

"She's become a human," I said.

Cass put her hand on my shoulder. "It'll work out."

You can boost me for the reunion, Amy offered. *Unless you'd rather boost Agatha.*

"Where *is* Agatha?" I said absently.

"Out with Gracie," Cass said. "She should be here soon."

I paced nervously, feeling wonderfully excited, but also scared. A short time later, Agatha and Gracie arrived. When we told them the news, Agatha seemed almost as excited as I.

We all waited anxiously. At last, Cindy's car pulled up in front of the house. Apprehensively, I watched from the window as Cindy and a stranger walked up the steps.

Her hair was blonde and short. She had blue eyes and very white teeth and she looked nothing like Billy.

"I was scared," I said. "It took you so long. I thought —"

"Oh, Jenna, is it really you?" She smiled through her tears. "You're so tall."

"But I . . . Billy, you do know that . . . that this is not my body. It belongs to a friend named Agatha."

"No, I thought . . . I assumed . . ."

I shook my head.

Cass moved forward and took Billy in her arms. "I'm Cass," she said. "I *have* permanated."

Billy clung to her. "You're beautiful."

Cass introduced Amy and Gracie, then guided us all to the living room. Billy and I sat next to each other on the sofa.

"Tell me what happened," I said. "What do you

think of Earth? Who was your first host? I want to hear everything."

"I still feel disoriented," Billy said. "The first human I entered was a child. It was in a cornfield. That's where I was stranded. Then from her, I shifted to her parent . . . her mother. The mother's name is Ella. She's a nurse. They live on a farm."

I stared at her. She looked and sounded like a stranger. The mannerisms were Billy, though, the way she cocked her head, how she leaned forward when she spoke.

"At the hospital where Ella works I met Deanna." Billy placed her hands on her chest. "This is Deanna's body. She was a patient on the psychiatric unit. I dipped and mind-tickled. Her pain was unbelievably intense . . . excruciating." Billy's eyes filled with tears. "She'd tried to kill herself. That's why she was hospitalized. She was all twisted up with guilt and misery. Despised herself. She longed for death. *I want to die. I want to die,* she'd think, over and over. She'd had years of treatment, but couldn't free herself. There was a baby . . . her baby. But . . . well, for whatever reasons — it had something to do with a man — it seems Deanna neglected the baby and the baby ended up dead. Deanna felt responsible. I guess she *was* responsible, at least that's what the court decided. She was jailed for a while. Deanna couldn't get over it; all she wanted was to die. She tried to kill herself, but her landlord found her. In the hospital, she pretended to feel better, to see some hope and a future for herself. But she was determined to die. They discharged her and I went home with her."

I glanced at Cass and the Earthlings. Their eyes were riveted on Billy.

"She was all alone," Billy said, "had cut herself off from everyone. All she had were her memories and the guilt." Billy was crying. So was I.

"She had a bottle of pills that she kept in the refrigerator. We'd been at her place only a short time when she poured the pills onto the kitchen table and one by one put them in her mouth. I knew I could boost and stop her." Tears streamed down Billy's cheeks. "But I didn't."

I reached over and took both of Billy's hands. They felt soft like her Allo hands.

"After she'd swallowed all the pills, she went into the bedroom. She laid on the bed and closed her eyes. Her thoughts were peaceful. She was completely calm."

I glanced at the others again — Cass, Amy, Cindy, Gracie. They were all crying.

"She pictured herself with the baby. They were together again, Deanna cradling the child . . . the two of them floating through the clouds." Billy's voice cracked. She took a deep breath. "That's when I switched to boost-blocking. I ran to the bathroom and threw up. Apparently very little of the drug had gotten into the bloodstream. I didn't feel groggy or anything, I just felt . . . strange . . . frightened . . . knowing what I was about to do."

"I think you did the right thing," Amy said.

Billy wiped her eyes. "I think so too." She looked at me. "This is hard."

"I know," I said. I squeezed her hand.

Cass handed Billy a glass of iced tea and she took a long drink. "It just happened yesterday," she said. "I was born yesterday." Her laughter caught in her throat.

"And then you found the ad and called," Cass said. "God, it's great to have you here."

"We can finally stop checking all those damn newspapers," Amy said, laughing tearfully.

Billy sighed again. She looked deeply at me. "I spent a lot of time with you in the void."

"Yes, I did the same thing," I responded. "I've missed you so much."

"Do you think you can adjust to my new body?"

I nodded. "I'll get used to it." I thought about asking her if she could adjust to my not having a body at all.

"So here we all are," Billy said. "On Earth. My head is still spinning. Do your friends know why we came?"

"Yes, they're part of ZET," I said. "The Zephkar Elimination Team."

Billy nodded. "I'm looking forward to getting to know all of you," she said to the Earthlings. "And Agatha," she added. "Is she in the void?"

"Yes," I said.

"Next to being alive, it's the best place to be," Billy said.

There was an uncomfortable moment of silence. I was thinking how much I wanted to be alone with Billy. I had the feeling Billy was thinking the same thing.

"Why don't you show Billy your room, Jenag?" Cass said.

Bless her heart.

"It's late," Cindy said. "I've got to get going."

"Yeah, me, too," Gracie said. She stood and took

165

Billy's hand. "Welcome to Earth, Billy. I hope to see you again soon."

Billy and I went to my room. It was a little awkward at first, but then I started telling her about my experiences on Earth and we both got more comfortable with each other. She told me more about her few days on our new planet.

We held hands and we embraced, but we did not kiss or make love. There was some adjusting to do before we'd be ready for that. I felt close to her and the loving feelings were there, but our contact seemed more like talking on the telephone than actually being together. Our bodies were strangers' bodies, our voices new, our language alien.

Before we fell asleep we talked about Allo and the people we'd left behind. We cried. We held each other. We each said how wonderful it was that we had all made it. We did not talk about my still being a DM. Not yet.

I was awakened the next morning by Agatha's thoughts. A spontaneous switch to unilateral boosting had taken place. I blocked her out. She had told me to keep her in the void as long as I wanted, just so I brought her back by Pit Flop day, which was the day after tomorrow. I'd told Billy of the plan. Like the rest of us, it disturbed her greatly that someone had to die, even a mutant like Joe Benninger.

I felt her lying next to me. Turning, I looked at her face, watching her sleep. This is Billy, I told myself again. This is the face I must learn to love. I lay back on the pillow. It would be harder for her, I thought. I have no face of my own for her to get used to. I wondered if I ever would. I went back to sleep and the next time I awoke I felt her arms around me.

"Good morning," she said. She scrutinized me. "You *are* Jenna, aren't you?"

"Yes," I said. "I dreamed about you, Billy. It was strange. You kept changing. One moment you were tall and very dark, then you'd shrink and your features would change, then you were you . . . the you from Allo."

"I'm still that *you*," Billy said reassuringly.

I caressed her cheek. "Soft skin."

She pushed herself up in the bed and leaned on her elbow. "You haven't mentioned anything about permanating, Jenna. About where you are with it."

"It's a touchy topic," I said. Then I added, "Disembodied minds need love too."

Billy laughed. I was starting to get used to the laugh. "I love your disembodied mind," she said. She looked into my eyes. "Do you doubt it?"

"I doubt that it's easy."

"It's always easy to love you. Do you intend to remain disembodied?"

"I don't know," I said.

"One day at a time," Billy responded. She chuckled. "That's an Earthian expression. I learned it in the psych ward."

"I've heard it. Can you wait?"

"Of course. We'll work it out."

"That's an Earthian expression too," I said.

"I'm full of them," she replied. "Jenna, I do love you."

"And I love you."

167

We looked at each other, into each other's tear-filled strangers' eyes, and we cried.

When we finally got up that first morning, I went to the kitchen to make breakfast while Billy showered. I overheard Cass and Amy arguing in Cass's bedroom. Cass apparently had plans with Cindy that day and Amy wanted to go along, but Cass said she wasn't invited. Amy acknowledged that she was jealous.

"No need," Cass said. She told Amy she had no romantic interest in Cindy, but I wondered if that was really true. On the Wraunkian spaceship, several Alloys had been pursuing Cass and she seemed receptive to all of them. Maybe she just likes everyone, I thought, stirring the oatmeal.

After breakfast, Billy and I went for a long walk along the lake. Later, we had lunch at an outdoor cafe. I was feeling very happy to be with her and even starting to get used to her new body with its pale skin and golden hair. When we got back to Cass's apartment late that afternoon, Amy was there alone. I asked her if she'd like a sojourn in dreamland and give Billy a chance to meet Agatha.

"Sure, but bring me back when Cass gets home," she said.

I asked Billy if she thought she could deal with the shift. "I'll deal with it," she said.

I contacted Agatha and told her what was going on, then I shifted into Amy, switching immediately to boost-blocking.

"You must be Billy," Agatha said. She was removing the jewelry as she spoke.

"Jenna told me you've been a good friend to her," Billy said.

As the three of us talked, it was obvious that Billy was working hard to adjust, to accept that I was now in Amy's body, and that the body she'd been relating to as me was now occupied by its rightful Earthian owner. I knew it wasn't easy. I wondered if I'd eventually end up finding some suicidal Earthling to permanate.

Cass and Cindy arrived about an hour later. I switched to maxi-riding. Amy was cordial to Cindy. I wondered what she was thinking, but, of course, did not dip to find out. Later in the evening we cooked fettuccine primavera. Billy had many questions for the Earthlings. At one point in the conversation, Amy asked Billy how Alloys deal with romantic triangles. Cass chuckled.

"Sometimes poorly," Billy answered. "In that regard, Allo certainly isn't a utopia. Sometimes tripling takes place, and that can be successful, but people do get hurt."

"Tripling?" Amy said. "What's that?"

"You don't have that here? It's when three people form a union together — you know, a romantic bonding . . . like your marriages, I guess. Sometimes they have children and raise them together."

Amy was incredulous.

"I was part of one," Cass said, "years ago. It worked pretty well for a while."

"What a weird idea," Amy said indignantly.

"We're a lot more flexible about such things,"

Cass said. "I suspect one of the reasons is that Alloys don't have any religious beliefs that get in the way."

"Fascinating," Agatha said.

When it was time to go to bed, Agatha volunteered to spend the night in the void. Billy and I went to my room. "So what do you think of my new friends?" I asked as we were getting undressed.

"They're weird," she said. "They eat flesh! Their whole structure is disgusting. Their bodies are revolting."

She started to cry. I put my arms around her and held her close to me.

"I miss home," she said, her voice muffled. "I miss my body. I don't like this body at all. It's deformed — one clitoris, no penis. You call that a body? I miss Jenna . . . your body. I loved your body."

I was crying with her. "Oh, hon," I said, "I know just what you mean. How many times I wished we'd stayed at your house that night instead of mine and then the Wraunkians never would have taken us."

"I thought it would help when I permanated," Billy said.

"But it didn't?"

She sniffed and wiped her nose. "A little."

"We have each other," I said. "And Cass. One of my fears was that I'd be the only one to make it out of the void."

"I worried about that too. To be the only one, it would have been so . . ."

"So horribly lonely," I said.

"Yes."

"I was lonely, Billy, before you came. Sometimes I got depressed."

"We have each other now," she said, clinging to me tightly.

"Repulsive bodies and all." I laughed weakly.

"Oh, they're not so bad," she said. "This one needs some tender loving care. I don't think Deanna treated it as well as she should have."

"It's in good hands now," I said, stroking her back.

"I love you, Jenag. Or whoever you are. You're my Jenna and I love you."

We kissed deeply, for the first time. It felt different. New. It felt good. She touched my breast. My borrowed body responded. "I think we'll make the best of it," I whispered into her ear. "Mm-mm-mm, I'm loving you, my love." And we kissed again.

There was nothing to compare it to. It wasn't like the first lovemaking with a new lover, nor like acting on an irresistible impulse with a desirable stranger. Billy and I had known and loved each other for years. It wasn't like it used to be when we made love at home. Her body was new and different; mine was not even my own. There was nothing to compare our lovemaking to. And yet there was. The arousal was the same. The excitement. Despite the absence of penises and the missing second clitorises, the climaxes were almost as good. We fell asleep in each other's arms.

The next night all the ZET members met at Cass's apartment to go over our plan for the final time. I was using Cindy as my host, unilaterally boosting so she could take part in the discussion. Cass had gotten another costume made and Billy tried it on. She looked divine.

Everything we needed was ready. Everyone knew her part.

"Nothing will go wrong," Cindy said encouragingly to Doris who seemed particularly nervous. "ZET is one well-oiled machine. I predict complete success."

Billy and I stayed in bed late the next morning. "I need to continue my examination," I said, running my fingers over her naked hip and thigh. "I have to familiarize myself with every inch of the new you."

She guided my hand between her legs. "This part needs special attention," she said.

"Perhaps the tongue test," I suggested, moving downward.

"Ah, yes," she purred.

I continued the exploration, concentrating on her warm, moist, delicious genitalia, probing and licking and sucking and tasting. Very interesting. After a while her back began to arch and then she was moaning delightfully in a low and growly way and squeezing my shoulders.

Sighing deeply, she pulled me up to her and kissed me. "I'm loving you," she said, her hand sliding downward, cupping my buttocks. Her fingers found my crotch.

Having orgasms in Agatha's body was definitely a different experience from what I'd known in my own. And yet the final moments were very much the same. Since Earthling bodies had no inner clitorises, Billy and I realized we really didn't miss each other's penises, though we did miss having our own.

"Less variety," Billy had said last night. "I guess I'll learn to live with it."

"We can't make babies together, you know," I had said.

"Unless you end up permanating a male," Billy replied.

That had led to a long discussion of sex roles on Earth and feminism and lesbianism. At the end, Billy said, "We could adopt."

"Or I could boost a genetically sound male," I said, "just for the occasion."

"I'd have to think about that," Billy had replied.

We'd gone to sleep then, our bodies intertwined, and when we awoke neither of us had been eager to get up. Our lovemaking was getting better each time. I had a little fear, however, that Billy was partly in love with Agatha, since I always used Agatha's body when she and I were alone together.

She was stroking my hair. "Would you like some fried slices of pig flesh for breakfast?" she asked. "And perhaps a couple of unfertilized bird ova?"

I laughed heartily. "I don't think we'll ever completely make it as Earthlings."

We ate fresh fruit and bowls of granola. At ten o'clock, the call came from Cass. She and Amy had been out tailing Calvin since early that morning. Cass told Billy he was in a restaurant on Broadway near Foster.

I went into our bedroom and switched to maxi-riding. I still had never entered Billy and I thought I probably never would. Neither of us had ever talked about that.

Good morning, I said to Agatha. *It's a little after ten, Thursday morning. We just heard from Cass. She and Amy followed Calvin to a restaurant. Billy will tell you where you're supposed to meet them.*

"Any new developments?" Agatha asked. "Any problems?"

Nope. Everything's fine. You better get moving. I'm projecting out.

"Enjoy the void," she said.

I did. The drifting seemed particularly wonderful that time. The music absorbed me and the images were all soft and sensual. I definitely felt some disappointment when I sensed the buzz. It was Amy, as planned. *Hello there, Earthling.*

"Hi, Disembodied Mind. Here's the update. Agatha got to the restaurant before Calvin left. We all followed him from there to that apartment building on Argyle, the one you told us about."

Yes, he has a girlfriend there, third floor.

"Grace's there now, outside the building."

He might stay there the rest of the day, I said.

"I hope so," Amy said as she walked to the living room. "I made some more labels for the video collection. I got them from that magazine Gracie found. One is called *Beneath My Feet,* and the other's *The Hour of Power.*"

Zephkar will love them, I said.

Cindy arrived at the apartment at two o'clock. She gave us each a hug and added a kiss for Cass. Cass kissed her in return. Amy watched silently.

"Jenna?" Cindy asked Amy.

"No, Jenna's maxi-riding," Amy said.

Cindy nodded. "Jenna," she said, looking at Amy. "I checked on Benninger's truck. It's there at the factory."

Doris, Billy, Amy and Cindy sat around talking and eating pizza, with me continuing to ride Amy. There was quite a bit of nervous joking among the group. At two-forty-five, I shifted into Cindy and maxi-rode. It was time to go. Billy and Doris wished us luck, and Cindy, Amy, and I went out to Cindy's car. Amy drove. She dropped us off a block away from the sausage factory, at a bus stop where I shifted into a sandy-haired man in his early thirties.

Boost-blocking, I walked his body to the rear of the factory. I checked out the parking lot and found Joe Benninger's blue pickup truck. Then I went over near the gate and waited for Joe's shift to end.

At three-thirty-five people started coming out of the factory. I spotted Joe, walking alone, smoking a cigarette. He was dressed in black pants and a WGN Rock T-shirt.

I walked up to him. "Got a match?"

He looked at me a little suspiciously. As he was reaching into his pocket, I shifted and went right to boost-blocking. The host I'd just left mumbled something I couldn't make out.

"Your bus stop is that way," I said, pointing.

Looking confused, he walked away.

The keys were in my pocket. I drove Joe's truck around the corner where Cindy was waiting.

"Who are *you?*" she asked, according to plan.

"Your favorite DM," I replied.

"So far so good," she said, climbing into the cab. She was wearing gloves so she wouldn't leave fingerprints on the truck.

On the way to Gracie's brother's, I stopped at a gas station to use the john. We had a covered bucket in the van but I figured it would make things easier if Joe didn't have to use it. That was a first for me, urinating through a penis. It didn't feel as weird as I'd expected. The men's washroom at the gas station was unbelievably filthy. There were many Earthling ways that I still found quite repulsive.

177

At Gracie's brother's house, the white truck, which Cindy had named *Whitey,* was parked in the driveway. I gave a short toot, and the garage door opened. Inside was the red van, *Van Go,* Cindy called it. Billy, Gracie, Amy and Doris were there.

Doris looked a little sick when she saw me. "That's you, isn't it, Jenna?"

"You bet," I said. "It's okay, Doris."

She kept her distance. Gracie didn't get much closer. Understandably.

I climbed into the van and got myself comfortably situated on the mattress. Billy put a leather cuff on each of my wrists. The cuffs were attached by leather straps to opposite sides of the truck. I gave them a tug. "Seem secure," I said.

Amy attached similar cuffs to each of my ankles. These also were connected by leather straps to the truck. When they finished with me, I was sitting spread-eagle, my arms resting on the mattress, my feet about a yard apart, my head on a pillow.

"Comfortable enough," I said.

"Ready for the gag?" Billy asked.

I told her to go ahead. She put a thick strip of silver duct tape over my mouth, then a couple more strips over that.

"Can you breathe all right?"

I nodded. Billy and Amy left the van, and a short while later, Amy returned wearing her costume, a gaudy silvery robe that came almost to her ankles. She slipped the rubber Cinderella mask over her head and pulled up her hood. "Okay, ready," she said. I shifted into her, and went to maxi-riding.

Joe Benninger immediately began to twist and

struggle against his bonds, making barely audible noises that sounded like angry humming. His eyes shot wildly back and forth.

"You're in no danger," Amy told him.

He glared hatefully at her, continuing to writhe and pull against the cuffs. Sweat was pouring down his forehead.

"Just relax," Amy said. "You're going to take part in an important religious ceremony. Now, just relax. We'll explain more later. Then, if you'll promise to keep quiet, we might remove the gag."

Amy left the van and closed the door behind her. We could hear Joe bumping around inside.

"Agatha called," Gracie said, coming back into the garage from her brother's house. "Calvin is at the pool hall."

That's better than his girlfriend's apartment, I thought. I shifted into Cindy. *Ready?* I asked.

"Let's go." She handed Billy the keys to Joe's truck. Billy was wearing gloves. While Cindy and I were taking care of Calvin, Billy and Cass would drive to Joe's apartment, pack up his stuff and dump it in garbage cans in uptown. Then they'd drive his truck to the west side, take off the license plates, and leave the truck. Doris would follow them in her car to give them a ride back to the garage.

Cindy parked half a block down from the pool hall. We saw Cass and Agatha across the street in Cass's car. They waved and then drove off, according to our plan. The neighborhood was pretty seedy, and even though it was only about four-thirty, Cindy and I remained in the car as we waited for a likely host.

I let several people pass. When a thin, six-foot white man in his mid-twenties came by, I left the car and walked behind him. I entered him before we got to the pool hall, and then, boost-blocking, walked Cindy back to the car.

"So far so good," Cindy said.

"Lock the door," I told her, in my new, raspy voice.

Inside the pool hall, I spotted Calvin hunched over a table making a shot. I bought a beer and leaned against the wall watching the game. I waited until Calvin hit the last ball, a black one, into one of the corner pockets, and then I entered him. I rode while he collected the money he'd won.

The thin guy I'd used to get into the pool hall looked around the room with wide eyes and a hanging jaw. I wondered again how seriously my unexplained body-borrowing affected my different hosts. Everything has its price, I thought guiltily.

"You OK, man?" someone said to the thin guy.

"I don't know how I got here."

The other man laughed. "The devil made you do it," he said.

I switched to boost-blocking and left the pool hall. "Got room for a boosting DM in there?" I asked Cindy. She unlocked the car door and I slid into the passenger seat. "I'd like to learn to play pool some day," I said.

Cindy started the engine. "I'd be happy to teach you, but you'd have to wear a better body than that one."

I laughed. "You mean I wouldn't be welcome in a lesbian bar looking like this?"

"As far as I'm concerned, you wouldn't be welcome anywhere looking like that."

She drove me to a barber shop and waited outside while I got Calvin's hair washed and cut to a neat, trim length.

"You're still ugly," Cindy said when I came back out.

When we got to the garage, all the other members of the Zephkar Elimination Team were there except Billy and Doris, who were still out getting rid of Joe's truck.

"Did Joe give you any trouble?" I asked Amy, gesturing toward the van.

Amy still had her robe on, but the mask was sitting on the stool near the drum set. "I took the tape off his mouth," she said, "but he wouldn't stop calling me obscene names and then he started yelling so I had to tape him again."

Cass handed me the pair of navy blue pants and I removed Calvin's wrinkled black ones and put the new ones on. They fit fine and so did the long-sleeved gray shirt. We'd gotten long sleeves to cover up Calvin's tattoo, an eagle surrounded by vines. The gray loafers turned out to be a little large, so I ended up wearing the tan lace-up shoes which fit perfectly.

"You look almost presentable," Amy said.

At six-thirty, Billy and Doris returned. No problems dumping the truck, they told us. Doris eyed me warily and stayed as far away as she could get. Gracie was keeping her distance too. I'm sure they were eager for me to get their would-be rapist's body the hell out of their sight.

In another fifteen minutes, Billy, Amy, and I would go to Zephjame's, and they'd get their wish.

* * * * *

Half a block before we got to Zephjame's, Amy and Billy got out of the truck, leaving me to drive the rest of the way alone. I parked in the driveway, then went and rang the bell.

"Mr. Lane," I said, holding out my hand. "I'm Carl Fairbanks."

Zephjame gave my hand a quick shake.

"I hope you don't mind that I parked back there," I said.

He grunted something and led me down the hallway, past the kitchen, and into one of the parlors. He took an easy chair and I sat about a yard away on a divan. He stared at me intensely for several seconds.

"This is really an honor for me," I said. "I certainly do appreciate your agreeing to see me like this."

He continued staring. "Do you have a twin brother?" he asked.

Obviously, he'd been trying to enter me. "Yeah, I do," I said. "My uncle must have mentioned it, huh?"

"Identical twin, right?"

"Right," I said.

"Interesting," Zephjame said pensively. He leaned back. "So you've got a questionnaire. Well, let's see it."

I opened my briefcase and handed him a folder. "I'm planning to get thousands of copies printed," I said.

Zephjame looked over the questions. All the ZET members had helped make them up. *Do you think that the high crime rate in the United States reflects a deterioration in the moral fabric of the country?* Doris had suggested that one. *Are you tired of godless liberals using the Constitution as a tool to further the de-Christianization of the United States?* That was Agatha's. There were thirteen others.

"Not bad," Zephjame said. "I could see a use for these. So what exactly is your plan, Carl?"

"To recruit volunteers to blanket the country with the questionnaires," I said. "Have people fill them out, then ask them to sign the petition for the New Direction Constitutional Amendments. I've got a lot of the members of the United Auto Workers behind me already."

Zephjame put the sheets back into the folder. "You have my approval," he said.

I smiled gratefully. "I was also thinking about making a video tape, sir. To show to different clubs and organizations. Something dramatizing the need for the new amendments."

Zephjame nodded. "Might be helpful." He searched through a box on the table, then handed me a business card. "Contact her. She's my Media Director. You're an ambitious kid," he said. "I like that. Loyal to the cause, eh?"

"Yes, sir!" I said enthusiastically.

"When you call Ms. Gendlin . . ." He gestured toward the card he'd given me. ". . . ask her about petitioning to become a Testee." He stood, obviously about to dismiss me.

"Video tapes are great for education," I said, standing also, "but even better for entertainment. The guy I borrowed that truck from is a movie collector. Mostly action and tough guy films. Most of them are kind of violent. He likes that. He's got a whole bunch of them in the truck, ones you can't get in the video stores. Some are a little on the porn side."

Zephjame looked interested. "What's your friend's name?"

"Jeff Eastwood," I said. "He was excited that I was going to meet you tonight. He's all for your movement too."

"And he collects videos."

"Yeah, especially the hard-to-get ones."

"And you've got some of them in the truck."

"That's right. Dozens of them. The boxes each have a description of what the movie's about. If you're interested, you could come and have a look."

Zephjame clearly was interested as ZET knew he would be. We walked out to the truck. I unlocked the rear door and flipped on the light. Zephjame stared at the rows of video tapes on the shelves. "After you," I said.

I closed the door behind us. As Zephjame took a couple of tapes and began reading the back of the boxes, I heard the faint click of the door being locked.

"This one looks good," he said. "Does your friend ever loan these out? Or sell them?"

"Sure," I said. I opened the cabinet in the corner. "Look what else he has." I held up a pair of silver handcuffs.

Zephjame cocked his head, narrowing his eyes. He smiled in a ghoulish way. "You like to play with toys like that, sonny?"

"Do you?" I asked. I had one of the cuffs open and was holding it in the air.

Zephjame started to reach for it and as he did, I

grabbed him and locked the cuff around his wrist. I went for his other wrist. He struggled, but Calvin was about three inches taller and twenty pounds heavier than James, so I was able to prevail. I got his hands cuffed together behind his back.

"You're making a mistake, kid," Zephjame said. "I'm not interested."

"Sit there." I gestured to the bench in the middle of the truck.

"Take the handcuffs off me, Carl. I mean it." He glared at me with penetrating eyes.

"Can't do that," I said.

I moved toward him, intending to push him down onto the bench, but he dodged and gave me a painful kick on the shin. I crumpled over and he took the opportunity to push past me to the door. He had to turn backwards so he could reach the handle with his cuffed hands. When he realized the door was locked, he came at me. This time I did better. I blocked his kick, swung him around, and pushed him down onto the bench. He tried to stand back up, but I held him down by pressing my hands against his shoulders and leaning on him.

"You're going to be very sorry for this," he said, struggling under the pressure of my weight.

Still holding him, I reached and got hold of the billy club stashed under the video shelves. "If you move, I'll hit you," I said. I glared menacingly at him.

"You're a dead man," he hissed, glaring back at me.

Still holding the club, I went behind him, reached beneath the bench and grabbed a piece of chain that was attached to the floor. The chain had a lock on

185

the end. I fastened it to the chain of Zephjame's handcuffs. Then I got the piece of rope from the cabinet.

Despite his attempts to kick me away, I managed to tie his ankles together.

"You are a fool," he said. "Obviously you have no idea what you're tampering with."

I laughed. "Not true," I said. "I know who you are."

"Then you know you're doomed," he answered.

"I know who you *really* are," I said, looking contemptuously at him.

His eyes narrowed. "What is it you think you know, punk?" I thought he seemed just a little nervous.

"That you, Mr. Zephkar, are no angel of God. You're the devil!" I hissed. "You've fooled most of them, but not me. Not the other Cimians. We are going to exorcise you. Your time has come."

He sneered hatefully, his eyes shooting hot fire. "You festering glob of sewer slime!" he said.

I almost laughed. That was a rough translation of a very strong Alloese curse. It sounded silly in English. "Vile talk," I said. "More proof of who you are."

Zephjame exhaled loudly through flared nostrils. "And who are you?" he demanded.

"Not Carl Fairbanks," I replied. "He's on a plane to California." I got the roll of tape from the cabinet and cut a strip. "My name is unimportant. What's important is my mission." I pressed the tape over Zephjame's mouth. Then I gave the signal, two short and two long raps on the front wall of the truck. "Relax now, Zeph," I said. "We're going for a ride."

The truck began to move. I sat on the stool near the door, about four feet away from Zephjame. He looked at me hatefully. After about five minutes the truck stopped, so Billy could phone Gracie at her brother's house, I knew, and tell the others to go ahead. Soon we began to move again.

I stared at Zephjame, wondering what was going on in Zephkar's mind, wondering if he realized how much danger he was in. So far, so good, I thought. Cindy's phrase. Then I thought of Billy up front in the cab. Very soon now, Billy. Soon this will be over, and I'll have to think about the next step in my life. It seemed that since Billy had arrived, thoughts about permanating were always somewhere in my mind.

"Renacim is our leader," I said to Zephjame. "She is a prophet. Wisest of the wise. Renacim communicates with the true God. It is God who guides me now, while your master, Satan, is powerless."

Zephjame shook his head. He began making nasal noises and gesturing with his chin, probably asking me to remove the tape.

"We are the Cimians for Christ," I said. "Perhaps you've heard of us. There are quite a few of us in Los Angeles. From the first moment Renacim learned of you, she knew who you were." I stretched my legs out in front of me. "This is a holy mission," I said.

It had been Agatha's idea to hide ourselves with costumes and to tell Zephkar we were part of a religious cult. Just in case something went wrong. So far everything was going so smoothly that I suspected the costumes and cult story would turn out to have been unnecessary. No matter, I thought. I was rather enjoying the charade.

"At our ceremony tonight," I continued, "we will disengage your energy and you will float harmlessly into the beyond. God will win again," I said smugly. I wondered if he was buying it. I couldn't tell from his eyes.

From the speed we were going now and the fact that we weren't making stops anymore, I figured we'd reached the highway. We were to go slowly, no more than fifty miles per hour, so the rest of ZET would be sure to arrive at the site first. Cass and Agatha were somewhere on the highway right now, I knew, driving the van, and Doris, Gracie, and Cindy were following them in Cindy's car.

"After the ceremony, James Lane will be free again," I said. "I suspect he will have no memory of anything since the time Satan sent you to take over his body. Or perhaps he'll remember everything. We'll see."

I began going over in my mind how it would go when we got to the site: I'll inject Zephjame, I thought. The truck door will open and Joe Benninger will be standing there. Zephkar will enter Joe, but then he'll realize he isn't free yet, that he's chained to the truck. I'll point the gun at Zephjoe and order him to go to the platform. He'll walk onto the chicken wire and down he'll go into the pit. Cindy will take my gun and mix it in with the others. Then she'll hand us each a gun and we'll all lean over the pit and fire. Joe Benninger will die and

Zephkar Tesot will be stranded at the bottom of the hole. Hopefully, forever.

I rubbed my sore shin. The plan seemed foolproof. I was feeling sure that everything would continue to go smoothly.

I wondered if everyone would fire her gun. Would I? We'd all promised we would. The eight guns were identical. Cindy had loaded two with bullets, six with blanks. No one would know who fired the live bullets. No one would know who did the actual killing.

And yet, we'll all be murderers, I thought, a sick feeling coming to my stomach. I took a deep breath and made myself think of other things.

I wasn't wearing a watch but I figured we must have been on the road for over an hour. About twenty minutes later I felt the truck leaving the highway. Fifteen or so minutes after that, we made a turn onto a bumpy road. I was pretty sure I knew where we were. The truck stopped, backed up a few feet, then forward a bit. Amy's maneuvering into position, I thought. Putting the truck at right angles to the van.

I got the syringe ready. The tapping on the truck came a few minutes later. I opened the bottle of alcohol, soaked some cotton, and sterilized the needle. I did all this with my back to Zephjame, hoping I could give him the injection without his squirming too much. I crouched behind him and plunged the needle into his biceps.

The drug, of course, would have no effect on Zephkar. Although James's mind would be asleep, Zephkar, fully conscious, would continue boosting and using James's body.

It was now time for me to dress. In a box in the corner of the truck was my robe, pastel blue with peach stripes. I put it on along with the white, china doll mask. I rapped on the door.

The first thing I saw when the door opened was someone in a glimmering robe walking away and out of sight. I knew that was Cass. Then, by the light of lanterns and torches, I saw Joe Benninger stumble out of the van. He was blindfolded. A rope was attached to one of his handcuffs, a chain to the other. He was unsteady on his feet; the drug Doris had given him apparently had not completely worn off. The four-foot rope that went from Joe to the van's bumper was to make sure Joe didn't stumble into the pit before Zephkar had a chance to enter him. The twenty-foot chain, locked to Whitey's bumper, was to make sure Zephjoe didn't run away.

About fifteen feet away, on the other side of the camouflaged pit, the line of robed women was visible, their figures illuminated by torch light. They stood on mounds of dirt, Agatha in the center wearing a milk white robe and golden mask. She was supposed to be Renacim. Next to her was a small wooden platform lit by two red flashlights. The whole scene looked eerily impressive.

Parked corner to corner, the rear ends of the truck and the van made two sides of a square. The other two sides were formed by the boundaries of the pit. That arrangement left a square-shaped segment of solid ground, about five feet to a side, as the stage. On that stage, Joe now stood, pulling off his blindfold. Behind Joe was the van. In front of him and to his right was the L-shaped pit, and on the other side of the pit, the women standing

190

solemnly in the torch light. To Joe's left was Whitey's rear end, door wide open, me and Zephjame still inside.

Joe rubbed his eyes groggily, looking around in all directions. "Those cunts are crazy," he mumbled, his speech slurred. "A bunch of fucking lunatics."

He began following the rope to where it was attached to Whitey, stopping a moment to stare at me and Zephjame. In that moment I raised my mask.

Joe's jaw went slack. "Calvin! What the fuck are you doing here?"

I beckoned him to come closer. He moved slowly toward me, blinking his eyes rapidly. I covered my face again with the mask. He came to the entrance of the truck, leaning part way in.

"They got you too, huh, buddy?" he said.

He was close enough now. I watched Zephjame. Suddenly James' eyes closed, the head slumped, and the body went limp. Zephkar had obviously made his move, leaving James Lane and entering Joe Benninger.

Within half a minute Joe was fully alert. Zephjoe did just what we had predicted — untied the rope from the van's bumper, then traced the chain to where it was locked onto the bumper of the truck.

"Time for the ceremony," I said.

Zephjoe looked into the barrel of my gun.

"Ahhh-ah, ooh, cimma-cimma, ohhh," the line of women chanted.

"You're to stand on that platform," I ordered, "between the two red lights."

We had little doubt that Zephkar would gladly do as I said since his goal would be to get near enough to the women to enter one of them and have an unchained body to use. I kept the gun pointed at him as I stepped out of the truck. He started to walk.

"Ohhh, ahhh, cim-cimma, eee-ahh . . ."

Two more steps and he'd go crashing ten feet down into the earth. I watched his feet, holding my breath; the gun was trembling in my hand. Time seemed suspended. Then the evil mutant took the fatal step. The chicken wire gave way, sinking downward. Twigs, dirt, and leaves flew into the air, and Zephjoe fell into the pit.

But something was wrong. He hadn't completely disappeared. Somehow he was managing to cling to the edge of the pit. The lower part of his body was dangling in the hole, but his head was out and his outstretched arms were on the ground, his hands clawing at the earth.

"Shoot him!' someone yelled. It sounded like Cindy.

Zephjoe's fingers dug into the ground, clutching handfuls of soil. I aimed the gun at his head. *Pull the trigger,* I told myself.

He had one leg up over the edge now and was making the final effort to pull himself completely out of the hole. *Fire now,* I told myself, *and he'll fall to the bottom. Shoot the mutant.*

But I couldn't do it. Zephjoe was on his feet. I stood frozen, the gun still pointed at him. He sprang at me with lightning swiftness and then we were both down, rolling on the ground. I felt his fingers squeezing my wrist painfully, bending my hand. Then a powerful explosion filled my whole head.

The music was beautiful. A symphony

accompanied the movement of the slow rolling surf. Billy and I strolled hand in hand along the shore. The sun was a low orange globe. "Another perfect sunset," Billy said. She handed me a large multi-colored shell. I stared at the complex design of its etched exterior. There was so much to see in the patterns of the shell. I wanted never to stop looking at it.

When the buzz came, I was still staring at the shell. Something told me not to ignore the buzz, that this was not a good time to remain in the void. I let the shell drop to the sand. *Go ahead,* Billy said. *We'll come back later.* I made myself concentrate. Zephkar. The Pit Flop. It was all coming back. He had tackled me. He'd tried to get the gun and . . . The buzz was quite distinct now. I pushed and instantly I was riding someone.

"Jen, you there?"

Yes, Agatha. What happened? I saw the knot of women huddled on the other side of the pit. The pit was covered with sheets of plywood. Billy walked toward us over the wood.

"Calvin's dead," Agatha said. "Zephkar got the gun from you and shot you — Calvin — in the head."

"Jenna, are you okay?" Billy stared into our eyes.

Tell her I'm fine.

"Why don't you take over?" Agatha said.

I switched to unilateral boosting, and took Billy into my arms. She was trembling. Then I saw Calvin's body lying on the ground. I realized I was shaking as much as Billy. Her arm on my shoulder steadied me. "Pit Flop was a flop," I said hollowly.

"There's more," Billy said. "Joe Benninger might be dead too."

"What?"

"We hit him on the head with a rock. After Zephjoe shot you — Calvin — he climbed over the van and started coming after us with the gun —

"Oh, no! Did he hurt anyone?"

Cass, Amy, and Cindy, maskless but still in their robes, had come across the plywood and were standing near us. Gracie and Doris were on the other side of the pit.

"No," Billy said. "Everyone's all right. Joe is lying over there." She pointed to a clearing beyond the van, about thirty feet from us.

"And he's dead?" I said.

"He might be. We don't know."

"We can't go find out," Amy said.

"Of course," I responded. "*I* have to do it."

"He hasn't moved since he fell," Cindy said. "Gracie and Doris are watching him now."

"I think he's dead," Cindy said.

I walked over the plywood to Gracie and Doris. Gracie was shining a flashlight on the form lying motionless on the ground twenty feet away.

"Any movement?" I asked.

"None."

I took the flashlight from Doris and went toward Benninger. Ten feet in front of him I saw the gun in the grass. Benninger was lying awkwardly on his stomach, one leg bent beneath him. I turned him over with my foot. There was blood on his forehead and lines of red dripping onto his face. I bent down and pulled back one of his eyelids and shone the flashlight into his eye. No pupillary response. I took his wrist and felt for a pulse. His hand felt clammy. My own skin felt pretty clammy too.

I returned to the waiting women. "He's dead," I said.

"I knew it," Doris said.

"And Zephkar's there somewhere," Billy said. "Somewhere within a six-foot radius of Joe's body."

"Zephzone," Cindy said. "The circle of death."

I looked at the area surrounding Benninger's body. There were a few shrubs, grass, some rocks. No trees. "Zephzone," I repeated. "Zephkar's there all right, somewhere in that circle, drifting in the void." I staggered toward a tree and leaned against it, feeling quite weak. Two corpses and an evil disembodied mind attached to some stone or piece of dirt, I thought.

"Luckily there's no breeze," Cindy said.

"What a night," I said. I noticed that Cass didn't look very well. "You look worse than I feel," I said to her. "Come here, share my tree."

"I killed him," Cass said numbly.

I put my arms around her and she immediately broke into sobs.

"You saved our lives," Amy said. "If you hadn't thrown that rock, he'd have killed us all."

"That's right," Cindy seconded.

Cass continued to cry, her breathing coming in loud wrenching gasps.

"I'm a murderer," she moaned. "First Veronica and now him."

"You're a hero," I said. I led her farther away from the body. The other women came also and we all sat on the grass some distance from the corpses.

"So, what now?" Doris said. No one answered. "I suggest it's time to call the FBI. This has gone far enough. Maybe they can figure out a way to keep Zephkar stranded. Build some structure around zephzone, maybe, and trap him."

"We're not calling anybody," Cindy snapped. "Dammit, Doris, use your brain."

"Cindy's right," Gracie said. "You know we can't do that."

"We have to figure out a way to trap him ourselves," Billy said.

"Before we do anything else, we should bury those bodies," Amy said.

Doris looked at her watch. "I better give James Lane another injection. He should be coming to any time now."

"No, wait," I said. "I'll use his body."

I tried not to look at Calvin's corpse as I went to Whitey and climbed in. James lay on the floor in the same position Zephkar had left him. I unlocked the handcuffs, removed the tape from his mouth, and entered him, going immediately to boost-blocking. The contrast with Agatha's body was striking. The first thing I always noticed when I was in a male was the feel of the pants crotch pressing against the unretractable penis.

Billy and Cindy pulled the plywood from the pit. I unlocked the chain from Whitey's bumper and Gracie drove Whitey forward a few yards to give us more room. We slid Calvin's legs over the edge of the pit, then Agatha and Amy, holding him by the wrists, lowered him down as far as they could, then let go. He landed with a gruesome thud.

After Amy moved the van out of the way, I went to get Joe Benniger. I removed the handcuffs, then dragged him slowly over the ground, pausing periodically to catch my breath. The other women kept their distance from zephzone.

"There's no chance Zephkar could be attached to Benninger's clothes, is there?" Doris asked as I got closer to them.

"No," Cass said. "The moment Benninger died, Zephkar's disembodied mind was propelled six feet away from the body, out of range."

"I know, but what if something went wrong? What if somehow he got onto the body."

"Wozar told us that never happens," Cass said. "Zephkar is attached to some piece of dirt or a rock within a six-foot radius of where Benninger fell. Count on it."

Despite the reassurance, Doris backed off as I came close with Joe's body. We dropped him into the pit the same way we'd done with Calvin. The thud was more muted this time. The two raping buddies, I thought, one atop the other for eternity. I returned for the gun and tossed it into the pit.

Cindy brought the shovels from the van. "Dig in," she said.

"Wait." Cass had a strange, determined look that I didn't like. "I'm going into the zephzone," she said.

We all stared at her.

"As soon as Zephkar enters me, I'll run and jump into the pit."

"What the hell are you talking about?" Cindy croaked.

"I'll stand in the middle of zephzone. He'll enter me right away, and then I'll have thirty seconds to get to the pit before he starts boosting." Cass was taking deep lungfuls of air. "I'll make it easily. You should probably shoot me once I'm down there — if you can — to be on the safe side, but also because I'd rather not die by suffocation if it can be helped."

I was speechless. So, apparently, were the others.

Cass looked at Doris. "I'd really prefer something less violent. If you have anything in that black bag of yours, Doris, that I could have in my mouth and swallow as soon as Zephkar enters, I'd prefer it. Something that will kill me fairly quickly and quietly, or at least put me into a deep sleep."

"Don't be asinine," Doris said.

"Oh, Cass, honey, what's wrong with you? Why are you talking like this?" Amy said.

"It's the only way," Cass responded flatly. "Zephkar will be stranded. This planet will be safe."

"That's insane," Billy said, shaking her head disgustedly.

"Come on," I said to Cass. "Let's sit and talk a minute."

"It's my choice. I want to do it," Cass said determinedly. "It's the perfect solution."

"To what, Cass?" I said. "Your guilt?"

She didn't answer. I made her sit on the grass next to me beneath a tree. The others stayed to the side.

"You had to stop him," I said. "By throwing that rock, you saved yourself and everyone else."

She was silent for a very long time. "What's happened to me, Jenna?" she said at last.

I knew exactly what she meant. "You're adapting to a different reality," I said.

"I've become a killer. First Veronica Bloom, now Benninger. I'm not me anymore." A moan escaped her lips. "I'm an alien. A mutant. I aimed for his head, Jenna. I wanted him dead. I felt . . ."

"Rage," I said.

"Yes."

"Fear and rage — at Zephkar for all the misery he's caused. And at Benninger for —

"But *you* couldn't bring yourself to kill," Cass said. "You haven't changed that much, Jenna. *You* couldn't do it."

"I'm not proud of that," I answered. "Look what it cost us. Calvin wasn't supposed to die. It's my fault that he did. Should I sacrifice myself then?"

"You don't need to," Cass said. "I'm going to do it."

"You are not! I want you to leave, Cass. Go with Amy or someone back to Chicago. The rest of us will finish up here."

Cass stood. Every eye was on her. Agatha moved a few feet and so did Gracie, blocking the path between Cass and zephzone.

"Don't even think it," Agatha said.

"I'm truly willing to do it," Cass replied. She looked at the line of women blocking her way. "I should have just gone ahead without telling you."

"Go home, Cass," Agatha said. "I agree with Jenna. You're too stressed out. You shouldn't be here anymore."

"I'll take you," Amy said.

"I'm not leaving," Cass protested. "If you won't

let me do it my way, then how else are we going to stop Zephkar? You saw that kids' tree house nearby and those gun shells. Obviously people come around here despite the no-trespassing signs. It won't take long for someone to come close enough for Zephkar to enter. Do any of you have a better solution than me?"

Cass remained standing where she was. The line of women did not move. I went over to Cass and put my hand on her shoulder. "We'll think of one," I said.

"Get another rapist," Cindy said. Everyone looked at her. "Jenna could go find some scumbag guy and boost him and bring him back here to zephzone."

Cass shook her head. "And how do we get him to jump into the pit? It won't work, Cindy. The one who's sacrificed has to be a volunteer."

"Maybe we actually could find a volunteer," Gracie said. "Someone with a terminal illness who would want to make a contribution before dying."

Billy shook her head. "Not necessary." She directed the beam of her flashlight into zephzone. "Look," she said. "The tallest object in zephzone is that rock that's about six inches high. That's the highest place Zephkar could be. No one else needs to die for us to strand him. We just cover over the whole zephzone with cement — build a cement pad, a square, twelve feet to a side. We make it thick enough to cover everything in the zone."

"Of course," I said, excitedly. I gave Billy's neck a squeeze. "That would do it, ZET. A DM can't go through solid matter. He'd be stranded there under the cement for as long as the pad survived."

"We could make sure it survives for a long, long time," Agatha said, her eyes glinting. "We could have a structure built over it."

"A tomb," Amy offered.

"Yes," Agatha said. "That's it. A mausoleum. We could have a nice inscription about resting in peace forever. No one would disturb a tomb."

"We'll have to come up with a good story for my sister," Cindy said.

"Tell her you had a dream," Amy suggested. "Your dream told you to build a mausoleum on that spot and that when you die, that's where your coffin's to be placed for all eternity."

"But I'm going to be cremated," Cindy said.

"Your urn of ashes then," Amy responded, chuckling. Her chuckle turned into real laughter that was on the verge of hysteria.

Cindy started laughing with her, and then so did Gracie and Agatha. I guess we were all pretty stressed out by that point. When they finally calmed down, we talked some more and agreed that covering over the area where Zephkar's disembodied mind was stranded was the best solution.

Cass still seemed somewhat shaky. Even though she also agreed with the plan, I would have felt more comfortable if she had gone back to Chicago instead of insisting on spending the night in the cabin with the rest of us.

On the small chance that somebody might trek through the area while we slept, we agreed to take turns guarding zephzone through the night. We flipped for guard duty but wouldn't let Cass participate. She objected at first then shut up, saying she understood our concern, but explaining that she really did prefer not to die if it wasn't necessary.

Agatha and Gracie drew first shift. Before the rest of us drove the quarter mile to the cabin, we all helped shovel enough dirt into the pit to cover over the two bodies. I marked the perimeter of zephzone with stones, and the others gathered wood so the guards could have a fire to sit by.

It was nearly three a.m. when we got to the cabin. Including the sofa and a folding cot, there were sleeping places for all of us. Even though we were exhausted, no one went to bed right away. Doris fretted about missing person's reports being filed on Joe Benninger and Calvin Magriel and the possibility of the police tracing them to us.

"We already went over that," Amy said. "People will just assume the two creeps took off. They've been known to take to the road, right Jenna?"

"Frequently," I said. "They're a couple of vagabonds. I agree that it's very unlikely any of us would be connected with Calvin or Joe's disappearance."

"We should probably pack up Calvin's things like we did Joe's," Billy said, "and dump them in the trash."

"Not necessary," I said. "He lives in a furnished room and owns next to nothing. Anyway, I think it's better if none of us goes near his place."

"The bodies will never be found," Agatha said.

Amy nodded. "A ten-foot-deep grave, on private property. Nothing to worry about."

Cindy brought a tray of drinks and a giant bowl of popcorn into the living room where we all huddled. As we ate and drank, we talked about how we'd build the concrete pad, about arranging to have the concrete delivered from nearby Racine, about the tools and supplies we'd need.

"And then eventually we'll have to get the mausoleum built," Cass said.

"It'll be a huge one," I said.

"I deserve space for my eternity," Cindy responded.

After that we lapsed into a long heavy silence. I was thinking about the two men in the pit and the fact that we were responsible for their deaths. From the others' faces, I imagined they were having similar thoughts. In my mind, I heard again the thuds the bodies had made when they'd landed in the pit.

"I'm going to bed," Doris said. "You better get some sleep too, Amy." Doris and Amy had the second guard shift.

Billy and I went to the slightly saggy bed on the front porch. I had drawn the third shift which meant I would be able to sleep until nine, a little over five hours. Billy had until noon. Despite the fact that I was occupying James Lane's body, Billy held me closely under the sheet and soft comforter. "What a night," I murmured before slipping into an uneasy sleep.

I dreamed I was shooting people with a huge, double-barreled pistol. Pieces of skull flew into the air, then each of the pieces turned into little Zephkars. I woke up moaning. Billy held me and listened as I described the terrifying nightmare. I had just drifted off again when Cindy shook my shoulder. "Time for our shift," she whispered.

Our sojourn at zephzone was as uneventful as Agatha's and Gracie's, and Doris's and Amy's had been. We sat on a pair of ratty lawn chairs several feet outside the marked danger zone. After awhile the sun was so warm we had to move our chairs to the shade. To make sure we didn't doze off, we tried to keep up a steady stream of conversation during our two and a half hour shift. Cindy spilled her heart out to me, about her feelings for Cass and her fear that Cass was unattainable. I thought she might be right about that.

By one o'clock everyone was up and about. Cindy had driven to a grocery store and gotten food. Doris had a meeting at the hospital that she couldn't miss, so after we ate, she and Gracie left for Chicago. Cass and Amy went to Racine in the van to get the cement and to buy tools and lumber. The rest of us stayed at the pit and shoveled. Getting the dirt in wasn't nearly as difficult as getting it out had been, but I still ended up with sore muscles. James Lane's body obviously wasn't accustomed to physical labor. We laid leaves and twigs and pine needles over the filled in pit, and then we sprawled on the grass. The sun blazed even though it was nearly four o'clock.

"There's a pond not far from here," Cindy said. "Anybody interested in a swim?"

Agatha agreed to stay behind to guard zephzone and Cindy promised to relieve her in an hour. Billy, Cindy and I drove Whitey to the cabin to get a blanket and some towels, then walked for a short distance through trees and a field of long grass until we came to a little hidden pond.

The water was cool and murky and it felt wonderful. Billy and I roughhoused and got pretty silly. After awhile Cindy left to take Agatha's place, and Billy and I spread out a blanket and laid down. Billy looked so beautiful, all wet and fresh. I wanted to make love with her but resisted since I was in James Lane's body. This was definitely one of the times when I fervently longed for a body of my own. I lay my head back, eyes closed, wondering if I should permanate soon now that Zephkar had been stopped and it was time to look to the future.

Cindy was leaning forward in her chair and staring intently into zephzone when Billy, Agatha, and I got back from the pond. "Some kids were here," she said.

"Where?" Billy said. "Not in zephzone?"

"I don't know. Do you see that shiny thing?" Cindy pointed. "To the right of that little birch branch."

"Yeah, I see it," Agatha said.

"Was that there before?"

"I don't know."

"I'll go get it," I said, walking into the area that only I could safely enter. I picked the object up. "It's a tiny pocket knife," I told the others.

"I heard some kids in the woods," Cindy said. "It sounded like they were coming this way so I went to cut them off before they got any closer. There were three of them, boys, maybe seven or eight years old. I told them this was private property, and that they couldn't play around here. After they left, I was on my way back here when I spotted some more kids.

Three of them were less than ten yards from zephzone. A fourth was walking away, up that path. I started toward them but as soon as they saw me they took off."

"Shit!" Agatha said. "So it's possible that while you were chasing away the first group, the other kids came and walked through zephzone. Shit!" She turned the knife over in her hand.

"The knife could have been there all along," Billy said.

"Maybe," Cindy responded.

"But maybe the kids entered zephzone," Agatha said, "and Zephkar entered one of them."

"Oh God, I don't want to think about it," Cindy said. "Damn! It's my fault. We had to go for that stupid swim. If we'd all been here, this never would have happened."

"We don't know that anything happened," I said.

"But we don't know it didn't," Billy retorted. "If Zephkar did enter one of those kids, he might come back here to . . ."

She didn't finish her sentence.

"Maybe we should get out of here," Agatha said. "He hasn't seen our faces and doesn't know who we are."

Just then we heard engine sounds and moments later Cass and Amy pulled up in the van. "Hope you weren't worried," Amy called. "We had a flat tire. Hey, what's wrong? You guys look terrible."

Agatha told them what had happened. Amy looked frightened but Cass seemed angry. "You shouldn't have picked up the knife," she said to me. "What if it *was* there all along and what if Zephkar was stuck to it."

I couldn't believe I hadn't thought of that.

"Well, obviously he wasn't," Billy said, defending me, "or he'd have entered one of us by now."

We discussed what to do, ending up deciding that there was enough uncertainty about whether Zephkar was still in zephzone that we should proceed with building the concrete pad.

"If he did enter one of the children," I said, "when he saw that the truck and van were gone, and that the pit was filled in, and that all that was left were a couple of discarded lawn chairs, he probably figured we'd all left, taking James with us."

"That could be," Cass said. "And since you can't see the cabin from here, hopefully, he'll never come back to investigate."

"I think Zephkar is still there," Amy said. "In zephzone."

We all hoped she was right.

The van was full of bags of cement, boards, hammers, trowels, a wheelbarrow, water containers, and the rest of the things we'd need to build the concrete pad. There was only enough cement to put down the first layer; the rest would be delivered in the morning.

We got started immediately. The boards were each thirteen feet long. The others laid them out in a square around zephzone and secured them with pegs pounded into the ground while I rested since I would have to do the actual laying of the concrete myself.

By the time it was too dark to see clearly, I had a thick layer of concrete over the whole area and globs of it piled atop the larger stones. If Zephkar was there, he was surely covered over and secured by the now-hardening concrete. We covered the area with a large sheet of plastic which we fastened to the ground with pegs.

Everyone ate heartily and slept deeply that night. The next morning, a truck arrived from town with the already mixed concrete. We had the man dump it right onto zephzone. We were hard at work leveling the concrete when Doris and Gracie arrived. Several of us took a break and told them about the children Cindy had seen. We were sitting and talking about it when a group of kids again appeared in the woods.

"Did someone lose a pocket knife?" Cindy called in a friendly voice.

Two of the children approached; two other littler ones hung back.

Cindy held the knife up. "This yours?"

"I think it's my friend's," a redheaded boy said.

"Here," Cindy said, "you can have it back then."

The boy approached. "You building a cabin here?"

"A tomb," Cindy said. She handed him the knife. "You know, something weird is going on around here. A gas in the air or something. It makes people sleepwalk."

The other children came closer and listened.

"They just suddenly fall asleep," Cindy continued, "and the next thing they know they wake up somewhere else and have no idea how they got there."

The kids looked at each other.

"It happened to me yesterday," one of them said. He was a rosy-cheeked child of about six or seven.

"Where's the gas come from?" the redhead asked.

"Tell me about what happened," Cindy said to the rosy-cheeked one.

"I was over right there where you're making the floor and then I wasn't there anymore because then I was with Mr. Gallagher in his yard. And he just walked away to his car and didn't say anything. And then he drove in his car and he was gone. But I didn't know how I got there. That's sleepwalking, I think. But I don't remember falling asleep."

A sinking feeling had come to the pit of my stomach.

"Where does Mr. Gallagher live?" Billy asked.

The boy pointed into the woods. "That way, not far. In the pink house."

"I know the place," Cindy said. She looked at the children. "I think the gas is gone now. There was just a little of it in the air. It doesn't hurt you anyway. But just to be safe, you probably shouldn't come back here for a few days. Maybe a week."

"I'm getting out of here," the redhead said. "I don't want no gas making me do weird things."

"Me neither," another said, and they all ran off.

"Son of a bitch," Cindy said.

Cass shook her head disgustedly. "That mutant is charmed. First he miraculously manages to avoid falling all the way into the pit . . ."

"It's because he walked so slowly," Doris said.

" . . .and then this little band of wood nymphs wanders right across his path," Cass continued.

"We've got shit for luck," Gracie said.

"I'm going to go talk to Gallagher," Cindy said.

Billy went with her.

"We might as well finish the job," Doris said, picking up a shovel.

We were hard at work when Cindy and Billy returned.

"He had a blackout," Cindy said. "In his back yard late yesterday afternoon. The next thing he knew, it was two hours later and he was in Chicago."

"The saga continues," I said disgustedly.

"At least Zephkar didn't stick around and find us," Agatha said.

"And he doesn't know what we look like," Amy added. "Thank God we had the costumes."

"He'll try to find out who we are. He'll get revenge," Doris said fretfully.

"He won't succeed," Agatha said. "We covered our tracks well. There's no way he can trace us."

"Let's finish up and get out of here," Doris said. "I'm getting a headache."

We completed the cement work, packed all our tools and equipment into the van, straightened up the cabin, and headed south. I rode in the back of Whitey with Billy. Cass and Amy were in the cab. Just outside of Chicago we stopped at a Howard Johnson's rest area to drop off James Lane. I went into the men's room and shifted into a black man with a very tiny prick, leaving James standing at the urinal.

Amy was waiting for me near the vending machines. *You are not alone,* I said.

* * * * *

I went to James Lane's house and mind-tickled Freddie.

Zephkar has his people searching for the Cimians in Los Angeles, I told Agatha when she came to pick me up. *It was a stroke of genius to come up with that cover story.* Agatha proudly agreed. *And Andrew Corrigan is out of town on a fishing trip.*

"Lucky for him," Agatha said, "and for us."

The apartment was empty when we got home. Billy was bicycling along the lake, Agatha told me, and Cass, Amy, and Cindy had gone to the park. "They're going to try to work things out," Agatha said. "At least that's what Cass hopes. It was her idea for the three of them to have a talk."

I was pretty sure I knew what Cass had in mind. I wondered if it would work.

"I had a nightmare last night," Agatha said, "about the guys in the pit."

They're haunting me too, I said. It was true. I kept hearing the thudding sounds they'd made when they landed.

"I've got something to distract you," she said. "Today's newspaper. It's disgusting, Jenna. Nearly every page has some reference to New Direction or something to do with Zephkar. *Theocracy: Its Time Has Come* was one of the headlines. And then there was a story about the effect on non-Christians. Lots of them are converting. Others are finding ways to integrate Zephkar's preaching into their own religions."

He's doing just what he set out to do, I said, *taking over.*

We heard the back door open. "Anybody home?" Billy called.

"Do you want the body?" Agatha asked. "I could use a little drift."

I shifted to boost-blocking and slipped on my jewelry just in time to take Billy into my arms and whisper love stuff in her ear.

"I don't think I could have gotten through the last few days without you," I said.

"You're dependent on me," Billy responded teasingly.

"I know. I love being dependent on you." I kissed her deeply.

When Cass and her two Earthling lovers returned from their serious discussion in the park, they looked unhappy.

"We need a consultation," Cindy said.

"What about?" Billy asked.

"Tripling," Amy said.

"I suggested an Alloy solution to the problem of our love triangle," Cass said. "Cindy called me a pervert."

"I did not!"

"Well, not in so many words," Cass said.

"I ended up agreeing to give it a try," Cindy said. "Even though I predict complete failure."

"And I said that with that attitude, it's bound to fail." Cass looked at me and Billy. "They want you to convince them that the whole concept isn't absolutely insane."

"What about you, Amy?" Billy said. "Are you as negative about it as Cindy?"

"I said I'll pull out. I told the two of them I

wouldn't bother them, that they could have each other and I'd take up knitting or something."

"I see. But Cass doesn't want that, does she?"

Amy looked petulantly at Cass. "No."

"I think you'd be a great knitter," Cindy said, chuckling. "You do have sexy eyes, though."

Amy batted her eyes.

"And I like your sense of humor," Cindy said.

"She has soft skin," Cass added. "Especially on her inner thighs."

"Oh?" Cindy's lips parted slightly.

"Cut it out, you two," Amy said. But she was smiling.

"I'd say the plan has potential," I offered.

"You're an extraterrestrial," Amy said. "What do you know?"

"I know about trying new things," I responded.

"Do you know about competition and jealousy and broken hearts?" Amy asked.

"It would be risky," I agreed. "It might not work."

"And then somebody ends up very hurt," Amy said. "Maybe all three of us."

"Are you really willing to bow out?" Billy asked her.

"I'd rather Cindy bow out. I already suggested she move to Alaska. I'm trying to help us find a solution."

"Cass, your love life is a mess," I said to my Alloy friend.

"I'm going tomorrow to buy a king-size bed," Cass said.

I laughed at that.

"I have a suggestion," Billy said. "I think you two have to spend some time together. Amy and Cindy. Just the two of you. Get to know each other better."

"That's just what Cass said," Cindy responded. "I'm willing."

We all looked at Amy. "This is weird," she said.

"So, what the hell," Cindy said. She held her hand out to Amy. "Let's go for a romantic stroll or something."

Amy shrugged. "What the hell," she said.

After they were gone, Billy wondered aloud whether it could really work when two of the triplers were Earthlings.

"Hopefully, we're going to find out," Cass said optimistically.

It crossed my mind that she and Billy and I would make a good tripling. But then I felt a sharp pang of jealousy at the thought of Billy and Cass together. Tripling was a very risky business for sure, even for Alloys.

The next morning when Andrew Corrigan arrived at his office I was waiting for him in the body of his secretary, C. W. Gatling. I shifted to Andrew, boost-blocked, and phoned Zephkar.

"I want to apologize for Carl missing his appointment with you last Thursday," I said. I explained how Carl had been taken against his will to the airport and put on a plane. "The kidnappers were obviously wearing disguises," I said. "And they stole Carl's briefcase. I have no idea what the whole thing was about. Do you, Mr. Lane?"

"Was your nephew harmed?"

"No sir, he's fine."

"Then forget about it," Zephjame said. "It doesn't concern you. The people who took him are part of a cult of fanatics. I'll deal with them."

After the call, I returned to Agatha and we hailed a cab.

I wonder what Zephjame will do if he finds out there is no Carl Fairbanks, Agatha said, *and that Corrigan has blackout spells.*

What could he do? I said. *Anyway, there's a good chance we'll be rid of Zephkar in a few weeks.*

Agatha wrote the note to Zephkar on perfumed stationery. *I'll be at the Ritz Carlton lounge at seven o'clock next Wednesday,* it said, *and it would please me if you would come by.* She signed it, Veronica Bloom. We felt fairly sure Zephjame would show up.

After finishing the note Agatha said she wanted to go back to the void.

"You in a bad mood? I asked.

"Not at all. I was in the middle of a great adventure. I want to continue it."

Shall I bring you back for the volleyball game tonight with those friends of Cindy?

"No, you go ahead. Keep the body as long as you want."

You're beginning to worry me, Agatha.

"I thought you liked using my body."

Is it the deaths? Is that what's bothering you?

"Really, Jenna, I'm fine. Do you think I'm depressed or something? I'm not. I'm just enjoying the void."

As much as I liked monopolizing her body, Agatha's attitude disturbed me. The others were concerned about her too. Agatha insisted on staying in the void most of that week and over the weekend as well. On Monday morning, I told her she was to have the body today.

Don't do it for me, she responded. *I'm doing fine.*

"Well, don't you want to hear about what's been going on? Aren't you curious about the volleyball game? And party we went to Saturday night? And what everybody did on Sunday? Don't you wonder how things are going with Amy and Cass and Cindy? And what about your writing? Aren't you interested in anything anymore?"

So how was the party? Agatha said flatly.

"I don't like this," I said. "You get the body whether you want it or not. I'm going to shift to riding."

Jenna, there's no need. Really, I want you to enjoy yourself. Go off somewhere with Billy. I truly am quite content in the void.

I was tempted to comply. Billy and I had talked about going to the zoo that day. "No," I said, "I'm going to shift."

As soon as Agatha had control of her body, she went to the bedroom and lay on the bed with her eyes closed. I was bored so I propelled myself into the void. For a while I just drifted with the images and the beautiful sounds. The music was a medley of all my favorite songs from Allo, but sung in English. The images included huge mountains and rushing waterfalls. Then Billy was there and she and I floated over an immense zoo and landed in the polar bear exhibit. Hanging onto the milky white fur of a big female bear, we dived and swam in the warm, crystal clear water. Then we were on an ice field, still mounted on the bear's back as she lumbered around on the glacier. The sun was bright. The music continued playing. Huge white mountain peaks rose on all sides of us. We climbed one, easily, for the bear was amazingly strong, and on the other side was a tropical jungle. Soon Billy and I were riding around on a huge elephant.

I found out later that I'd stayed in the void for six hours. Occasionally I'd listened for the buzz but there was nothing until finally Amy was there. *DM on board,* I said. *Hi, Amy Klein, how's your love life?*

"Have you been snooping, Jenna?" she asked indignantly. "You're supposed to let me know when you're riding me."

Hey, guilty conscience, or what? It was just an innocent query. I haven't been in you for days.

"Oh."

So, how is your love life? I said, chuckling.

"We had a threesome."

Mm-m. And?

It was pretty good. She smiled. *I've grown rather fond of Cindy actually, and being with her like that, with Cass and . . . it was . . . very nice.* I could feel her blushing. "You missed the picnic today," she said aloud. "So did Agatha. She went out somewhere

217

by herself this morning and we assumed you were with her. It's four o'clock now and she just got back. She told me you were probably in here in the void."

How does she seem to you? I asked.

"Agatha? A little withdrawn," Amy said. "She says everything's all right, though. Is she angry at you for some reason?"

I don't know. She wanted to stay in the void today and I insisted she take over her body. Does she seem angry at me?

"A little. Do you think she's become addicted to the void?"

That's what I'm afraid of, I said. *I probably shouldn't boost-block her anymore for a while.*

"That'd be hard on you, wouldn't it? Since you like using her body best. Billy likes it too."

Next thing you know, she'll tell me I can use her body permanently, I said.

The next day that's exactly what Agatha did. I was boost-blocking Amy when she broached the topic. "What's the harm?" she said. "You want a body, I like the void; so let's make a deal."

"Oh, come on, Agatha. What about your life? Don't you have things you want to do in the real world?"

"Sure, but relatively speaking, I prefer the void. No pain, no frustration. In the void I create a world exactly the way I want it to be. And it seems as real as this one, Jename. You know that. I have a new lover."

"Oh?"

"She's my dream woman and she's as real to me as any flesh and blood person. We have wonderful times together. And I'm an established author too. My works stimulated a lot of social change that's now made our world close to a utopia. There are still things I need to do though. I want to get back to it, Jename. Check with me every month or so if you want. I'm sure I'll be content, though, that I won't want to come back."

"Wouldn't you miss us?" I asked. "Your friends?"

"You're all with me," Agatha responded. "You and Billy have a farm."

I shook my head angrily. "That's it," I said, "no more void for you. You're cut off, girl."

Agatha stared at me incredulously. "You *are* kidding," she said.

"Agatha, you have a real life. If you stay for a long time in the void, that life could disintegrate. You need to be here. To interact. To be a person."

"One year," Agatha said. "Give me one year. Then we'll renegotiate. It should be my decision, shouldn't it? How I choose to spend my time? What I'm proposing wouldn't harm anybody. It would be good for you and good for me. I know you like my body. And I trust you to take good care of it. Why pass up an offer like this?"

Agatha's proposal was making me very upset, yet, in a sense her arguments were reasonable. But while the idea attracted me, it also repelled me. "It's escapism," I said.

"So what?" she retorted.

I knew what she was proposing was wrong, yet I couldn't think of any powerful arguments to support my position. "We need you to help us stop Zephkar,"

I said at last. "I have to ride Cass when she's with him, so you have to be in the real world then."

"That's fine. But in the meantime and afterwards . . ."

"Agatha, this is pissing me off."

"Well, I think that's your problem," she said. "Because you don't like the void, you're deciding it isn't healthy to like it."

"I do like the void, but I like the real world better."

"So we have a difference of opinion; why impose your values on me?"

The argument went on and on but we didn't come to any resolution. I finally said I needed to think about it and that we could talk later.

"All right," Agatha said, "but unless you boost-block, I'd rather you didn't use my body anymore."

"Fine," I said. But I didn't feel fine at all.

Later, still boosting Amy, I discussed the situation with Billy.

"Maybe she's right about there being no harm in giving it a try," Billy said. "She doesn't have a lover. Her parents are both dead and her siblings settled around the country. Her career as a free-lance writer could easily be put on hold, I imagine. Why not give her the year, Jenna? She obviously wants it badly and it seems like it would certainly benefit you, unless you've changed your mind and plan on permanating."

"But don't you think it's unhealthy for her?" I said.

"How so?"

"To want to stop living?"

"It's not like dying."

"In a sense it is."

"There's nothing comparable to it," Billy argued. "Nothing we knew on Allo and nothing here on Earth. There was never this option before."

I was quiet for a while. "What if I agree and then every time I check back with her she says, 'More, more, I'm having a great time,' until finally after five years or something she decides she's had enough."

"So you're worried that it would end up being hard on you?"

"Yes. That's one of my concerns. And on you. And probably on her too, to re-enter after being gone that long. It could be a tough readjustment."

"Nothing compared to what we've had to adjust to. I think it would be harder on us than on her. It's like we'd be living on borrowed time."

"Exactly."

"Knowing any moment she could demand her body back. That would be rough, hon, but what about the alternatives? You borrowing bodies if and when people let you. Both of us having to adjust to that all the time. Is that better?"

"Well, since she offered to let me keep her body permanently," I said, "then maybe I should get her to commit to it. Tell her she can't change her mind."

Billy looked at me. "That wouldn't feel right to you."

"No," I said.

"That's basically what they do on Wraunk except they don't bother getting the host's permission."

"Yeah, and when the body starts breaking down the DM's give it back. Is that what you're suggesting I do?"

"I'm not suggesting anything. None of this was my idea."

"What you want is for me to permanate, isn't it?"

"Yes," Billy said, "when the time is right. You know I feel like a real jerk for not waiting myself. Cass does too. Neither of us thought it through. We didn't think about how much easier it would be to get rid of Zephkar as DM's. Luckily, you did."

"Not really," I said. "That wasn't my reason for not permanating."

"Well, it's part of your reason now, I assume."

"Yes, of course." Persephone nuzzled my hand and I scratched her behind the ears. "Agatha is offering me a perfect solution," I said. "Maybe I feel guilty about it. Maybe it's exactly what I hoped for all along and I feel guilty about using her that way."

"She's the one who suggested it. The void is wonderful. She's not making the offer as a favor to you, Jenna."

"Why aren't you calling me Jename."

"Because I hate that."

"See? You can't stand my not having my own body. I knew it."

"Oh, give me a break."

"You've picked up all the Earthling expressions. That gets on my nerves."

"You do the same thing and you know it. We're part of this culture now."

"Well, I hate it here. I suspected you'd get sick of

222

dealing with me as a DM. I feared it from the moment I learned you permanated."

"Oh, Jenna." She pulled me to her arms. "What are we doing? I love you so much. It's the pressure. There's just too much pressure on both of us, and Agatha has brought it to a head by suggesting a way to relieve some of it, a way that just doesn't feel right to you."

I kept myself rigid in her arms. "How does this sound?" I said. She let go of me. "I tell Agatha that she and I can both continue thinking about her proposal and maybe discuss it together and with other people, but that we won't even consider acting on it until Zephkar is stranded."

"Sounds reasonable."

"And that I'll continue boost-blocking her from time to time, but not for long stretches."

"All right."

"And that she continue to have a life when she's not in the void. Relate to people and do her writing. That she can't just sit around waiting for her times in the void."

"Yes, I think you should tell her that," Billy said. "And Jenna . . ."

"What?"

"I love you."

I started crying. We reached for each other and cried together.

Zephjame arrived at the Ritz Carlton lounge five minutes after we did. He was dressed in a smart-looking steel-gray suit and vest. I was riding so Cass had the responsibility for handling the conversation. I would coach her, we'd agreed, if it seemed necessary.

Their conversation flowed easily. Zephkar apparently needed no convincing that Veronica Bloom was a devoted Christian who was sincerely intrigued by the work of New Direction. At one point, he tried to enter her. Unable to, he said, "Tell me about your background, Veronica. You come from a large family?"

"Two sisters," Cass responded. "One is my twin. Most people don't know about that; I used to keep it secret."

"An identical twin, I suspect," Zephjame said.

"Yes. She lives in Paris."

Zephjame nodded. "You've heard, I assume, that I can transport my divine spirit into the souls of others."

"I've heard."

"The only exception seems to be with identical twins," Zephjame said pensively, "though interestingly this is not true with all twins." He continued staring at her. "You have very lovely eyes."

Her gaze didn't waver. "Thank you."

"Let's go somewhere for dinner." He called for the check.

A Mercedes Benz, with Freddie at the wheel, was waiting in front of a fire hydrant on Michigan Avenue. Freddie drove us to Como Inn where the conversation continued over eggplant Parmesan and wine. During dessert, Zephjame began stroking Cass's hosiery-encased leg. She removed his hand.

"My body is a temple," she stated with great sincerity. "It took me a long time to learn that."

A flash of irritation crossed Zephjame's face, but then a smile. "And now you have even more to learn. Inhibition is insufficient, my dear. To transcend your desires, you must fully indulge them."

"Oh, really?"

"This is one of the new messages I bring."

"From God?"

"Of course. Did you know that you are being tested this moment?"

Cass cocked her head coyly.

"Does it please you to be a personal Testee of Zephkar?"

Cass scrutinized him. "They say Zephkar's spirit dwells within you, Mr. Lane. If this is true, then being your Testee, being with you at all, is definitely quite . . . pleasing."

"We'll go to my home now," he said, "where we can be alone and get to know each other."

"I'm flattered," Cass responded. "Yet, despite my . . . attraction to you, you see, my morality . . . my faith forbids me to —"

"Ideas like that are obsolete," Zephjame snapped. "To become a Full Christian, you have to give vent to your impulses, not inhibit them."

"This is difficult for me," Cass said in a faltering voice. "I finally let in God's truth and now you tell me there's another truth."

"Yes, yes, that's right. Another truth. Let it in, my sweet. If you do and if you pass my test, you'll become an Initiate. This is quite an opportunity for you, Veronica. I thought you understood that."

You better back off, Cass, I warned.

"An Initiate?" she said.

"Yes, and then a Disciple. In your case, becoming an Apostle might even be a possibility. Are you familiar with the hierarchy?"

"I've read some accounts of it," Cass said.

"Then you know that before tonight you were what we call a Fish — one of the many swimming in the sea of uncertainty."

"Not yet a Full Christian," Cass said.

"That's right. People who claim to be converts and who want to work actively with us petition to be Testees and then —"

"And you saw my notes to you as a petition?"

"No. Until this evening you were still a Fish. But now that I've met you, I consider you a Testee. Even though I'm not able to enter you and check the purity of your heart, I've decided to speed you along. That *is* acceptable to you, I assume."

"I think it is," Cass said. "And the testing involves . . ."

"In your case, it involves becoming known to me . . ." He smiled seductively at her. ". . . being with me in ways that I can assess your sincerity and your true potential."

"You test everyone yourself?"

"Of course not. That would be impossible. The Disciples handle most of it."

"But you're . . . testing me now," she said coyly.

She was doing well, I thought, even though her playing up to Zephkar disgusted me.

"I certainly am. Testees who are judged unready

226

become Fish again. I doubt very much that this will be your fate. After tonight, I'm sure you'll be elevated to Initiate."

"I hope my celibacy won't interfere with my progress," Cass said.

That was risky, I thought.

"You're not listening to me, Veronica."

"I'm listening," she responded, holding his eyes. "I'm just not sure I'm buying it."

Oh oh, I thought, now she's blown it. But Zephjame burst out laughing.

"You're a rare one," he said, his eyes on her breasts. "In many ways."

"And what about Cadreers?" Cass asked. "I know these are people who help with the work of New Direction. Must all of them first be tested?"

Zephjame leaned back. "I'd be happy to explain the whole process to you, my sweet, if that's what you want."

She had succeeded in distracting him, I thought, for the moment, at least.

"You know what Fish and Testees are. When the Lord sent me to Earth, all humans were Fish. Some heard my message and claimed to be New Direction converts. Those who petitioned were then tested. Testees who pass the testing stage become Initiates. But the majority aren't ready yet. They become Cadreers, or sometimes Fish again. Would you like some more wine?"

"No, I'm fine."

"Cadreers," Zephjame continued, "are Full Christians who are not yet ready to become Initiates.

They join cadres and work for the cause. That's what happens with most Testees. Eventually they can petition again and become Testees again."

"And the Testees who pass?" Cass asked. "The Initiates?"

"A select group," Zephjame said. "They make the journey to St. Thomas for the Test of Divinity. From there they either return to being Cadreers, or even Fish occasionally, or they become Disciples. I think you would make an excellent Disciple. Are you in favor of the Christianization of the world, Veronica.

"Of course," Cass said immediately.

"And do you wish to dedicate yourself to this purpose?"

Cass frowned. "I think I do." Looking sincerely into Zephjame's eyes, she asked, "What would it involve?"

"Accepting the truth of my divinity, for starters. Knowing that I'm sent by God."

"You, meaning Zephkar, not James Lane."

"Of course."

"But because I'm a twin, you can't enter my soul and speak to me from within my own body. If that happened, then for sure I'd —"

"Because you are a twin, that will not happen. A deeper faith is required of you. You've read of the many miracles."

"Yes."

"And mostly you believe, yet a little doubt remains."

Cass held his eyes, not speaking.

"I respect that," Zephjame said. "You'll have your proof." He smiled with self-delight. "Look around the room, Veronica. Choose someone, a patron, a waiter, it doesn't matter. I will enter that person's soul and take over his or her body. Tell me what you would need to see that person do in order to be convinced of my powers."

"Hmm-m," Cass said. "Well . . . if that man over there were to come and sit at this table and . . . let's see . . . and if he were to tell me exactly how you and I came to be together here tonight . . . yes, that would convince me."

"Done," Zephjame said, and he left the table.

He's loving this, I said.

Big show off, Cass responded.

Several feel from the targeted man's table, Zephjame stopped as if to tie his shoe. He then sat down with the man and a half a minute later the man rose and came to our table. "We didn't exchange a word, did we?" he said.

"No," Cass replied, her eyes appropriately wide.

"Now, your request is that I tell you how you and James Lane over there happened to be here together tonight."

"This is amazing," Cass responded, looking appropriately amazed. "Is it you, Zephkar? Are you . . . in there?"

"Of course, my sweet."

Cass kept her mouth slightly open.

"You wrote me a note, Veronica Bloom, several weeks ago, and then another this week. You told me you wanted to meet me and would be at the Ritz Carlton lounge tonight. We had a nice little talk there, one drink for you — a Manhattan, and part of another; two vodkas for me. Then Freddie drove us here. I was recognized at the door . . . James Lane was, that is."

Cass looked toward James who sat quietly at the other table.

"James is now controlling his own body," Zephkar said.

"And you . . ."

"I am being hosted by . . . just a second, I'll read his mind . . . ah, by Mr. Ronald Winston. At the moment he's drifting happily in the heavenly preview."

Cass took a deep breath and let out a long sigh. Very convincing, I thought.

"Do you need more proof?" Zephron asked.

Cass shook her head. Zephron began to rise. "Wait! One more thing," Cass said. "In the car on the way over here, what did Freddie say when the taxi cut him off?"

Zephron smiled. "Wasn't once enough? Freddie does get vulgar when he's angry. I believe *cocksucker* was the word he used."

Cass folded her hands on the table, as if praying, and looked adoringly into Ronald Winston's watery eyes. "I'm in the presence of an angel of the Lord," she said, her voice dripping with awe.

Zephron smiled condescendingly. "Excuse me while I return Mr. Winston to his meal."

Don't overdo it, I said to Cass.

When Zephjame returned, he again invited Cass to his home. Again Cass declined. "I'm not ready," she said. "Perhaps another time."

I waited anxiously for his response. He frowned momentarily, but then smiled. "You're the first," he said, looking quite pleased, "to know who I am and yet to turn me down."

"I hope I haven't hurt your feelings," Cass said sincerely.

Zephjame laughed heartily. "After I got your last note, I read some old newspaper and magazine articles about you. From what I perceive, your character has indeed undergone a radical revision — in some ways, but in some ways not, I think. You intrigue me, Veronica Bloom." He took her hand. "And so we shall follow your timetable. With you," he added, "I suspect the waiting will only serve to intensify my ultimate pleasure in being with you."

"We'll see," Cass said, gently pulling her hand away.

"So we shall," Zephjame responded. He signaled the waiter then said to Cass, "I'm giving a dinner party Saturday night, a social affair, no business. I'd like you to come."

Cass nodded. "All right."

When we got to the street, Cass insisted that she take a cab home.

"It will be no trouble to drive you," Zephjame protested.

"I'd prefer the evening to end like this," Cass said.

"You're a willful woman despite your transformation," Zephjame observed. "I like it." We were at the Mercedes by then. Zephjame beckoned a nearby cab. "Until Saturday then," he said. "People will begin arriving at eight."

"I'll be there," Cass said.

The moment the cab was on the move, Cass sighed audibly. *Oh Lordy, am I glad that's over.*

You did a terrific job, I told her. *The boy is*

hooked. The trick's going to be to keep him that way without letting him into your pants. What a lecher. Somehow you're going to have to convince him that you do want to go to his place in St. Thomas, even though you don't want to have sex with him.

I suppose I could have sex with him if I had to.

I didn't respond. I'd been having the same thought, as repulsive as it was. *Luckily he didn't ask where you live,* I said.

Maybe Doris was right and I should get a cover apartment. I hope it won't be necessary though. Cass sighed again. *The mutant certainly has picked up some superficial charm since arriving on Earth.*

All part of his act, I said. *The President of the United States probably has to have at least some social skills.*

I'm not looking forward to Saturday night. How about you taking over for round two?

I couldn't possibly do it as well as you, I said.

Cass wore a dusty pink silk dress to the dinner party; she looked gorgeous. Zephjame's other guests included a columnist with the *Chicago Tribune,* an aide of the mayor, a well-known local artist, the chancellor of the University of Chicago, a televangelist whom I'd seen once or twice on TV spouting New Direction garbage, and a half-dozen others.

After the food, people were milling and chatting when Zephjame maneuvered Cass into a side room that contained, among other beautiful furnishings, a very large sofa. *The better to ball you on,* I thought, wondering if there was any way Cass could get out of this without blowing the invitation to St. Thomas.

He sweet-talked and Cass countered playfully but she ended up laying out her bottom line again — that her morality forbade her to indulge her carnal desires, despite the new message. "To me it would feel sinful," she told him, gently pulling his paw from her breast.

"New converts to Christianity are often the most rigid," Zephjame said. "The ideas you learned recently are correct in principle," he continued patiently, "and they do apply to most people. The human body is indeed a temple and should be treated as such. But what you're still not letting yourself understand, Veronica, is that to be truly moral, the desire itself has to be overcome. Simply disallowing the behavior by repressing the impulses or inhibiting the actions is a shallow accomplishment. Of course it's as much as can be expected from most people. But to be truly evolved, the diabolical desires have to be exorcised, not just submerged. And to exorcise them, they must first be fully and uninhibitedly indulged. *Exercise to exorcise,* we say. Only then will you be in a position to transcend the desires."

Cass smiled. "Sounds like a bunch of rationalizations to me," she said playfully.

Be careful, Cass, I warned.

"I should know what is true, shouldn't I?" Zephjame said.

"Yes, of course." Cass lowered her head.

Zephjame raised her chin with the tip of his finger. "For most people the journey to the transcendence of their animalistic desires is a long one. Many of those who have made it then choose to help others on the path. I am offering to help you, Veronica."

Cass laughed. "If I didn't know you were an angel, I'd say you had quite a line, Zephkar."

Zephjame laughed with her. "You delight me," he crooned, squeezing her arm. "Never before has a believer shown such resistance. You are true to yourself. A rare quality, Veronica."

I felt tremendous relief. He really was enjoying the game. I remembered how eager the Testees on the yacht had been to jump into bed with him. That reminded me of my own behavior that day and I started to feel ashamed.

Zephjame went to a bookshelf and got a pamphlet. He wrote a phone number on it and handed it to Cass. "I'm returning to my guests now," he said. "Take this home with you and read it. Afterwards, if you think you're ready, then consider yourself an Initiate and come to the Palace at St. Thomas. I'd like you to come when I'm there, the week of October eighteenth. Call Freddie and let him know if you'll be joining us."

With that, he turned and left the room.

Whew, Cass said.

You did it, I said. *Mission accomplished.*

Let's get out of here.

"*Exorcism by Indulgence,*" Billy read aloud.

The Zephkar Elimination Team, with the exception of Doris, was sitting around the kitchen table, cups of coffee in front of us. I was riding Amy.

"Read some more," Amy said.

Billy set her cup back on the table. "*You have heard it said that carnality must be suppressed, but Zephkar says that the test for Full Christians is more difficult than that. To become pure of heart and eligible for Induction into Divinity, all Initiates first must succumb to the extremes of hedonistic temptation, indulging freely in every pleasure of the flesh.*"

"That's one way to get converts," Cindy quipped.

Billy shook her head. "What a crock, huh? You're probably right, Cindy. Making virtue out of self-indulgence is bound to be attractive to a lot of people."

"Sounds good to me," Cindy said.

"You might not think so when you hear the rest." Billy read some more sections of the pamphlet including a description of the Palace of Pleasure in St. Thomas and the steps to becoming a Disciple. "It even has an application form," Billy said. "Anyone want to apply to be a Testee? They guarantee that every applicant will be contacted by a Cadreer for a screening. Then if you're one of the lucky few, you get to be *tested* by a genuine Disciple. That takes place in person."

"Preferably in a bedroom," Cass said.

"What a con game," Agatha said.

"Right," said Gracie, "especially the part about the Penitents. Recruiting guilt-ridden, incredulous people to serve as sexual slaves."

"There are worse ways to make a living," Cindy

cracked. "Seriously, this crap is unbelievable. Do people really buy it?"

"By the thousands, according to their statistics," Billy said. "The ranks of Cadreers are growing geometrically. So Cass, what do you think? Want to push on or should we try to strand Zephkar some other way?"

"Do you have some other way in mind?" Cass asked.

"No," Billy answered. "Unless anyone wants to take another crack at dumping him into a pit."

"No way," Gracie said.

"Or trying to push him out of an airplane over some remote mountains," Billy added. "Or lure him into an abandoned coal mine."

"We already decided stranding him in the ocean is our best bet," Cass said. "I'm willing to proceed."

"If you're going to indulge your flesh I want to be there with you," Cindy declared.

"Me too," Amy added, leering at Cass.

"And when Zephkar mind-tickles you?" Cass responded.

"We'll stay out of his way," Cindy said.

"And the testing? You're willing to let one of the New Direction Disciples *have his way with you?*" Cass chuckled.

"Don't they have women disciples?" Cindy wanted to know.

"Cindy, you're not going to the Palace. It's much too risky," Cass said.

"I know, I'm just kidding."

Cass smiled at her. "What I'm hoping is that I can get Zephkar to go scuba diving *before* my

Induction into Divinity begins. Which reminds me, I have to learn how to scuba dive. Some of you should, too. In fact, in case anything goes wrong, I think all of us should know how to dive. And Agatha, we're counting on you to handle the boat. You *are* experienced, right?"

"I'm a pro," Agatha said.

"I've got some bad news," Gracie said. "Doris won't be going to St. Thomas. She can't take the time." Gracie stared at her hands. "And I might not be going either. Doris doesn't want me to go and I told her I wouldn't unless I was really needed. According to our plan, all we actually need is four people — Cass and Jenna, of course, and then Agatha to drive the boat and the fourth person to go underwater to set up the shells and shackle. Since there are eight of us in ZET, I figured without me and Doris you'd still have two to spare."

Cass nodded. "OK, Gracie. We'll miss you but you're right, we could manage it without you."

"I wouldn't miss it for the world," Cindy said.

"Doris gets freaky when I'm away. She hardly has any time for me but she still wants me around."

"We understand," Agatha said. "It's all right, Gracie."

Gracie looked from face to face.

"No problem," Billy said. "Doris will still get the drugs for us, won't she?"

"Of course," Gracie said.

After reassuring Gracie we weren't mad at her and Doris, the rest of us agreed we should learn how to scuba dive. It would have to be a crash course since we only had a couple of weeks.

* * * * *

We didn't see much of Doris after that, although Gracie got together with us from time to time. The scuba lessons were fun. Even Agatha seemed to be enjoying herself, despite the fact that she was still annoyed at me for refusing to go along with her proposal. When I had presented my compromise idea to her, she'd gotten huffy and I ended up refusing to boost-block her at all. She'd responded by saying then I couldn't ride her. Since then, she'd gotten back into spending time with people and doing her writing.

Cindy and Amy and Cass continued their tripling and it actually seemed to be working. I was impressed. Even on Allo, successful triplings were difficult and rare.

A short time before we were to leave for St. Thomas, Billy said something that took me completely by surprise. I was boosting Amy at the time, and was planning to stay with her when she went to band practice with Cindy and Cass. "Why don't you stay with me instead?" Billy said.

"What do you mean?" I asked.

"Enter me. It's about time, don't you think?"

"I didn't think it would ever be time," I said.

"It's time. Come on in."

I felt scared, but I brought Amy back and told her what I was about to do. She wished me luck, and I made the shift.

"Want me to hang around awhile to see if it's OK?" Amy asked.

What do you think, Billy?

"Not necessary."

Amy and the others left. Agatha was out by herself somewhere, the Art Institute, I think she'd said. Billy and I were alone at the apartment, about as merged now as two lovers could be. I was maxi-riding. *You feel good,* I said.

Billy began to cry.

It's all right. I'll propel to the void.

"No, no, don't," Billy said. "It's just the weirdness of it. It's okay, I want you to stay."

Reminds you of the Wraunkians, doesn't it?

"It's not that so much . . . it's the idea . . . you being . . ." She wiped her tears.

I know.

Can you hear me now?

Yes, love.

Don't dip, all right?

I won't.

She sighed loudly, wiped her eyes again. "Well, how about going out for lunch?" she said aloud.

Fine, I said.

We could go to that health food place in Rogers Park you like so much.

Shall we take Amy's bike?

Amy had bought a motorcycle the week before and said anyone was free to borrow it. Billy had owned a motorcycle for a while on Allo. She'd ridden around on Amy's a few times and said it worked pretty much like hers. She changed into jeans, got the helmet and a jacket and we took off. It was a crisp October day but the sun was bright and we were warm. We chatted as we drove and we delighted in the fact that we had no problem hearing each other. We used to have to yell to be heard on Billy's bike.

This is great, I said. *Shall we get a motorcycle when we move to San Francisco?*

Maybe two of them, Billy replied. I knew what she meant. She frequently hinted about my permanating.

At the restaurant, we had fun talking about the people around us, Billy never saying a word out loud. *Look at that one,* I said. *He's got more hair on his face than you have on your head.*

I still can't get used to the two sexes, Billy said. *It's such a stupid arrangement.*

They can't help it, I replied. I realized that from time to time I found myself defending Earthlings. I wondered if I was starting to identify with them.

I guess I could get used to this, Billy said at one point, meaning my riding her. *If I had to,* she added.

After eating, we rode north on Sheridan Road, stopping at several beaches along the way. *The lake is pretty,* Billy commented.

Yeah, but it can't compare to San Francisco Bay. I can't wait until you see San Francisco, hon. Honestly, parts of that city are almost as nice as Allo.

That's hard to believe, Billy said.

Keep your mind open, I reminded her.

After our scuba lesson that evening, Billy and I and the triplers gathered around the dining room table to play Hearts, a card game Cindy had taught us. Agatha was stretched out on an easy chair reading the newspaper.

"Oh God," Agatha moaned. "Listen to this." She read aloud.

There had been a bombing. Several hundred New Direction opponents had been meeting at a high school auditorium in Madison, Wisconsin, when a bomb was tossed through a window. Fifty people had been killed and scores of others injured. The man who threw the bomb had been caught.

"He claimed amnesia for the incident," Agatha read, "and said he had absolutely no reason to do such a thing. He's being held at a maximum security psychiatric facility."

Cass shook her head disgustedly. "I wonder how many more Zephkar will kill before we strand him."

"One more week," Amy said.

The following Wednesday, Billy, Agatha, Amy and Cindy flew to St. Thomas. Two days later, Cass and I arrived at the Astor house. Zephjame greeted Cass warmly.

"I'm a little nervous," Cass said.

"You'll have the time of your life," Zephjame assured her. He said the same thing later when we were about to enter the Pleasure Palace.

On the flight to St. Thomas, Cass had tried feverishly to convince him that she needed to adjust to being on the island before going to the Palace, that she would stay at a hotel the first night or so.

"Nonsense, my dear," Zephjame had said pleasantly. "We have a beautiful room set aside for you."

"But I can't wait to see the coral reefs," Cass

had objected. "I'd really prefer to do some scuba diving before my Initiation." She told him about having taken the crash course and how eager she was to test her skills in beautiful waters.

"Don't worry," Zephjame had replied, "you'll get your chance to scuba dive. But first things first. Other Initiates have been reluctant too," he added.

A limousine was waiting at the airport. Besides Freddie and Zephjame, an Apostle named Emmett had flown to the island with us as well as another Initiate, Caroline, also hand-picked by Zephjame. On the flight, Zephjame had divided his attention between Cass and Caroline.

We drove along a palm-lined road through green countryside until we came to a fenced-in estate. Once inside, we rode through beautifully-landscaped grounds with lush vegetation and brilliant flowers, past several white buildings of varying sizes, and then arrived at the huge Palace itself. Zephjame had Cass on one arm and Caroline on the other as he escorted us into the Pleasure Palace's elegant marble lobby.

"My friends," he said to the two Initiates, "you are about to have the time of your lives."

Christian symbols abounded, huge golden crosses, paintings depicting scenes from the Bible. There were two sculptured angels over the arched entryway doors.

"May I present Veronica Bloom," Zephjame said to a pretty, raven-haired woman wearing a short, white silky dress. "And, Veronica, this beautiful lady is Theresa, your guide."

"Welcome to the Palace of Pleasure," Theresa said, her smile revealing straight, glistening teeth.

"Take good care of her," Zephjame said to Theresa.

Theresa led Cass up winding stairs, through a long, curved corridor lined with sculptures and paintings, and into a luxurious suite, complete with a stocked kitchenette.

"Please make yourself comfortable," Theresa said. "Everything you will need is here." She swung the closet door wide revealing racks of pants, dresses, robes, and other clothing. "There is a little gathering beginning now in the center room on the main floor. Rest a while if you choose, take a bath, a nap if you wish, or relax on the balcony. When you're ready to join the others, pick up the phone and ask for me. I'll accompany you to the party. Wear anything you want from the closet. Nothing would be considered inappropriate."

"Is it all right if I use the phone to call the States?" Cass asked.

"Of course. Everything here is for you to use. I will see you soon," Theresa said pleasantly.

Should I tip her? Cass quipped.

I chuckled.

Theresa closed the door quietly behind her.

What a place, I said. I was truly impressed by the beauty of the furnishings and decor. *Smell the flowers, will you?* Cass went to the vase and sniffed. *Ah, beautiful,* I said. *Well, what now? Do you want to sneak out of here or risk having* the time of your life?

This isn't going how I wanted it to go.

I know. Looks like you have to play Zephkar's games for a while before the big swim.

Easy for you to be so flippant.

Do you want me to take over, I asked. *I will if you want. I can boost-block and you can drift while I have the time of my life.*

They have orgies here, Cass said.

So I've heard. What do you think would happen if you refused to participate?

What do you think?

I think you'd be dismissed. Demoted to Fish. And I definitely doubt that Zephjame would go scuba diving with an Initiate who chickened out.

I wasn't supposed to have to go through with it.

We knew there was a possibility. Seriously, Cass, I'll do it if you can't.

Maybe we can take turns. Let's play it by ear.

Cass phoned our apartment in Chicago and left a message on the answering machine. "Hi ZET, this is Veronica calling as promised. It's one-fifteen p.m., day one. I'm in my suite at the Palace. No scuba diving scheduled yet. So far everything is fine. Talk to you soon."

Gracie would pick up the message and call Billy and the others at their St. Thomas hotel, the Royal George.

So you want a bath or nap or what? I asked.

I want to go for a bike ride on the trail in Polmoir Woods.

I laughed. *Right. I wouldn't mind being on Allo now either. Your second choice?*

Stay here until they drag me out kicking and screaming?

I decided Cass's attitude needed work. *Maybe we should just let ourselves get into it,* I tried. *Experience whatever they have in store for us. It's*

*bound to be interesting and maybe even pleasurable.
What do you say?*

*I shouldn't fight it, huh, coach? All right. Let's
take a bath in that huge marble tub, then summon
Theresa.*

Our gorgeous guide to carnal bliss.

An hour later, dressed in a sleeveless lavender
pantsuit and wearing the wristband of gold Theresa
had given her, Cass walked into a large circular hall
on the main floor of the Palace.

What appeared to be an ordinary cocktail party
was in progress. Music played, people were talking
in groups and pairs, some were dancing. In one
section people played cards; in another, a game of
pool. Everyone, male and female, was dressed in
colorful clothing — sexy, sensual costumes made
from rich-looking fabrics.

"You are to choose three Tempters," Theresa told
Cass." Two women and one man. You can tell who
they are by the gold collars."

Cass scanned the room. Some of the people wore
narrow golden bands around their necks. Others, like
Cass, wore them on their wrists.

"Choose two women and one man," Theresa said.
"There's no rush. Talk with people. Eat. Dance. Take
your time. Choose three who appeal to you."

"For what purpose?" Cass asked.

"To begin the sensual journey," Theresa
responded. "The Tempters are here to please you and
the other Initiates in every way. They're skilled and
knowledgeable. They'll take you through the first two
pleasure rooms. Come, let me introduce you to some
people and get you started."

For the next couple of hours, Cass talked with one Tempter after another. She danced with some of them. All were charming and attractive people who related to her very warmly. Each Tempter Cass talked to seemed totally absorbed by her, as if she were the most beautiful and interesting person in the universe.

Finally, after discussing it with me, Cass made her choices — Angela, Anna, and Adam. *The three A's,* I said. Angela was tall and narrow-hipped with very short blonde hair; Anna was shorter with an angular face and dark brown skin; Adam was clean-shaven, slim and muscular with sandy brown curls. Cass found Theresa and let her know she had made her selections.

Theresa gathered the three and accompanied them and Cass down the corridor to *Room One,* the *Silk Room.* The main pieces of furniture in the room were several wide contour lounges, each covered with soft fabric. Thick mats were arranged in semi-circles around each lounge. There were vases with birds of paradise and other exotic flowers whose names I did not know. The dim, soft lighting gave the room a rosy amber hue.

Following the others' lead, Cass removed her shoes. Her bare feet sank deeply into the lush carpeting as Theresa walked her to a little alcove formed by a set of fabric-walled screens.

"Slip into this," Theresa said, taking a silvery garment from a hook on the screen.

The garment was silky to the touch with wide sleeves, no buttons, and just one thin tie at the waist. It came only to Cass's thighs. "Too short," Cass said.

"*Au contraire*. It fits you perfectly," Theresa insisted.

Adam, Anna and Angela had donned similar garments, one a shade of magenta, one turquoise, the other black. Angela wore the black one and it contrasted strikingly with her blonde hair and pale skin.

"You look beautiful," Angela said to Cass, taking her hand and leading her to one of the lounges.

Soft music filled the room. The ambience was undeniably sensual.

"Would you like to start with a mind-unwinder?" Anna asked. "Lawrence will discuss the menu with you." She beckoned the barefoot young man in a mauve pants outfit sitting at the other end of the room. He came instantly and sat himself on the edge of a mat next to Cass who was reclining on the lounge.

Lawrence went on to list the many euphorics Cass could choose from and what each of their effects would be. He assured her he would control the dosage and could guarantee she would have a pleasant experience no matter what she chose.

Do I have to choose something? Cass asked me.

Take a little hashish, I suggested. *To be cooperative. A friend of mine tried it on Allo. It won't harm you.*

Lawrence hustled to bring Cass the "mind-unwinder" she had chosen. As Cass smoked the hash from a little pipe, the Tempters gently stroked her arms and legs and massaged her feet. Soon the room seemed even more lovely, the music more sensual, the beautiful Tempters even more beautiful and tempting. I was enjoying the

247

light-headed, floaty feeling. It reminded me of the void although it wasn't quite that good. The stroking of Cass's skin felt very pleasant. The Tempters, I realized, had begun applying fragrant oils to Cass's skin. It felt slippery and warm. Someone untied Cass's belt and the silky fabric tumbled to her sides. The sensual caressing now included Cass's belly and breasts. I was becoming quite aroused.

Cass laid her head back and closed her eyes. Soft fingers meandered over her body. Someone's tongue moved slowly back and forth along her shoulder then across her chest, slowly approaching her breast. Warm liquidy lips enclosed her nipple. Cass gave a weak moan. Her eyes remained closed. A smooth hand slipped between Cass's legs, gently stroking the bare inner thigh. Cass's breathing grew deep and audible. The music spun in our head. I felt delightful goosebumps as fingers caressed and tongues slid and the sucking on Cass's nipple continued. I felt Cass's panties sliding slowly down her legs. Then someone blew a soft stream of warm air around her labia. Cass's back arched. Soft fluttering came across her skin. Feathers, I thought, and perhaps fur. Cass's hand found someone's back. She stroked the flesh sensually, with her palms and her fingertips.

"Wonderful . . . mm-mm, yes-ss," someone crooned appreciatively. Anna, I thought. I sensed slowly shifting bodies, numerous limbs undulating around Cass's legs and torso like large lazy snakes on tree branches. A thigh moved in a slow rhythm against Cass's buttocks. Soft caresses covered every part of her slick oiled skin. Another low moan gurgled in Cass's throat as something soft and smooth purred between her spread legs.

A tiny vibrator. It was nearly soundless and felt pleasantly soft. The gentle sucking continued on her nipples, both of them now, as paper light fingers fluttered over her forehead and down her cheeks and along her neck. The purring vibrations continued over her wet labia. Cass's breathing had become more rapid. The skin sensations and the undulating music seemed to be seeping inside of us, entering us, filling up my mind, and circulating around and around in our body. Cass's hips moved rhythmically. Silky fingers and silky limbs wove themselves over our skin.

Cass's climax was wonderfully slow in coming, rising like a helium-filled balloon, with me along as a passenger, rising higher and higher, taking us on a floating journey to the cusp, an ascent into wispy clouds and twinkling stars and then at last the sunburst of dawn, a long, slow explosion that lasted until the sky was aglow with pinks and purples and lavenders and we were left panting. Undulating fingers still caressed, lighter now, slower, soothing, as we lay spent and content.

Cass opened her eyes, half-lidded. "Did I die and go to heaven?"

"You are wonderfully alive," Angela crooned. She stroked Cass's forehead. "Sleep if you wish. Letting yourself drift . . . glide."

"Drifting . . ." another voice said.

"Feeling yourself sliding away . . ."

I slid and I suspect Cass did also. I don't know how long we slept but Cass apparently awakened first. *Are you there, Jenna?*

Mmm-mm, I purred hazily. *I don't know where I am.*

Cass's naked body was covered to her shoulders with a light silken comforter. Adam held a bowl of cut fruit. Anna brought a slice of melon to Cass's lips. Juicy and sweet. The music made me think of wood nymphs playing flutes beside a gurgling brook. A wedge of orange came next. Anna wiped a drop of juice from the side of Cass's mouth.

I could get hooked on this, Cass said.

I already am, I responded, as a sweet strawberry slice was slid between Cass's lips.

It's like a dream.

I know. So, did we pass the test?

Cass smiled. *This is only Room One.* Angela was massaging one of Cass's feet. *There are three more rooms to go,* Cass said. "Exorcism by indulgence," she said aloud.

"Exactly," said Anna. "You indulge quite beautifully, Veronica."

From the Silk Room we were escorted to the Water Room. There were three marble swimming pools, linked together by tiled waterways and surrounded by life-sized statues of graceful nudes romping in a jungle of huge plants and marble antelope and gazelles. A semi-naked, marble statue of Jesus stood smiling beneath two palms.

Cass was now wearing a gauzy two-piece swim

suit. After soaking in one of the hot tubs, she went to a lukewarm pool where we drifted on a chair-like inflated float. The music was light and airy. Huge windows lined three walls of the spacious room allowing a view of endless gardens with their brilliantly hued flowers and umbrellas of palm. Dusk was coming, the sky an orange and pink glow.

Other Initiates were in the pools and stretched out on padded lounge chairs along the shores. They too were being "indulged" by their trios of Tempters.

As Cass was eating and taking sips of a chilled fruit drink, she spotted James Lane basking in one of the hot tubs. Their eyes caught and Zephjame smiled and winked. Cass returned the smile. *Quite an improvement over his life on Allo,* she said.

He should enjoy it while he can, I responded.

A while later Cass stretched out on a padded chair near one of the windows and was chatting with the three A's when Theresa came. "You seem to be enjoying yourself so far," she said.

Cass smiled. "I guess I am."

"And are you aware of any inner rebellion against the pleasuring? Feelings of doubt or guilt?"

Cass laughed. "Not so far. A couple of times it crossed my mind that all this was decadent and depraved, but then I thought about the purpose."

"Exorcism by indulgence."

Cass smiled. "What if I get hooked by the indulgence, Theresa, and don't want to be exorcised?"

Smiling, Theresa told her, "At the end of your time here, you will have an interview with a Rater to determine your status. I very much doubt that you will be ranked a Fish or Cadreer. Mr. Lane has expressed a particular interest in you. If you end up a Disciple, you will be able to return to the Palace from time to time."

"I see."

"Of course, it's still early in your initiation. There's much more for you to experience."

"Are you a Disciple?" Cass asked.

Theresa smiled indulgently. "I'm a Penitent," she said. "Until I discovered New Direction, my life was . . . well, let me put it this way, I have much to atone for."

"And your penance is to work here at the Palace?"

"That's right. All the Guides and all the Tempters are Penitents. In six more weeks, I'll apply to be an Initiate."

"Good luck to you," Cass said.

"Thank you, Veronica. I think you're ready for the next step. Shall we go?"

Cass wrapped herself in her thigh-length silken robe and she and the three Tempters followed Theresa to an adjoining room. It was a tropical paradise. A waterfall tumbled from above into a clear, rock-lined pool. Palm trees, plants and vines were everywhere. Shallow rivulets of water streamed in meandering paths across the floor. There were several two-foot high, padded platforms set beneath semicircles of palms. Coils of narrow, brightly colored hoses sprouting from brass-ringed holes in the tiled floor lay in coils near the head and foot of each platform.

Cass was led to one of the platforms. The moment she sat, a young woman in a white tunic approached her. "Beer, wine, liquor," she said sweetly. "Cocaine, marijuana, hashish, LSD, PCP,

Ecstasy, mushrooms, peyote, heroin, demerol, codeine, speed, ludes, valium." She smiled warmly at Cass. "My name is Belinda," she said. "There are other mind-unwinders if none of those appeal to you."

Cass said nothing.

"Shall I explain the effects?" the lovely Belinda asked.

"I'll have some cocaine," Cass said.

I was surprised. *Be careful,* I warned.

I did some with Cindy once.

Oh?

You'll like it, she said.

You're still a little buzzed from the hash.

We have to cooperate.

Cass lay back and Adam immediately placed a pillow beneath her head. The cocaine took effect quickly, the rush of excitement, a happy revved feeling that grew to delightful euphoria. After a few minutes, Cass sat up and began chattering. I tuned in and out of what she said.

". . . and then he just decided to donate this place to New Direction, huh?"

"Yes," Anna said. "It belongs to the movement now."

"Terrifically generous fellow."

"He's a developer," Adam said. "Shopping malls and suburban housing complexes. He built this palace ten years ago. He used to use it for private parties." Adam smiled. "His goals are bigger now."

"The Christianization of the world," Angela said.

"Here, here," said Cass. "Peace on Earth and joy to the world." She was up and walking. She went to the waterfall and stared up at it. Then she tossed her robe aside, slipped out of her swimsuit, and stepped naked into the shallow pool. A spray of water wet her face and shoulders. She moved closer to the gently falling water, laughing delightedly as the cool liquid poured over her face and body.

Angela and Adam were waiting with big fluffy towels when Cass emerged from the pond. They dried her and wrapped her and led her back to the padded platform. Cass stretched out languorously.

Anna pulled back the towel. "Joy water," she said, directing a soft stream from a bright purple hose onto Cass's shoulders and chest. From the other hoses, the Tempters sprayed more streams of warm water onto other parts of Cass's body. They sprayed her belly, and then her silken-haired triangle. Cass spread her legs slightly as the warm, stimulating spraying continued, and warm, stimulating fingers caressed her wet skin everywhere.

When Cass was finally ready to stop, Theresa took her to a small alcove where Cass dried off and dressed in magenta satin pants and a matching scooped-neck tunic. We were then escorted to a cafe on the second floor, a large, multi-leveled room of wood and beveled glass. Conversations buzzed from the scores of brightly dressed people gathered around tables and booths. Classical music played softly in the background.

Theresa led Cass to a corner table and introduced *Veronica* to the half-dozen people seated there. One of them was a handsome, middle-aged man named Jefferson Riley.

He took Cass's hand. "We've met before," he told Theresa. "I'm delighted to see you here, Veronica," he said to Cass.

"Hello, Jefferson," Cass said nonchalantly.

Cass and I had talked about the possibility of her someday running into someone who had known Veronica Bloom. I wondered if she was feeling as nervous as I.

"We've all made so many changes in recent months," Jefferson said. He pulled an upholstered chair toward Cass.

Remaining standing, Cass glanced at Theresa.

"I must take her from you, Jefferson," Theresa said, taking Cass's hand. "I just wanted her to meet all of you."

"We should get together sometime," Jefferson said to Cass.

"Perhaps." Cass let herself be led away by Theresa.

"Did I read you correctly?" Theresa asked when we were out of Jefferson's earshot. "I sensed you didn't want to stay and talk with Mr. Riley."

"You read well," said Cass.

Theresa smiled with satisfaction. "My mission is to ensure that you don't have a second of unpleasantness here."

Sometime after midnight Zephjame joined us at our table. "You have a glow on your cheek and a gleam in your eye," he said, taking Cass's hand and pressing her fingers to his lips. "She's doing well?" he asked Theresa.

"Quite."

"I'd never say, *I told you so*," he said to Cass.

"You're a wise man," she said, "though I am beginning to feel a bit overwhelmed. I think a look at a coral reef is just what I need as a break from all this . . . indoor activity. Do we have a date? Tomorrow morning?"

"She's obsessed with scuba diving," Zephjame said to Theresa, winking. "Your happiness is my happiness," he said to Cass. "The trip is all planned for you, my sweet. But not tomorrow. Monday."

"That's three days away," Cass protested.

"You see what I mean?" Zephjame said to Theresa. "Be patient," he told Cass. "I want you to indulge in all four rooms first. You're just getting started. Tomorrow you'll do the Leather Room, then on Sunday, Room Four."

"Leather Room?" Cass said.

Zephjame nodded. "Once they allow themselves to get into it, it turns out to be many people's favorite." He chuckled lasciviously. "Monday on the boat you can tell me all about your adventures there. Just keep reminding yourself, *Indulgence is good for the soul.*" He touched her cheek. "Go rest now, Veronica Bloom. Take it slowly, bask in your experiences here. Relish them."

We watched him cross the room and join a group near the mind-unwinder bar.

"I guess Mr. Lane thinks you've had enough for one day," Theresa said. "Come, I'll walk you back to your suite."

Despite how long a day we'd had, Cass and I did not sleep right away. First Cass called home and left another message: "Hi, ZET. Having quite a time; wish you were here. So far I've just been hanging around the Palace but Monday I'll be going scuba diving. It's actually more enjoyable here than I'd anticipated. I'll be in touch."

Cass got between the satin sheets of the huge water bed and she and I talked, about the Palace mostly, but we also reviewed our scuba plan. *Foolproof,* Cass proclaimed after we'd gone over each step, then she fell asleep.

We rose late Saturday morning and fixed breakfast in our kitchenette. As we ate, we watched a movie on the huge TV.

Theresa came to our suite at noon. "Leather, anyone?" she asked.

Tell her you have a headache, I said.

"I'd like to spend some time outside first," Cass said, "if that's all right."

After a period of sunbathing, Theresa again suggested the Leather Room, but Cass said she'd prefer spending some time in the cafe first. Theresa willingly took us there and introduced us to a group sitting on easy chairs in one corner of the huge room.

"Deportation is preferable to mass executions," a redheaded woman named Claudia said. "If they won't join us, then they must leave us."

"But wherever they go, they'll make trouble," an anemic-looking man named Philip responded. "New Direction ultimately will be spread throughout the world. We'd be asking for trouble later if we simply ship out the Incorrigibles. Exit Parlors, that's the solution."

"A fancy name for execution chambers," the woman protested.

"They'll be given humane exits to the next world," Philip said. "At least that's more Christian than using gas chambers. You'll see; it will be necessary."

"Mr. Lane is correct in saying there are far too many people on earth. Some Zephians are talking about eliminating the social parasites in addition to the Incorrigibles. I'd be opposed to that as well as to the mass sterilizations."

"Be careful what you say, Claudia, or you may put *yourself* in jeopardy."

The redheaded woman looked distressed. "Don't be absurd. I'm a Disciple."

"Our status as Disciples isn't immutable," Philip responded. "Because you have strong opinions about the Incorrigibles, I'd recommend that you get yourself appointed to the Purity Committee. They're the ones who'll be making the final decisions about the Incorrigibles and other undesirables."

"Perhaps I should," Claudia said.

This is making me sick, I told Cass. *Can we get out of here?*

She glanced at Theresa who immediately rose and excused us.

Theresa again suggested that it was time to go to Room Three.

Agree to go, I told Cass. *We might as well get it over with.*

"All right," she said to Theresa. "Leather, it is."

Agatha and our other Earthling friends had told us of a sexual practice called S and M, engaged in by some Earthlings, including some lesbians. The moment we walked onto the darkened observation deck of the Leather Room and looked into the first cubicle, the memory of those conversations came back to us.

Cass stared silently at the scene below. Four people were in the room. One stood with his arms stretched above his head, shackled to a chain that hung from the ceiling. He was naked. Sitting on a stool was a woman wearing a leather contraption that circled her exposed breasts. She was in handcuffs. The other woman, dressed entirely in black leather, held a leather strap. So did the other man, also dressed primarily in leather.

Theresa flipped a switch beneath the window just in time for us to hear the sound of the strap lashing across the naked man's buttocks.

Ask her why they're doing it, I said.

"What's the purpose?" Cass asked, as another blow struck the man's buttocks.

"Pleasure," Theresa answered. "Strictly pleasure, just like everything here." The man's moan was a mix of ecstasy and pain. "The Initiates can call it off or change what's happening whenever they want."

"And the Penitents?" Cass asked.

"They're here to please the Initiates," Theresa said. Another blow fell and we could see red welts forming on the man's rear. "We encourage the Initiates to explore every potential pleasure source, to let their imaginations go free and to live out even their most submerged fantasies."

"And this is what these people came up with?" Cass asked incredulously.

"The man being whipped is a CEO at a computer company. A very conservative person. It took him a long time to allow himself to indulge in this repressed desire. He spent hours talking with his Guide first."

"His desire to be beaten?"

"Yes. Shall we move on? You look a little shaken."

Cass nodded. Theresa flipped the switch, and then moved us along the platform to the next window that had open drapes. A man dressed in a polo shirt and short pants was on his hands and knees, his shorts pulled part way down. A woman wearing silver-studded leather wristbands and a white uniform was smacking his bare buttocks rhythmically with a wooden paddle.

Theresa flipped a switch and we could hear the man moaning in ecstasy.

I don't get it, Cass said. *He's enjoying it?*

Apparently.

The man called the woman "nurse" and the woman referred to him as a "naughty little boy." We didn't stay long at that window.

At the next, a naked woman was lying, stomach-down, over a high leather hassock, her wrists and ankles secured by straps to rings on the floor. Another woman, dressed in leather pants and a T-shirt stood over her.

"Let's go," Cass said immediately.

"To the next room?" Theresa asked. "Or would you like to go somewhere and talk?"

"Talk," Cass said.

In a small parlor on the first floor, Theresa tried to explain. "Every human being has dual power needs, the wish to exert power over others and the wish to be overpowered."

"You don't say?" Cass said.

"Many of us suppress these needs because we have other values which conflict with them."

"Like mutual respect," Cass said.

Cool it, Cass, I warned.

"Yes, among others. As you know, here at the Pleasure Palace, we allow our desires and impulses to come out of their prison. We vent them — safely, pleasurably. No one gets hurt. Everyone gets satisfied."

Jenna, how should I handle this? I'm not going to go into one of those rooms.

Tell her what you saw is way too intense for you.

Good idea. "What I saw in those rooms," Cass said, "that was not a bit attractive to me. It was much too intense. I would get no satisfaction from anything like that."

Theresa laughed. "Nearly all the Initiates you were watching said similar things at first. You believe that such acts are morally wrong and that's why you reject them. But no one does anything against his or her will, Veronica. Don't get the Leather Room confused with the violence of the real world. These are games."

"They're not my kind of games," Cass said. "I don't have power needs."

"But of course you do," Theresa responded. "They're submerged in you, but you started out as a child like everyone else. We all had powerful adults to deal with when we were little and powerless. So we all developed needs related to power — needs to exert power like mommy and daddy did, needs to be overpowered by towering figures to whom we attribute omnipotence. Believe me, any physical pain that's inflicted only serves to augment the recipient's psychological pleasure."

Cass looked pointedly at her Guide. "You seem like an intelligent person, Theresa. Do you actually believe what you're telling me?"

"Of course. And you'll end up believing it too. But first you have to allow yourself to let go, to take the shackles off your mind."

Yeah, and put them on my body, Cass said to me.

"You must let go of those old ideas," Theresa continued. "Let go of the confusion of one thing with another." She opened a drawer in the table and removed a tray of pills and vials. "Since your defenses are so strong, I suggest this." She held a green capsule between her fingers. "Take this and you'll feel a pleasant loosening, an easy, gradual lowering of those defenses of yours. Then as we continue our talk, you'll be able to tap the submerged parts of your psyche."

Cass shook her head.

"The parts that you don't want to admit having," Theresa added, "that you feel shame or guilt about."

No way, Cass said to me.

Theresa scrutinized her. "No harm will come to you, I guarantee it. Your inhibitions will be lowered, that's all."

"I'd really rather not."

Theresa nodded. She put the capsule back on the tray. "A drink then?" she asked.

Cass shook her head.

"All right, we'll try it without." Theresa leaned back on her easy chair, looking somewhat disappointed in Cass, I thought. "To complete this phase of the initiation, Veronica, you must partake in an experience that involves power exploration — domination or submission, or both, if you choose. The experience has to include both power and sex. The two must be linked as they are in our psyches. I've shown you some examples of other people's choices. Now, we have to come up with yours."

"I can't imagine what it could be," Cass said. *Do you think it's true,* she asked me, *that all Earthlings crave this kind of thing?*

All of Zephkar's graduates, probably, I replied.

Theresa asked, "Does the prospect of someone being awed by you, trembling in your presence, seeing you as all-powerful, but at the same time adoring you and craving erotic contact with you — does that idea hold any appeal to you? Think about it, Veronica. Don't answer too quickly. Forget your old ideas of right and wrong. They don't apply in this context. Forget any associations of this pleasuring with actual oppression. Just let yourself tap your fantasies, free of rules, free of guilt, free of values, free of social implications."

I'm not going to do it, Jenna. It's repulsive.

I know.

"Theresa, I understand your rationale," Cass said, "but even if I do have the sorts of needs you talk about, submerged somewhere deep in my psyche, I have no wish to tap them." Theresa started to say something. "I mean it," Cass interrupted. "No amount of persuasion will change my mind."

Theresa shrugged. "All right," she said. "Of course, Initiates are always free to choose not to participate in Pleasure Palace activities."

"That's what I choose," Cass said.

Theresa nodded. "Then you're on your own for the rest of the night. Of course, the Tempters are available if you wish them."

"Thanks, Theresa. I think I'll just go to my suite."

"Fine," Theresa said. "Be sure to let me know if you want anything." She left the room.

She seems annoyed, I said.

So it goes, said Cass.

When Cass and I awakened the next morning, she rang for room service. Trays of delicious foods were brought — no meat or animal products.

Theresa stopped by as we were eating. "Feel free to spend the day however you want," she said. "Wander the grounds, play tennis, return to the Silk Room or Water Room if you wish, or the pools. Or you might want to go into Magens Bay for some shopping and sightseeing."

Tell her Magens Bay, I said, hoping I'd get a chance to see Billy.

"Sightseeing in Magens Bay sounds good," Cass said.

A Penitent gave us a lift to the town in one of the Palace jeeps. She said she'd be back for us at six o'clock. We went to the Royal George and found Billy and Agatha in their rooms.

"Feel free to enter and boost me, Jenna," Agatha said. "I'll just listen."

I shifted immediately. "Thanks, Agatha." It was the first time she'd allowed me to unilateral-boost since I'd confronted her about the void.

"Jenna, hon, are you okay?" Billy asked. "Is it awful?" She held me. "We were worried. It's taking so long."

"I know. They're insisting Cass go through with the whole initiation first, but the scuba excursion is all set for tomorrow at noon."

"Were you able to get another diver?" Billy asked.

"Yes, one of the Tempters," I said. "His name is Adam. He's strong enough, and he'll make a good witness."

"Tempter?" Billy said.

Come on, Jenna. Tell us about it, Agatha said. *Are there orgies?*

"Is the Palace as bizarre as the pamphlet made it seem?" Billy asked.

"More so," Cass said.

Cass and I took turns telling them about the elegance of the palace, about Theresa, the food, the drugs, the beautiful Tempters, the Silk Room. We had just started describing the swimming pools when Cindy and Amy came back from the beach. They insisted on hearing it from the beginning so we started over. When we told them about the Leather Room and Cass's refusal to participate, Amy said, "Good for you, Cass."

"Were you able to get the boat all right?" I asked.

"Yes, and all the scuba gear," Cindy said. "Hey, why don't we go for a boat ride?"

"Maybe we could do a dress rehearsal," I said. Everyone thought that was an excellent idea.

We took the boat to a deserted spot about forty minutes out of the harbor. The day was perfectly beautiful — sunny, in the low eighties, a slight breeze. After we anchored, Amy and Agatha put on their gear and went in the water to set up the shackle and the shells.

When they returned, Billy said, "Okay, you three," indicating Cass, Cindy and Agatha, "you're the divers from the Zephkar boat. Our boat is anchored fifty yards from yours. Are you ready?"

"Ready, Captain," Agatha said.

"You all know your parts," Billy said. "Go on in. Amy will be down in five minutes."

Cass (with me riding), Cindy playing the role of Zephjame, and Agatha as Adam all dropped into the water. We swam around, pretending we were at a reef, pointing things out to each other. We did see some fish and a few shells. It was amazingly peaceful down there, far better than the swimming pool in Chicago where we'd had our lessons.

Cass found the pile of huge, beautiful shells Amy had planted. She beckoned *Zephjame* and *Adam* over. When they were close enough, I shifted into *Adam*, and immediately went to boost-blocking. Cass moved out of *Zephkar's* range. As *Zephjame* was admiring one of the shells, I slipped the shackle from under the shell pile. The rope was visible but at the real dive it would be concealed among the coral. Swimming down behind *Zephjame*, I quickly

266

locked the shackle around *his* ankle. *He* began kicking and squirming, but I still managed to go through the motions of injecting *him* with the syringe I'd had hidden in my belt. The drug would make James unconscious for hours.

I pulled on the rope, three long jerks, and the boat began moving, tugging *Zephjame* behind it. The weight attached to the shackle made it impossible for *Zephjame* to rise to the surface.

I shifted from *Adam* into Cass. Agatha acted bewildered, as Adam surely would be after just spending time in the void. Cass acted bewildered also. She and *Adam* went up.

"What happened?" Cass asked when they reached the surface. "I blacked out or something," she said. "I was having these beautiful visions."

"Me too," *Adam* said. "It was the strangest thing."

"Where's Mr. Lane?" Cass asked.

"He must still be down below."

Cass and *Adam* dived again. They searched the area but, of course, did not find Zephjame. They went up to their boat to see if Zephjame was there. Of course he wasn't. "We had blackouts," Cass said to the imaginary people on the imaginary boat. "Something very odd is going on. We can't find Mr. Lane."

"So now the crew would dive and search for him," Agatha said. "Ultimately, they'd have to conclude that he drowned."

On the horizon we could see our boat returning. We dived again to retrieve the shells and when we surfaced the boat was there. The others helped us on.

"So are you stranded, Zephkar?" Cass asked Cindy as she pulled off her wet suit.

"You bet your sweet little ass I am. I will drift in the sea forever."

"And James?"

"Deceased," Amy said. "After enough time went by that we knew he was out of air, we pulled his body up. I think he died peacefully and painlessly."

Cass nodded. "So then you took the shackle off and dumped the body?"

"That's right," Billy said. "Not too far from the site of your dive."

"Should we run through our reactions when the police question us?" Billy asked.

"I doubt that they will," Cindy said, "but, yeah, just in case, let's practice that too."

Cass pretended to be the cop, questioning each of the others. Everyone played her part well.

When they finished, Cindy said, "They'll think whatever made Adam and Cass have those blackouts also affected James and caused the drowning. They'll have no reason at all to suspect us."

"I hope everything goes as smoothly tomorrow," Billy said.

Tell them the hardest part was giving Zephjame the injection, I said.

Cass told them.

"If you can't pull that off, then you'll just have to skip it," Cindy said, "and James won't have such an easy death."

"Everything else went beautifully," Cass said. "Those shells are so spectacular, Zephjame's bound to be entranced by them."

We had drinks and munchies to celebrate, then

Agatha let me use her body again and Billy and I went to the bedroom below.

When we got back to the Palace, Theresa was at the entrance. She asked Cass whether she needed to rest up from her sightseeing or was ready now for the Wrath Room.

Cass and I had agreed to get the final room over with as soon as possible. "I'm not tired," Cass said. "Let's go ahead." As we walked through the elegant corridor toward the elevator, Cass asked, "So is everything all set for the scuba trip?"

"All set," Theresa assured her. "I understand you invited Adam. He's excited about going."

"Who else will be there?" Cass asked.

"Just the crew," Theresa responded, "unless you want other divers."

"No," Cass said quickly. "That's fine. And we'll be casting off at noon, right?"

"That's the plan." Theresa opened the door to our suite. "You certainly are eager to get to those reefs," she said. "Maybe you're more an outdoor type than indoor," she added, chuckling. "The more pleasure, the better, we say, on the road to Full Christiandom. Go ahead and get dressed, I'll wait."

The Wrath Room made the Leather Room seem like a picnic.

"Initiates are encouraged to get involved in the activities here," Theresa said, "but only up to their own level. The initiation does require, however, that you at least get a feel for what goes on here and that you try to keep an open mind about joining in."

Located in the basement of the Palace, the Wrath Room was a huge open space containing several arenas with viewing stands. Theresa took us to the smallest arena which was enclosed by a wire fence. Two dogs were going at each other viciously, teeth bared, fur flying. A crowd of human observers cheered and yelled.

This is horrible, Cass said, turning her head away. *I think I'm going to be sick, Jenna.*

Try to get out of here fast, I said.

"All the dogs except the pit bulls belong to Incorrigibles," Theresa said. "There's a group of Incorrigibles over there." She pointed to a cluster of people in normal street clothes. "Their dogs are here too. The collie that's in the process of being destroyed by our pit bull belongs to an Incorrigible."

"I find this disgusting," Cass said flatly.

The crowd went wild as the pit bull came in for the kill.

"Place your bets, ladies and gentlemen," the announcer said. "The next contest will begin in five minutes."

"Bet something," Theresa said. "It'll help you get more involved."

"I don't want to get more involved," Cass responded.

The next battle began. It was even worse than I'd expected. I don't know how they got two house pets to fight so ferociously, but fight they did. It must have lasted ten minutes. I felt totally drained and ill. So did Cass. "I can't take one more minute of this," she said to Theresa.

"Fine," Theresa replied. "Let's move on then."

The next arena was surrounded by a five-foot cement wall. Theresa led us to seats with a clear view. "The Incorrigibles themselves battle it out here," she said, "though not to the death, of course. The winners get to go immediately to the Truth Center to be instructed and then are held for their *Minute with the Mighty.*"

"Zephkar, you mean," Cass said.

"Yes, in the body of James Lane. After the Truth Center, the Incorrigibles are held until Mr. Lane's next visit to the island. The ones who are here now are lucky since they won't have to wait very long."

"So the Incorrigibles are kidnapped?" Cass said, "and brought here for this?"

"They're taken against their will, yes," Theresa said.

"Don't the police do anything about it?"

Theresa shook her head. "You still have a lot to learn about the power of New Direction. Your own instruction will take place at the Truth Center after you complete the program here. All Initiates finish up with our brief education course. You'll enjoy it."

I'm sure, Cass said to me.

"As harsh as it may seem," Theresa continued, "the taking of certain Incorrigibles is a necessary means to our end." She smiled. "They inevitably end up thanking us. Many apply to return to the Palace as Initiates. Several have even become Disciples."

Cass did not respond.

"The Incorrigibles who lose the battle in the

arena," Theresa said, "stay on for more Wrath Room activities."

We watched as the *Incorrigibles* were paraded around the ring and their *evil* deeds described. It was clear that no one would get seriously hurt with the weapons they were using, but the whole exercise was repulsive nonetheless. As soon as we could, we left that arena.

The third and final event of the Wrath Room included audience participation. Within a walled ring, Initiates and other guests used cloth bats, bean bags, switches, and hoses to beat, hit, whip, and spray the Incorrigibles. The Incorrigibles had no weapons, only circular shields with which to try to protect themselves.

The Incorrigibles stood in the center of the ring while their sins were read, then the guests were unleashed upon them. Theresa encouraged Cass to participate, telling her she might be surprised at how enjoyable this physical expression of wrath could be.

"This does nothing but repel me," Cass said.

"It's your choice," Theresa said. "I'm going to leave you now. Stay as long as you want. When you're finished here, feel free to go anywhere you wish in the Palace and to get involved in whatever activities you choose. Enjoy yourself, Veronica, that's what this is all about. If you want me, just pick up any phone."

"Thanks, Theresa."

"By the way, Mr. Lane has arranged for a little brunch to be held on the yacht tomorrow before the scuba diving. Adam will come by for you in the morning, around ten o'clock."

Moments after Theresa left, Cass got us out of the Wrath Room and to the refuge of our suite. We didn't emerge until Adam tapped on the door the next morning.

On the ride to the yacht we were both very nervous. *Not to worry,* I told Cass. *Nothing will go wrong.*

This day is the turning point for the future of this world, she responded.

Don't say that. You'll make me more nervous than I already am.

Not to worry, she said. *Nothing will go wrong.*

Zephjame's yacht was even more impressive than his Chicago one. He was already on board when we arrived. "Your big day," he said laughingly, taking Cass's hand as she walked onto the boat.

A tall, very attractive woman was leaning on the railing. I got a sick feeling when I realized who she was. Theresa had pointed her out to us in the Wrath Room and told us she was in charge of the Incorrigibles.

"Nellie," Zephjame said, "this is the famous Veronica Bloom. Veronica, meet Cornelia Harper."

The woman held out her hand to Cass. "I've heard a great deal about you," she said, her smile revealing beautiful white teeth. Her handshake was firm and warm.

Cass nodded to her. *Maybe we could get Zephkar to boost her for the dive,* Cass said to me, *then we could "kill two birds with one stone" as the Earthlings say.*

Act friendly, I told Cass.

"Will you be scuba diving today also?" Cass asked the woman, in an almost pleasant tone.

"Oh no, not me. I think you divers are all a bit crazed to trust that tanked air."

"Chicken, huh?" Cass said playfully.

Cornelia Harper laughed. "I guess I am," she said unapologetically. "Come on over here where the food is. There's quite a spread."

That was an understatement. It was a feast fit for the Highest Tribunal. Cass ate sparingly and sparred with Zephjame as she did, nondefensively telling him where he could stuff both his Leather Room and Wrath Room. He laughed. "To each her own," he said.

Zephjame was his usual flirtatious self during our two hours of brunching and chatting. Although Adam made occasional pleasant contributions to the conversation, he stayed mostly in the background, hovering around Cass making sure she had everything she wanted. Zephjame monopolized the conversation and no one seemed inclined to try to grab the spotlight from him. After all, Cornelia and Adam thought the spirit inhabiting James Lane's body was sent by God and destined to become the king of Earth. We did learn a few things about Cornelia Harper, though — that she was an Apostle, that she lived in Chicago and coordinated Incorrigible abductions from there, that before joining New Direction, she had worked for the CIA. She'd be a good one to permanate, I thought.

Finally one of the crew members brought out the scuba equipment. Zephjame looked at his watch. "It's noon," he said, "and I'm a man of my word. Time for the big event." He gave Cass's cheek a tweak. "Bring me back a shell or two, will you, sweetheart?"

"I'm sure you'll find your own," Cass said.

Zephjame shook his head. "I'll not be going."

"What?"

"I know you'll manage without me."

"You're not going?" I could feel Cass's heart pounding. "You *have* to go."

"No, my dear." He gave Cass a pleased smile. "You really are disappointed. How flattering."

"Well, yes, I . . . I was looking so forward to our doing it together." *Help, Jenna, what else can I say?*

"Isn't she a charmer," Zephjame said to Cornelia.

Tell him the main reason you came to St. Thomas was to go scuba diving with him.

Cass said it.

"Oh, my dear, now you're making me feel guilty. Believe me, I'll make it up to you. We'll have plenty of opportunities to enjoy each other's company. Dinner tomorrow night for starters. Now you go ahead. Go commune with the fishes. Take care of her, Adam." With that he went to the walkway and exited the boat, Cornelia at his side.

"I can't believe it," Cass said aghast, watching them leave.

The son of a bitch, I said.

"I guess you didn't know," Adam said. "Mr. Lane no longer goes out on the water."

"Shit."

"I'm sorry you're disappointed, Veronica. Is there anything I can do?"

"Why doesn't he go on the water?" Cass snarled.

"I'm not sure exactly," Adam said in his smooth, soothing way. "Something happened last month. I've heard rumors. I think it might have been an attempted assassination, but I don't know for sure. Anyway, he told us he wouldn't be scuba diving anymore and that, in fact, he wouldn't be going out on the boat at all. No one's exactly sure why."

No one but us, I said. *Damn!*

Cass was slumped on a deck chair. She didn't move as the crew cast off and the boat headed out toward the coral reef.

Ever-sensitive Adam obviously was concerned by Cass's mood. He sat on a cushion next to her. "Is there anything at all I can do for you, Victoria?"

"I'm okay," she said. "I just need a minute alone."

"Of course," he said, and left her immediately.

All for nothing. We failed again, Jenna.

You know, I replied. *It crossed my mind that if I were Zephkar, there's no way I'd go anywhere I could be stranded. I wouldn't go hiking in the wilderness, or explore a cave, or go anywhere that an enemy might try to kill my host and leave me stranded. That would certainly include the sea.*

It never crossed my mind.

You forgot what it's like being a DM, I said.

I guess I thought Zephkar considered himself invulnerable, that he didn't think any precautions were necessary.

He probably didn't until the Pit Flop, I said. *He must have realized what would have happened if the Cimians had succeeded in getting him to the bottom of the pit.*

Do you think he knew that was our intention? To strand him?

No, not to strand him. I don't think he has any

idea anyone knows he's strandable. But he knew damn well that if we had killed and buried his host he would have been stranded.

True. He must have thought of that. Shit! So what do we do now?

Go scuba diving, I said.

And that's what we did. Despite our intense disappointment, diving at the coral reef was wonderful. Billy and the others showed up a few minutes after we did. Adam and Cass were just putting on their gear and getting ready to go down when we saw our friends' boat, Agatha at the wheel.

"Hi, are you all going to dive?" Cass called out as they were passing by.

Amy was at the bow in her wet suit. She looked shocked when Cass spoke to her. "Uh, yeah we are. Is there anything wrong? This is a good spot for diving, isn't it?"

"It's supposed to be beautiful. That's what I'm out here for, to dive and nothing else."

"I see," Amy called. "Well, have a good time."

"You too." *Do you think she got the message?* Cass asked me.

If she didn't, they'll figure it out when they don't see Zephjame.

Not long after we submerged, Cass and Adam came fairly close to Amy. Cass caught Amy's eye and shook her head slowly back and forth. Amy got a disgusted look, nodded her understanding, and swam away. A short time later, we saw that Billy and Cindy were diving also.

I guess they decided to make the most of it, Cass said.

* * * * *

Several hours later, in our Pleasure Palace suite, Cass and I brainstormed. *Maybe you can get him to take you somewhere in his private plane,* I said.

That's a possibility. A trip to St. Croix, maybe. Theresa mentioned that he sometimes flies there to go to some restaurant he likes.

And we could push him out over the ocean somehow.

How?

Well, I said, *if there's someone else on the plane besides the pilot, a co-pilot maybe, then I could boost the co-pilot and overpower Zephjame. You could get the door open and I could push Zephjame out.*

Risky, Cass said. *Much riskier than the Pit Flop or the scuba washout. You could end up falling out of the plane too.*

Without totally rejecting the airplane possibility, we moved on to another. Pit Flop number two. We'd find a piece of land in some deserted spot on the island, buy it, hire a construction company to dig a big hole for a swimming pool, lure Zephjame out there, push him into the hole, then shoot him and bury him.

We kept playing with different possibilities. After an hour or so, Cass called Theresa and asked if she could borrow a Palace car to take to town.

As she drove, Cass kept looking into her rearview mirror. *No one's following us,* I said. *They have no reason to suspect you,* Veronica.

At the Royal George, after hearing why the scuba plan had failed, Cindy said, "Well, you might as well get the hell out of the Palace then."

I think we should stay, I told Cass.

"Jenna thinks we should stay. She's having a great time there."

"Oh, yeah?" Billy said.

"Jenna and I have been talking about other ways to strand the slimy mutant," Cass said.

"So did we for a while," Amy said, "but all of our ideas were really far-fetched so we gave it up."

"My initiation is supposed to last for four more days," Cass said. "Maybe I should stay on and try to become a Disciple. That would probably give me more leverage for future plans."

We went out for dinner at an open-air restaurant which had a beautiful view of the sea. Agatha let me open-boost again. After dinner I offered to boost-block.

Really? Sure, she said, *I'd like that.*

I figured she would. After I launched her into the void, Billy and I walked along the shore.

"I was relieved," Billy confessed, "when the plan was called off. Jen, hon, I was so worried about you. I kept thinking that something could go wrong, that Zephkar would turn the tables somehow and you'd be the one to get stranded."

I touched her cheek. "You would have found me, my love."

Billy nodded. "I wouldn't have left until I did, even if it took the rest of my life."

I believed her and felt very loved. "I was worried too," I said. "But I was convinced we'd succeed this time."

"I wonder if we ever will."

* * * * *

279

Cass and I stuck it out at the Palace for the rest of her initiation. She had already met the main requirement, being exposed to all four rooms. Except for the instruction sessions on Thursday and then the meeting with the Rater, Cass was free to spend her time however she pleased. Well, not completely free. Zephjame continued courting her.

The dinner on Tuesday night was tolerable. Besides Zephjame and Cornelia Harper, there were four other guests. After eating, people dispersed to visit their favorite rooms. Cass chose the Water Room intending to swim in the pools, but Zephjame persuaded her to go into the adjoining room, the one with the hoses. Cornelia Harper came also. In addition to Angela, Adam and Anna, a half-dozen other Tempters were there.

Cornelia settled onto one of the platforms, snorted some cocaine and uninhibitedly let the Tempters pleasure her. She had a very attractive body. Cass told Zephjame she was uncomfortable participating in the water games when there were so many people around.

"I'll reserve this room for just the two of us," he said. "Tomorrow night."

He had come on to her several times during the evening. This time Cass spelled it out. "I understand the need for Full Christians to indulge our passions," Cass said, "and I've come to accept the idea, agree with it, actually, and certainly enjoy it." She was sitting on a chair near the waterfall, fully clothed. "But I would not want to do any of the activities in these rooms with someone I have special feelings for, or who I might have a relationship with."

Zephjame nodded. "Some of the Disciples feel the same," he said. "That's fine."

Whew, I said. *I wasn't sure you'd get away with it.*

"Those *special feelings* you mention," Zephjame continued, "you're feeling them for me, I take it."

"I have so many feelings for you," Cass responded. "It's very complicated, a little confusing."

"Let's get out of here," he said. "We'll go to my suite and discuss it further."

Help! Cass pleaded.

Tell him you're a lesbian, I said.

Really? Cass said. *Yes, of course.*

Zephjame's suite was similar to ours, maybe a tad more luxurious. He offered Cass a drink. She chose a glass of lemon Calistoga. He sat next to her on the sofa stroking her forehead and fluttering his fingers over her hair. When he was moving in for a kiss, she turned her head away. He glared angrily and grabbed her jaw jerking her head back. "Enough cat and mouse," he said. "I want you, Veronica, and I'm going to have you. You've put me off long enough."

"There's something I have to tell you," she said, her voice strained.

"Don't give me any crap about your morality," Zephjame hissed.

"It's not that, it's . . ."

He released his grip on her jaw. "Go on."

"I'm very attracted to you . . . to your . . . your spirit, your energy and your charm, but . . ."

"Go on, go on."

"It's . . . well . . . I'm a lesbian, James. Hardly anyone knows it, but it's true. It always has been."

Zephjame was motionless for a few moments. Then he threw back his head and laughed. "Yes, yes," he said, "that explains it. But why didn't you tell me sooner? No, I take that back. I'm glad you didn't. The buildup has been marvelous."

I realized what he was thinking. I should have thought of it myself. We'd lost again.

"How about Angela?" he asked. "She has a perfectly lovely body. Does she appeal to you?"

Jenna, we're in trouble.

My mind was racing. There was no way out of it now, I thought. No way without destroying any possibility of getting to Zephkar through Cass. Ideas flew through my mind one after another. I had a flash of a bulldozer, a car, the woods, those people in the Wrath Room being attacked with whips and water hoses. *Cornelia Harper,* I said to Cass. *Tell him you're attracted to her.*

Don't make me puke.

Do it, Cass. I have a plan. Trust me.

As soon as she told him, a smiling Zephjame jumped up and left the suite. I offered to boost-block for what inevitably was coming next. Cass said she wasn't going to cop out because the going got rough. I argued but she insisted. A few minutes later, Cornelia Harper came into the suite, or rather Zephkar in Cornelia's body, with Cornelia, of course, enjoying her drift in the *heavenly preview.*

I had planned to switch to mini-riding as soon as

the lovemaking began, but I didn't. This was the second time I experienced sex with Zephkar Tesot while he was boosting a very attractive woman. This was the second time I felt the guilt.

Pretend you're into it, I told Cass as Zephcorn began unbuttoning Cass's blouse. *Remind yourself it's all for the greater good.*

I didn't have to give her any more advice. She played her role beautifully and her orgasms definitely were not faked. We didn't talk about it afterwards.

It was nearly two a.m. when Zephcorn walked Cass to our suite and gave her a final goodnight kiss. "Until the next time, my sweet. Welcome to my life."

As soon as he was gone I told Cass my idea for the stranding. She nodded as she listened. *Yes, it could work,* she said excitedly. *This one might do it.*

There were two more lovemaking sessions with Zephcorn before Friday finally came and the initiation was over. One of the rendezvous took place in his suite again, the other in the Silk Room. Again, Cass and I did not talk about it afterwards.

On Thursday, Cass had her indoctrination session. The goals and strategies of New Direction were explained to her in grisly detail. Zephkar's plan did seem diabolically inspired. After becoming President of the United States and changing the Constitution to fit his needs, he would begin converting world leaders. The most important resisters in the U.S. and abroad would be converted by Zephjame personally via the *Minute with the Mighty.* Those opponents who didn't follow their converted leaders would be eliminated or enslaved.

283

"A necessary means to the goals God wants for the Earth," Cass's instructor said.

"Yes," Cass replied. "It has to be done."

Apparently she had convinced her teacher she had fully understood and digested her training. The final step of Cass's initiation took place Friday morning before our flight back to Chicago. In a small lounge in the Palace, Cass met with a Rater. He asked her question after question about her views regarding New Direction, about her wish to be involved in the movement, about the contributions she might make. Between the two of us, I thought she did okay.

"You did very well," the Rater said at the end of the interrogation. "Ordinarily I would now arrange a meeting with Mr. Lane, but that has been waived in your case. He told me that if I rate you as Disciple material, then Disciple you shall be." He took a paper from his desk drawer, filled it out and signed it. "You are a Disciple of New Direction," he said, showing her the form. "This will be officially recorded." He held out his hand. "Congratulations."

"Thank you," Cass said.

"Welcome to the future," he said as he walked her to the door. "You'll be contacted by our Chicago Liaison Officer within the next month to discuss your assignment."

When Zephjame said goodbye to Cass under the arch of angels at the Pleasure Palace entryway, he assured her they would be seeing a great deal of each other in Chicago.

Cass will be the last person Zephkar *ever* sees, I thought.

During the two weeks following our return from St. Thomas, I spent some time riding Cornelia Harper. She was thirty-four years old, divorced, childless, lived alone in a condominium on Lake Shore Drive, drove a brand new Saab, was fluent in German and Russian, played the piano, and enjoyed very dry white wines. She had season tickets to the opera and usually went with her friend, Leona Tyler, a buxom woman in her early forties who had also once spied for the U.S. government. Most of Cornelia's time was spent in the foul business of coordinating the capture, transporting, punishment, and indoctrination of the "Incorrigibles."

During one of my visits, on a gloomy Sunday afternoon, Cornelia dozed off while reading the newspaper, giving me an opportunity to boost-block. I got her Saab from the garage, drove to a hardware store some distance from her condo, and had a duplicate of her car key made. I dropped the extra key off at Cass's apartment before returning Cornelia to her condo.

Several times when I was with Cornelia, Zephjame summoned her to the Astor place so he could use her body for his evenings with Cass. Cornelia enjoyed her sojourns in the "heavenly preview," and found it amusing that Zephkar needed her body in order to carry on his love affair with the ex-entrepreneur, Veronica Bloom. Wrong, I thought, an idea hatching. No, Cornelia Harper, you don't find it amusing at all. In fact, you hate it.

"I hate it," I said to Leona Tyler one night on the telephone. Cornelia had fallen asleep early and I was boost-blocking her to make the call. "I pretend it's fine but actually it enrages me to have him use my body that way."

"I'm not surprised," Leona responded. "If ever there was someone who needs to be in control, it's you."

"But of course I can't say anything to him."

"That wouldn't be wise."

"So I'm thinking of leaving. I didn't want you to worry, Leona. I'm thinking of taking on a new identity and disappearing."

"It's that bad?"

"It's intolerable. Each time I get the call from him, I want to kill the sonofabitch, angel of God or not."

"Maybe the affair won't go on too much longer," Leona said.

"I don't agree. This isn't a fling. He's hooked on

the bitch. I considered eliminating her, or at least maiming her so he wouldn't find her so desirable."

"But he'd know you did it," Leona responded, apparently not shocked by the idea.

"He trusts me completely now, never reads my mind anymore, but if anything happened to his lady, my thoughts would get very close scrutiny, I'm sure." I paused. "I'm having a passport made. I'm also considering plastic surgery once I get to my destination."

Leona sighed. "I understand," she said. "I'll miss you, my friend."

Cass bought a new car, a compact blue Volvo. Billy bought another one exactly like it. Each day, we parked the one Billy had bought on different streets in various quiet, middle-class neighborhoods. One day when Billy and I went to move the car, we saw a woman walking a beagle. "I wonder how many dogs have been killed since we left St. Thomas," Billy said.

The stranding has to work this time, I responded.

In fact, I was so sure we'd succeed that I told Agatha it was time to discuss our futures. *Amy and Cindy want to be in on the talk too,* I told her.

The next evening, the three Earthlings and I gathered around Cass's kitchen table. I was maxi-riding Amy.

"Here's the deal," Cindy said, directing her words to Agatha. "We all take turns. You, me, and Amy. Three months each. Three months in the void each year and nine months in the real world. That way all of us have a real life and we each get to drift too."

Agatha looked skeptical. "You'd want that?" she said. "I thought you were opposed to long stretches in the void."

"Not if we do it this way," Amy said. "Cass and Billy think it's a good idea. So does Jenna."

"How come I didn't hear anything about this?" Agatha said.

"You're hearing now," Amy responded. "We've been talking about possibilities ever since you got addicted."

"We'll have a schedule," Cindy said. "Each of us will know in advance when it's her turn for the void. We already worked out the first few years, dividing each year into quarters. Our void periods will vary, falling in different quarters of different years."

"So we each get to be around during all the seasons," Amy said.

"You've worked out all the details," Agatha responded.

"Not all of them. It's just a proposal so far. We're still thinking about it."

"What if one of us gets sick or something?" Agatha asked. "Gets injured or has to have surgery or something?"

"Whoever's controlling the body during that time deals with the illness," Cindy said.

"That's acceptable to you, Jenna?"

Tell her it's the fairest way," I responded.

"Jenna says that's the fairest way," Amy said.

Agatha nodded contemplatively. "And if one of us dies?"

Cindy shrugged. "We haven't talked about that. I guess Jenna would try to find another volunteer."

After a period of silence, Agatha said, "If you're doing this for me, it's not necessary."

"We'd be doing it for all of us," Amy said.

Again Agatha had become pensive. "I don't think it would work," she'd said at last. "How would we explain our dramatic shifts in personality? Take you, for example, Amy. For part of the year you're a graphic artist and a musician, then suddenly you lose those talents? And you shift lovers from Cindy and Cass to Billy? How would you explain that to people?"

Amy laughed. "It'll be a challenge."

Agatha was not smiling. "Billy really thinks this is a good idea? I thought she wanted Jenna to permanate."

"She knows that's up to Jenna," Amy replied.

"And what about when we all grow old and die, Jenna? What then for you?"

I don't know, I said.

"She'll make new friends," Cindy said. "Jenna wants to do this, Agatha. She could permanate if she wanted to. Obviously she doesn't."

"Don't you see, Agatha," Amy said, resting her hand on Agatha's arm, "it's the best possible solution, the best for everybody."

Cass had suggested to Zephcorn that they spend Friday night at his friend Peter's place at Lake Geneva. Zephcorn thought it was an excellent idea.

At six o'clock on Friday, we picked up Zephcorn in Cass's new Volvo. Zephcorn had brought a hand-drawn map to Peter's summer house which he put in the glove compartment.

As we got further north, Cass, from time to time, would look at Zephcorn with half-lidded eyes, and run her tongue slowly over her upper lip. Perfect, I thought. After one of those seductive glances, Zephcorn's hand wandered to Cass's thigh. Cass kept her eyes on the road but began breathing heavily as Zephcorn moved his fingers closer to her crotch. "If you don't stop I might have to pull over and ravage you right here in the car," Cass said. We were near the Wisconsin border at that point, about thirty miles from Lake Geneva.

Zephcorn laughed. "I'd love it," he said with Cornelia's throaty voice.

Grinning lustily, Cass shifted to the right lane then exited the highway. Soon we were parked under a cluster of evergreens at the side of a moonlit country road. Cass turned to face Zephcorn. Slowly, she lifted up her sweater, holding Zephcorn's eyes with her own. Beads of sweat glistened on Zephcorn's forehead as he stared at her breasts. Cass pulled the sweater off and tossed it into the back seat.

We referred to Cass's lovemaking with Zephcorn as her "noble sacrifice for the cause." "You truly are a martyr," Cindy once said. "I don't think I could do it." Cass had remained silent. She and I never talked about it, but I knew that the lovemaking sessions with Zephcorn, though definitely distasteful in one sense, were also strangely exciting to her.

As Zephcorn sucked her left nipple and Cass

stroked his hair with her right hand, her left hand found the syringe we had stashed under the seat. She had practiced many times.

He was sucking vigorously, his hand simultaneously rubbing her still-clothed crotch. Cass got the needle into position against the soft flesh just below his belt. He continued sucking and rubbing. *Now,* I said, and Cass shoved in the needle and pushed the plunger.

"Ouch!" He pulled back. "Something stung me."

"Really? What could it be, my love?"

He rubbed his hip. "A bee, maybe."

"Where, darling? Let me see."

"Oh, it's okay, it doesn't hurt now." His speech was already beginning to slur. His eyelids fluttered. Seconds later he slumped over on top of Cass. When she pushed him away his slack head rolled to one side.

Do you think she's dead?

See if there's a pulse, I said.

Cass put her fingers over Cornelia's wrist. *I don't feel a thing.*

Cass's heart was thumping madly. *Relax, hon,* I said. *Take a deep breath. It's almost over.* She was shaking. *Put your sweater on,* I said, but she didn't move. *Cass, are you okay?*

No response.

I'm going to boost. Still no answer. *Cass, can you hear me?*

"Do it," she said aloud. "Boost-block."

I shifted. As soon as I was controlling the body, I got the sweater from the back seat and slipped it on over my shivering torso. When I had the car moving, I turned the heat on full blast. I got to the highway and headed north again, forcing myself to concentrate on the road and not think about the body slumped on the seat next to me. Another forty-five minutes and we'll be there, I thought. I was sweating. I turned the heat down. There was more traffic than I'd expected. Don't think about having an accident, I told myself, and, of course, that made me picture a crash in gory detail.

I turned the radio on to distract myself. ". . . making Colorado the eighth state to ratify the new constitutional amendments," the announcer said. "The Theocratic Party continues gaining . . ." I switched the station until I found some music. I wondered where Zephkar was. Stuck on the car ceiling, perhaps, or the dashboard. Adhering to one of the windows, maybe. Nothing will go wrong this time, I told myself. "Three strikes and you're out, Zephkar," I said aloud.

I took the turnoff to Cindy's sister's cabin. Cindy's car was there and so was the twin Volvo. Through the rearview mirror I saw my friends coming out of the cabin, Billy in the lead. I drove on to the hole and pulled up at the deep end, parking parallel to the edge. The hole was rectangular in shape, twelve feet deep at the diving board end, tapering to four feet at the shallow end.

The other ZET members parked their cars. I took off my sweater, shoes, and socks, then wiggled out of the slacks. I tossed all the clothes in the back seat, including the underpants. Although there was no chance Zephkar would be adhering to my body, I

292

shook my hair anyway and brushed my skin with my palms.

I was about to leave the car when I remembered I had to get the map to Peter's house and the house keys. The map was in the glove compartment. As I was reaching across Cornelia's body, my arm brushed against her hair and a chill ran up my naked spine. I felt claustrophobic, as if the sides of the car were crushing in on me. I have to get out of this coffin, I thought, feeling panicky. As I was turning the body to get the keys from the pocket, my head began to spin; my ears were ringing. Then I was with Billy at my farm at home. We were swinging in the hammock, singing silly songs in the language I could no longer remember.

Then I became aware of being in the car, slumped over Cornelia Harper's dead body. I must have passed out. I felt weak and nauseated, but I made myself fish through Cornelia's pockets until I found the key. Slowly then, using one finger, I pulled on the handle and opened the door. Very carefully, I backed out of the car. The ground was hard and cold on my bare feet. I closed the door.

I stood unsteadily, leaning on the car. Then again my consciousness seemed to slip and I was once more with Billy on Allo. This time we were swimming in Sumikuya Lake in the Yallali Territory. I shook my head vigorously from side to side. Gone, I told myself angrily. All gone. This is the only reality. The cold ground stung my feet. Earth. My bodiless mind participating in killings, burying bodies, trying to prevent this disgusting planet from being taken over by a mutant and becoming even more disgusting than it already was.

I saw my friends waiting in a huddle on the cement pad we'd built two months before, Billy holding a pair of jeans, Agatha a sweater and jacket. I was tempted to brush off my skin some more but reminded myself that DM's do not adhere to living organisms. "It's all right," I said aloud, more to myself than the others. "He's inside the car." I walked to my friends.

"Did everything go okay?" Doris asked.

I handed her the map and keys. "So far." I shoved a leg into the jeans.

"Is it you, Jenna?" Billy asked.

"Yes."

The moment I was dressed, Billy took me into her arms. The warmth of her body warmed me, and I had an image of us lying on the beach at home, the sun warm, a cool breeze whispering over our skin.

"Come on, hon, let's go help them," I heard her say.

It was not difficult for seven women to push the car over the edge. The shiny new Volvo landed on its side with a grating thud.

"Now comes the fun part," Amy said, picking up a shovel.

"You two should get going," Agatha said to Doris and Gracie. Doris was examining the map by flashlight.

"It's about forty minutes from here," I said.

Gracie and Doris got into the other Volvo. "See you tomorrow," Gracie said nervously, and they drove away.

"Billy, why don't you take Jencass to the cabin?"

Cindy suggested. "She's done enough. We can bury the car without her."

"I'm okay," I said, putting on a pair of work gloves. I grabbed a shovel. "The exercise will do me good."

We shoveled and shoved the dirt for hours, no one speaking. The only sounds were the scraping of the shovels and the thuds made by clods of dirt landing on metal. When the Volvo was completely covered, we piled into Cindy's car and drove the quarter mile to the cabin. Cindy darted to the shower and I collapsed on the sofa next to Billy. Nobody had much to say.

"I want to celebrate, but I don't feel like it yet," Agatha said.

"I know," said Amy, "not until the hole's completely filled in. I won't feel safe until then."

"Do you want to talk about what happened?" Billy asked me.

"It went exactly as planned," I said. "Cass did everything perfectly, down to the glint in her eye. He didn't suspect for one second."

"Even when she injected him?" Amy asked.

"He thought it was a bee sting."

"How come Cass is in the void?" Agatha asked. "I think I know."

"She'll be okay," I said. "We owe her a lot, you know."

"The world does," Agatha said.

"She's been through more than any of us," Amy said. "She truly is a hero."

"If you want to bring her back, Jenna, you can boost me," Agatha offered. "Open boosting."

I switched to maxi-riding. *Cass, we're in the cabin,* I said. *The car is buried. Are you OK?*

I was at the sea with my birth parent, Cass replied dreamily. She took a deep breath. *Yes, Jenna, I'm fine.*

I'm going to shift to Agatha.

"All right," she said numbly.

The moment Cass was controlling her body, she reached toward Amy and clung to her, then burst into tears. I guess that gave us all permission because every one of us began to cry. When Cindy came into the room, she went to the sofa with Amy and Cass and cried also.

"It's hard to save the world," Amy finally said, and that made the crying turn to hysterical giggling.

And then we talked. It seemed each of us had so much to say, so many feelings to vent, especially Cass. *Remind her that we're all equally responsible for the deaths,* Agatha said at one point. I told Cass what Agatha had said.

"That's right," Billy seconded. "We did what we had to do."

We knew that was true, but we all felt terrible anyhow. The talking did seem to help a little. It was almost daybreak when we finally went to bed.

My dreams were all of Allo, pleasant dreams, wispy and nostalgic. When I awoke, Billy wasn't in the bed. I found her in the kitchen with Doris and Gracie who had returned at ten-thirty that morning.

Amy, Cass, and Cindy joined us in the kitchen. After her wakeup coffee, Cindy made the call to the construction company. She told the contractor she ended up not getting the money after all and would not be able to complete the pool. "Some friends and I tried to fill in the hole," she said, "but it was just too much work. We'll need you to come out and finish the job."

"So how did it go at Lake Geneva?" Amy asked Gracie and Doris.

"Smoothly," Doris said. "We didn't see a soul but I'm sure Peter's neighbors heard the car. There were lights on in the house next door when we arrived."

"Outside the houses, though, it was real dark," Gracie said, "so it's very unlikely anyone could have gotten a good look at us."

"How about in the morning?" Cass asked. "When you left? Did anyone see you then?"

Doris shook her head. "The neighbors' drapes were all closed. I think we're fine. They'll tell the police they heard a car arrive at about nine p.m., then leave the next morning. Hopefully someone noticed the car was a blue Volvo."

"That would help," Cass said, "but it's not crucial."

When the bulldozer arrived, we all went and watched as the driver maneuvered the huge machine, picking up giant shovelsful of dirt and dropping them into the hole. It was near dusk when the ground was level again.

"You gals ought to learn to make up your minds," the man said, chuckling, as he took the check from Cindy.

As soon as he was gone, the celebration began. Gracie and Doris had bought great quantities of food. It reminded me of the Pleasure Palace. We danced and sang and ate and toasted our victory. At one point, we all quieted down while Cass phoned the Astor house.

"James Lane is here, Ms. Bloom," Freddie told her, "but Zephkar is not with him."

"I see. Hmm-m, well, all right, tell him I called, will you?"

The party continued. Bit by bit we let the full reality sink in — that the disembodied mind of Zephkar Tesot was neutralized, incapacitated, stranded deep beneath the soil of the planet whose spine he had hoped to crush.

"Gone forever," Amy said, holding her glass of wine high in the air.

Maybe forever. Surely, at least for your lifetimes, I thought, looking around at my friends, wondering sadly if someday, long after they were gone, I would have to fight the battle again.

The next afternoon, boost-blocking a passed-out junkie in Uptown, I called the Astor house. "Zephkar speaking," I said. "Get James for me, will you, Freddie?"

I told James Lane where I was and what I looked like. Fifteen minutes later he arrived. I shifted into him and immediately boost-blocked.

Freddie was clearly relieved to see me when I arrived at the house. I accepted the drink he brought me, a Bloody Mary, Zephkar's favorite.

"I expected you yesterday, Mr. Lane. I know you don't like it when I worry, but you usually let me know if you're going to be delayed. Is everything all right?"

I took a sip of the drink, trying not to grimace at the unpleasant taste. "Something important is developing, Freddie." I put my feet up on the footstool as Zephjame always did. "I want you to cancel all my appointments for the next few days."

"Ms. Bloom, I assume," Freddie said.

I shook my head. "This is far larger than my love life."

Freddie waited expectantly.

"After Veronica dropped me off yesterday at Cornelia's, there was a contact." I stared pensively out the window.

"From . . . you mean . . .?"

"Yes, from the Lord God." I looked at Freddie. "He pulled me home, the first time He's done that since my coming. I was with Him through the night. I'm not sure what will happen yet, but He's preparing me. There will be a message. Soon. I want you to alert the others. Contact all the Apostles and the key Disciples and have them stand by. When I come again, I'll want to meet with them."

"Yes, sir. Can you give me any idea what it's about?"

"You'll find out when the others do."

"Shall I tell people —"

"Just tell them to stand by."

"And Veronica? She called last night. What should I tell her if she calls again?"

"Nothing," I said. "She'll just have to stand by too. There are going to be some big changes. There might have been some with Veronica and me anyway. It seems that Cornelia resents my using her body."

"Resents it?"

"She pretends not to but I tuned in the other day. She's not content with the arrangement."

"How dare she," Freddie said indignantly.

"It's of little consequence anyway," I said, placing my unfinished drink on the table and rising from the chair. "I'm leaving now. I'll be back soon, probably within a week." I left a very worried-looking Freddie standing at the back door.

I parked the Mercedes in a lot near the Holy Name Cathedral, then walked a few blocks until I came across a ragged-looking woman dozing on a bench. After laying some coins on the bench, I shifted into her and immediately boost-blocked. James blinked his eyes a few times, looked around, then started walking. I watched him hail a cab. He's like a homing pigeon, I thought. Wherever he is when he suddenly finds himself pulled from the void, unless told otherwise by Zephkar, he heads right for home.

Taking a quarter from the bench, I found a phone booth and called the apartment. "This is Jenbaglady," I told Agatha. After telling her where I'd be waiting and the interesting outfit I was wearing, I went back to the bench to wait for her to come and take me home.

Two days later, when the police questioned Cass about the whereabouts of Cornelia Harper, Cass told the following story: Saturday evening, she and Cornelia drove to Lake Geneva in Cass's Volvo. They spent the night in Peter Gustufson's house, had a leisurely breakfast the next morning, then drove back to Chicago. Cass dropped Cornelia off at her apartment, then went home where she remained the rest of the day with her roommates, Agatha Tarlton, Billy Apeldum, and Amy Klein.

I maxi-rode Cass throughout the interrogation. She didn't have to pretend to be deeply distraught about Cornelia's disappearance. I wondered if she'd ever get over the reality of what we'd done, if any of us would. When the detective finished with Cass and asked to speak with the roommates, I shifted into him. By dipping and mind-tickling, I learned that Leona Tyler had done her job. When informed that Cornelia had disappeared, Leona had told the police that Cornelia was planning to leave the country. The detective didn't doubt that Leona was telling the truth, especially after he received the report that Cornelia's Saab was found in the O'Hare Airport long-term parking lot.

On Sunday evening, nine days after the stranding of Zephkar Tesot, I stood before a packed house of Apostles and Disciples in the Holy Name Cathedral.

"The Lord called me to Him," I said, in as deep and somber a voice as I could muster in James Lane's throat, "and has sent me back with His message." I lowered my head and said the next sentence softly. "I have failed."

There was murmuring in the crowd.

"I have failed," I repeated loudly. "God gave me free reign to work as I saw fit and I misjudged. The fault is mine; I led you astray. The fault is yours; you followed me, allowed yourselves to be misled."

I waited until the noise died down.

"We all were being tested — you and I and the world, and we failed." I paused, looking over my audience. "God is calling me back. To stay. He has let me know that my approach, and yours — the involvement of believers in worldly politics . . . is not the way! We have all gone astray. There is to be no takeover of governments. No constitutional amendments. No theocracy. No James Lane for president. New Direction is to be disbanded."

The response was loud enough to drown me out. I waited. "The Theocratic Party is no more!" I declared, emphasizing each word. "It is over."

I left the podium and walked down the center aisle of the church. Every eye was on me. I went up to a man I recognized, a high-ranking Apostle. "You," I said. "God will speak through you." I shifted into him.

Boost-blocking, I returned to the pulpit. "Zephkar speaks," I said through the Apostle's mouth. "He is in me, saying farewell, directing me to say farewell to all of you. God is angry with us, Zephkar says. The way we have treated those we called the Incorrigibles is an abomination." I closed my eyes as if listening to something. "Wait!" I said, alarmed.

A hush came over the huge chamber.

"I'm getting a message . . . It . . . it's coming directly from God. Yes, Lord, I hear Your voice." I raised my arms high into the air. "Yes, yes, I understand. I will tell them. Three golden values. Yes, Lord, I've got it. I will speak your words."

I looked at my rapt audience. "This is what the Lord said to me." I took a deep breath. "We must be compassionate to our fellow beings. We must be aware of their needs and feelings, and do unto them as we would want done unto us, treating each fairly and kindly. Compassion is the first Golden Value. So says the Lord."

I closed my eyes, nodding as if listening to something from afar, then spoke again. "Sharing, the Lord says, the second Golden Value. We must insure an equitable distribution of goods and of liberties to all people."

Again I closed my eyes. "Respect, the Lord God says, the third Golden Value. To respect is to truly value ourselves and every other human being. To respect is to make room for differences, accepting the diversity among us that God and the course of our lives have jointly created."

I breathed heavily as if exhausted. "These are the Three Values of Gold," I said. "Values that God wants us to live by." I held my mouth agape as if astounded by what I was experiencing.

Many of the people in the audience also had open mouths.

"There's more," I said, my voice quaking. "Abominations . . . yes, Lord, I hear you." I paused for a good ten seconds. "The Lord says that the use of physical force against another is an abomination. Never to be initiated. Warranted only to contain those who use violence themselves, and then only to the degree needed to stop the violence. Never cruelly, never in vengeance."

I did some more nodding with eyes closed, then said, "This ban on physical force is called God's Holy Prohibition." I was breathing heavily. "From the Holy Prohibition and from the Golden Values, God gives to us the duty of deducing the rest — how to live, how to treat ourselves and all the others of the world."

At that point, I collapsed over the podium. Several people ran up to me. I shifted to maxi-riding. The man I'd been boosting looked around, clearly confused and astounded. "What happened?" he mumbled.

"God spoke through you," someone said.

"His will be done," said another.

Cindy pushed her way through the Cathedral crowd until she was near enough to my host for me to shift into her. As we headed for the exit, she was laughing.

What's so funny? I asked.

You, she said. *How you hammed it up. You were great.*

Do you think I overdid it?

Of course. That's the way the game is played.

That night our celebration was ecstatic. The band shook the walls — Amy on drums, Cindy playing guitar. Cass sang from the depth of her being. It was November seventeenth. I was still shifting around from host to host, but on December first, I would enter Cindy and boost-block her continually for three months. Amy's turn would be next, then Agatha's. After that, on September first, I would have my turn in the void, if I wanted, or I could spend that quarter-year shifting around among different hosts. I probably would do some of both, I thought.

The party finally ended and Agatha offered me her body for the night. I accepted and took it to bed with Billy.

"So, it's really over," Billy said, lying back on the pillow, her hands behind her head. "Will we wake up now, Jenna, and be back home?"

"Don't I wish. I keep having flashes of Allo."

"Me too."

"But I'm getting used to Earth."

"What choice do we have?"

I kissed her tenderly. "I love you more today than I did yesterday," I said.

"You always say that."

"It's always true."

She kissed me softly, then laid her head on the pillow again, and stared at the ceiling. "Is San Francisco really that pretty?"

"Parts of it are."

"I think Cass and Amy and Cindy should get the top floor apartment of our Victorian house, don't you? After all, there are three of them. We'll take the middle floor and Agatha can have the bottom."

"Whatever," I said lazily. "Or we could just flip a coin like Cass suggested."

Billy yawned.

"I wonder if my Golden Values and Holy Prohibitions will do any good," I said.

"Agatha doubts it. You heard her, she said they'll distort what you said, twist it to meet their own needs."

"Probably," I said. "There are so many *true* incorrigibles on Earth."

"What a pit."

"You know," I said, "Zephkar's plan had some clever elements to it, don't you think?" I sat up. "Maybe we should start a new political party, Billy, and a new movement. Only no God stuff. We could call it the Feminist/Humanist Party."

I chuckled and lay back down, putting my arms around Billy, my cheek against her neck. "I think I'll ask Agatha if she'd like to be president."

A few of the publications of
THE NAIAD PRESS, INC.
P.O. Box 10543 • Tallahassee, Florida 32302
Phone (904) 539-5965
Mail orders welcome. Please include 15% postage.

IN THE GAME by Nikki Baker. 192 pp. A Virginia Kelly
mystery. First in a series.   ISBN 01-56280-004-3 $8.95

AVALON by Mary Jane Jones. 256 pp. A Lesbian Arthurian
romance.   ISBN 0-941483-96-7   9.95

STRANDED by Camarin Grae. 320 pp. Entertaining, riveting
adventure.   ISBN 0-941483-99-1   9.95

THE DAUGHTERS OF ARTEMIS by Lauren Wright Douglas.
240 pp. Third Caitlin Reece mystery.   ISBN 0-941483-95-9   8.95

CLEARWATER by Catherine Ennis. 176 pp. Romantic secrets
of a small Louisiana town.   ISBN 0-941483-65-7   8.95

THE HALLELUJAH MURDERS by Dorothy Tell. 176 pp.
Second Poppy Dillworth mystery.   ISBN 0-941483-88-6   8.95

ZETA BASE by Judith Alguire. 208 pp. Lesbian triangle
on a future Earth.   ISBN 0-941483-94-0   9.95

SECOND CHANCE by Jackie Calhoun. 256 pp. Contemporary
Lesbian lives and loves.   ISBN 0-941483-93-2   9.95

MURDER BY TRADITION by Katherine V. Forrest. 288 pp.
A Kate Delafield Mystery. 4th in a series. ISBN 0-941483-89-4   18.95

BENEDICTION by Diane Salvatore. 272 pp. Striking,
contemporary romantic novel.   ISBN 0-941483-90-8   9.95

CALLING RAIN by Karen Marie Christa Minns. 240 pp.
Spellbinding, erotic love story   ISBN 0-941483-87-8   9.95

BLACK IRIS by Jeane Harris. 192 pp. Caroline's hidden past . . .
             ISBN 0-941483-68-1   8.95

TOUCHWOOD by Karin Kallmaker. 240 pp. Loving, May/
December romance.   ISBN 0-941483-76-2   8.95

BAYOU CITY SECRETS by Deborah Powell. 224 pp. A Hollis
Carpenter mystery. First in a series.   ISBN 0-941483-91-6   8.95

COP OUT by Claire McNab. 208 pp. 4th Det. Insp. Carol Ashton
mystery.   ISBN 0-941483-84-3   8.95

LODESTAR by Phyllis Horn. 224 pp. Romantic, fast-moving
adventure.   ISBN 0-941483-83-5   8.95

THE BEVERLY MALIBU by Katherine V. Forrest. 288 pp. A
Kate Delafield Mystery. 3rd in a series. (HC) ISBN 0-941483-47-9   16.95
                  Paperback ISBN 0-941483-48-7   9.95

THAT OLD STUDEBAKER by Lee Lynch. 272 pp. Andy's affair
with Regina and her attachment to her beloved car.
ISBN 0-941483-82-7   9.95

PASSION'S LEGACY by Lori Paige. 224 pp. Sarah is swept into
the arms of Augusta Pym in this delightful historical romance.
ISBN 0-941483-81-9   8.95

THE PROVIDENCE FILE by Amanda Kyle Williams. 256 pp.
Second espionage thriller featuring lesbian agent Madison McGuire
ISBN 0-941483-92-4   8.95

I LEFT MY HEART by Jaye Maiman. 320 pp. A Robin Miller
Mystery. First in a series.   ISBN 0-941483-72-X   9.95

THE PRICE OF SALT by Patricia Highsmith (writing as Claire
Morgan). 288 pp. Classic lesbian novel, first issued in 1952 . . .
acknowledged by its author under her own, very famous, name.
ISBN 1-56280-003-5   8.95

SIDE BY SIDE by Isabel Miller. 256 pp. From beloved author of
Patience and Sarah.   ISBN 0-941483-77-0   8.95

SOUTHBOUND by Sheila Ortiz Taylor. 240 pp. Hilarious sequel
to *Faultline*.   ISBN 0-941483-78-9   8.95

STAYING POWER: LONG TERM LESBIAN COUPLES
by Susan E. Johnson. 352 pp. Joys of coupledom.
ISBN 0-941-483-75-4   12.95

SLICK by Camarin Grae. 304 pp. Exotic, erotic adventure.
ISBN 0-941483-74-6   9.95

NINTH LIFE by Lauren Wright Douglas. 256 pp. A Caitlin
Reece mystery. 2nd in a series.   ISBN 0-941483-50-9   8.95

PLAYERS by Robbi Sommers. 192 pp. Sizzling, erotic novel.
ISBN 0-941483-73-8   8.95

MURDER AT RED ROOK RANCH by Dorothy Tell. 224 pp.
First Poppy Dillworth adventure.   ISBN 0-941483-80-0   8.95

LESBIAN SURVIVAL MANUAL by Rhonda Dicksion.
112 pp. Cartoons!   ISBN 0-941483-71-1   8.95

A ROOM FULL OF WOMEN by Elisabeth Nonas. 256 pp.
Contemporary Lesbian lives.   ISBN 0-941483-69-X   8.95

MURDER IS RELATIVE by Karen Saum. 256 pp. The first
Brigid Donovan mystery.   ISBN 0-941483-70-3   8.95

PRIORITIES by Lynda Lyons 288 pp. Science fiction with
a twist.   ISBN 0-941483-66-5   8.95

THEME FOR DIVERSE INSTRUMENTS by Jane Rule. 208
pp. Powerful romantic lesbian stories. ISBN 0-941483-63-0   8.95

LESBIAN QUERIES by Hertz & Ertman. 112 pp. The questions
you were too embarrassed to ask.   ISBN 0-941483-67-3   8.95

CLUB 12 by Amanda Kyle Williams. 288 pp. Espionage thriller
featuring a lesbian agent!   ISBN 0-941483-64-9   8.95

DEATH DOWN UNDER by Claire McNab. 240 pp. 3rd Det.
Insp. Carol Ashton mystery.   ISBN 0-941483-39-8   8.95

MONTANA FEATHERS by Penny Hayes. 256 pp. Vivian and
Elizabeth find love in frontier Montana.   ISBN 0-941483-61-4   8.95

CHESAPEAKE PROJECT by Phyllis Horn. 304 pp. Jessie &
Meredith in perilous adventure.   ISBN 0-941483-58-4   8.95

LIFESTYLES by Jackie Calhoun. 224 pp. Contemporary Lesbian
lives and loves.   ISBN 0-941483-57-6   8.95

VIRAGO by Karen Marie Christa Minns. 208 pp. Darsen has
chosen Ginny.   ISBN 0-941483-56-8   8.95

WILDERNESS TREK by Dorothy Tell. 192 pp. Six women on
vacation learning ''new'' skills.   ISBN 0-941483-60-6   8.95

MURDER BY THE BOOK by Pat Welch. 256 pp. A Helen
Black Mystery. First in a series.   ISBN 0-941483-59-2   8.95

BERRIGAN by Vicki P. McConnell. 176 pp. Youthful Lesbian —
romantic, idealistic Berrigan.   ISBN 0-941483-55-X   8.95

LESBIANS IN GERMANY by Lillian Faderman & B. Eriksson.
128 pp. Fiction, poetry, essays.   ISBN 0-941483-62-2   8.95

THERE'S SOMETHING I'VE BEEN MEANING TO TELL
YOU Ed. by Loralee MacPike. 288 pp. Gay men and lesbians
coming out to their children.   ISBN 0-941483-44-4   9.95
                                           ISBN 0-941483-54-1   16.95

LIFTING BELLY by Gertrude Stein. Ed. by Rebecca Mark. 104
pp. Erotic poetry.   ISBN 0-941483-51-7   8.95
                                           ISBN 0-941483-53-3   14.95

ROSE PENSKI by Roz Perry. 192 pp. Adult lovers in a long-term
relationship.   ISBN 0-941483-37-1   8.95

AFTER THE FIRE by Jane Rule. 256 pp. Warm, human novel
by this incomparable author.   ISBN 0-941483-45-2   8.95

SUE SLATE, PRIVATE EYE by Lee Lynch. 176 pp. The gay
folk of Peacock Alley are *all cats*.   ISBN 0-941483-52-5   8.95

CHRIS by Randy Salem. 224 pp. Golden oldie. Handsome Chris
and her adventures.   ISBN 0-941483-42-8   8.95

THREE WOMEN by March Hastings. 232 pp. Golden oldie. A
triangle among wealthy sophisticates.   ISBN 0-941483-43-6   8.95

RICE AND BEANS by Valeria Taylor. 232 pp. Love and
romance on poverty row.   ISBN 0-941483-41-X   8.95

PLEASURES by Robbi Sommers. 204 pp. Unprecedented
eroticism.   ISBN 0-941483-49-5   8.95

EDGEWISE by Camarin Grae. 372 pp. Spellbinding
adventure.   ISBN 0-941483-19-3   9.95

FATAL REUNION by Claire McNab. 224 pp. 2nd Det. Inspec.
Carol Ashton mystery.   ISBN 0-941483-40-1   8.95

KEEP TO ME STRANGER by Sarah Aldridge. 372 pp. Romance
set in a department store dynasty.   ISBN 0-941483-38-X   9.95

HEARTSCAPE by Sue Gambill. 204 pp. American lesbian in
Portugal.   ISBN 0-941483-33-9   8.95

IN THE BLOOD by Lauren Wright Douglas. 252 pp. Lesbian
science fiction adventure fantasy   ISBN 0-941483-22-3   8.95

THE BEE'S KISS by Shirley Verel. 216 pp. Delicate, delicious
romance.   ISBN 0-941483-36-3   8.95

RAGING MOTHER MOUNTAIN by Pat Emmerson. 264 pp.
Furosa Firechild's adventures in Wonderland.   ISBN 0-941483-35-5   8.95

IN EVERY PORT by Karin Kallmaker. 228 pp. Jessica's sexy,
adventuresome travels.   ISBN 0-941483-37-7   8.95

OF LOVE AND GLORY by Evelyn Kennedy. 192 pp. Exciting
WWII romance.   ISBN 0-941483-32-0   8.95

CLICKING STONES by Nancy Tyler Glenn. 288 pp. Love
transcending time.   ISBN 0-941483-31-2   9.95

SURVIVING SISTERS by Gail Pass. 252 pp. Powerful love
story.   ISBN 0-941483-16-9   8.95

SOUTH OF THE LINE by Catherine Ennis. 216 pp. Civil War
adventure.   ISBN 0-941483-29-0   8.95

WOMAN PLUS WOMAN by Dolores Klaich. 300 pp. Supurb
Lesbian overview.   ISBN 0-941483-28-2   9.95

SLOW DANCING AT MISS POLLY'S by Sheila Ortiz Taylor.
96 pp. Lesbian Poetry   ISBN 0-941483-30-4   7.95

DOUBLE DAUGHTER by Vicki P. McConnell. 216 pp. A Nyla
Wade Mystery, third in the series.   ISBN 0-941483-26-6   8.95

HEAVY GILT by Delores Klaich. 192 pp. Lesbian detective/
disappearing homophobes/upper class gay society.

                                         ISBN 0-941483-25-8   8.95

THE FINER GRAIN by Denise Ohio. 216 pp. Brilliant young
college lesbian novel.   ISBN 0-941483-11-8   8.95

THE AMAZON TRAIL by Lee Lynch. 216 pp. Life, travel & lore
of famous lesbian author.   ISBN 0-941483-27-4   8.95

HIGH CONTRAST by Jessie Lattimore. 264 pp. Women of the
Crystal Palace.   ISBN 0-941483-17-7   8.95

OCTOBER OBSESSION by Meredith More. Josie's rich, secret
Lesbian life.   ISBN 0-941483-18-5   8.95

LESBIAN CROSSROADS by Ruth Baetz. 276 pp. Contemporary
Lesbian lives. ISBN 0-941483-21-5   9.95

BEFORE STONEWALL: THE MAKING OF A GAY AND
LESBIAN COMMUNITY by Andrea Weiss & Greta Schiller.
96 pp., 25 illus. ISBN 0-941483-20-7   7.95

WE WALK THE BACK OF THE TIGER by Patricia A. Murphy.
192 pp. Romantic Lesbian novel/beginning women's movement.
ISBN 0-941483-13-4   8.95

SUNDAY'S CHILD by Joyce Bright. 216 pp. Lesbian athletics, at
last the novel about sports. ISBN 0-941483-12-6   8.95

OSTEN'S BAY by Zenobia N. Vole. 204 pp. Sizzling adventure
romance set on Bonaire. ISBN 0-941483-15-0   8.95

LESSONS IN MURDER by Claire McNab. 216 pp. 1st Det. Inspec.
Carol Ashton mystery — erotic tension!. ISBN 0-941483-14-2   8.95

YELLOWTHROAT by Penny Hayes. 240 pp. Margarita, bandit,
kidnaps Julia. ISBN 0-941483-10-X   8.95

SAPPHISTRY: THE BOOK OF LESBIAN SEXUALITY by
Pat Califia. 3d edition, revised. 208 pp. ISBN 0-941483-24-X   8.95

CHERISHED LOVE by Evelyn Kennedy. 192 pp. Erotic
Lesbian love story. ISBN 0-941483-08-8   8.95

LAST SEPTEMBER by Helen R. Hull. 208 pp. Six stories & a
glorious novella. ISBN 0-941483-09-6   8.95

THE SECRET IN THE BIRD by Camarin Grae. 312 pp. Striking,
psychological suspense novel. ISBN 0-941483-05-3   8.95

TO THE LIGHTNING by Catherine Ennis. 208 pp. Romantic
Lesbian 'Robinson Crusoe' adventure. ISBN 0-941483-06-1   8.95

THE OTHER SIDE OF VENUS by Shirley Verel. 224 pp.
Luminous, romantic love story. ISBN 0-941483-07-X   8.95

DREAMS AND SWORDS by Katherine V. Forrest. 192 pp.
Romantic, erotic, imaginative stories. ISBN 0-941483-03-7   8.95

MEMORY BOARD by Jane Rule. 336 pp. Memorable novel
about an aging Lesbian couple. ISBN 0-941483-02-9   9.95

THE ALWAYS ANONYMOUS BEAST by Lauren Wright
Douglas. 224 pp. A Caitlin Reece mystery. First in a series.
ISBN 0-941483-04-5   8.95

SEARCHING FOR SPRING by Patricia A. Murphy. 224 pp.
Novel about the recovery of love. ISBN 0-941483-00-2   8.95

DUSTY'S QUEEN OF HEARTS DINER by Lee Lynch. 240 pp.
Romantic blue-collar novel. ISBN 0-941483-01-0   8.95

PARENTS MATTER by Ann Muller. 240 pp. Parents'
relationships with Lesbian daughters and gay sons.
ISBN 0-930044-91-6   9.95

THE PEARLS by Shelley Smith. 176 pp. Passion and fun in
the Caribbean sun.   ISBN 0-930044-93-2   7.95

MAGDALENA by Sarah Aldridge. 352 pp. Epic Lesbian novel
set on three continents.   ISBN 0-930044-99-1   8.95

THE BLACK AND WHITE OF IT by Ann Allen Shockley.
144 pp. Short stories.   ISBN 0-930044-96-7   7.95

SAY JESUS AND COME TO ME by Ann Allen Shockley. 288
pp. Contemporary romance.   ISBN 0-930044-98-3   8.95

LOVING HER by Ann Allen Shockley. 192 pp. Romantic love
story.   ISBN 0-930044-97-5   7.95

MURDER AT THE NIGHTWOOD BAR by Katherine V.
Forrest. 240 pp. A Kate Delafield mystery. Second in a series.
                                      ISBN 0-930044-92-4   9.95

ZOE'S BOOK by Gail Pass. 224 pp. Passionate, obsessive love
story.   ISBN 0-930044-95-9   7.95

WINGED DANCER by Camarin Grae. 228 pp. Erotic Lesbian
adventure story.   ISBN 0-930044-88-6   8.95

PAZ by Camarin Grae. 336 pp. Romantic Lesbian adventurer
with the power to change the world.   ISBN 0-930044-89-4   8.95

SOUL SNATCHER by Camarin Grae. 224 pp. A puzzle, an
adventure, a mystery — Lesbian romance.   ISBN 0-930044-90-8   8.95

THE LOVE OF GOOD WOMEN by Isabel Miller. 224 pp.
Long-awaited new novel by the author of the beloved *Patience
and Sarah.*   ISBN 0-930044-81-9   8.95

THE HOUSE AT PELHAM FALLS by Brenda Weathers. 240
pp. Suspenseful Lesbian ghost story. ISBN 0-930044-79-7   7.95

HOME IN YOUR HANDS by Lee Lynch. 240 pp. More stories
from the author of *Old Dyke Tales.* ISBN 0-930044-80-0   7.95

EACH HAND A MAP by Anita Skeen. 112 pp. Real-life poems
that touch us all.   ISBN 0-930044-82-7   6.95

SURPLUS by Sylvia Stevenson. 342 pp. A classic early Lesbian
novel.   ISBN 0-930044-78-9   7.95

PEMBROKE PARK by Michelle Martin. 256 pp. Derring-do
and daring romance in Regency England.   ISBN 0-930044-77-0   7.95

THE LONG TRAIL by Penny Hayes. 248 pp. Vivid adventures
of two women in love in the old west.   ISBN 0-930044-76-2   8.95

HORIZON OF THE HEART by Shelley Smith. 192 pp. Hot
romance in summertime New England.   ISBN 0-930044-75-4   7.95

AN EMERGENCE OF GREEN by Katherine V. Forrest. 288
pp. Powerful novel of sexual discovery.   ISBN 0-930044-69-X   9.95

THE LESBIAN PERIODICALS INDEX edited by Claire
Potter. 432 pp. Author & subject index.   ISBN 0-930044-74-6   29.95

DESERT OF THE HEART by Jane Rule. 224 pp. A classic; basis for the movie *Desert Hearts*. ISBN 0-930044-73-8   8.95

SPRING FORWARD/FALL BACK by Sheila Ortiz Taylor. 288 pp. Literary novel of timeless love. ISBN 0-930044-70-3   7.95

FOR KEEPS by Elisabeth Nonas. 144 pp. Contemporary novel about losing and finding love. ISBN 0-930044-71-1   7.95

TORCHLIGHT TO VALHALLA by Gale Wilhelm. 128 pp. Classic novel by a great Lesbian writer. ISBN 0-930044-68-1   7.95

LESBIAN NUNS: BREAKING SILENCE edited by Rosemary Curb and Nancy Manahan. 432 pp. Unprecedented autobiographies of religious life. ISBN 0-930044-62-2   9.95

THE SWASHBUCKLER by Lee Lynch. 288 pp. Colorful novel set in Greenwich Village in the sixties. ISBN 0-930044-66-5   8.95

MISFORTUNE'S FRIEND by Sarah Aldridge. 320 pp. Historical Lesbian novel set on two continents. ISBN 0-930044-67-3   7.95

A STUDIO OF ONE'S OWN by Ann Stokes. Edited by Dolores Klaich. 128 pp. Autobiography. ISBN 0-930044-64-9   7.95

SEX VARIANT WOMEN IN LITERATURE by Jeannette Howard Foster. 448 pp. Literary history. ISBN 0-930044-65-7   8.95

A HOT-EYED MODERATE by Jane Rule. 252 pp. Hard-hitting essays on gay life; writing; art. ISBN 0-930044-57-6   7.95

INLAND PASSAGE AND OTHER STORIES by Jane Rule. 288 pp. Wide-ranging new collection. ISBN 0-930044-56-8   7.95

WE TOO ARE DRIFTING by Gale Wilhelm. 128 pp. Timeless Lesbian novel, a masterpiece. ISBN 0-930044-61-4   6.95

AMATEUR CITY by Katherine V. Forrest. 224 pp. A Kate Delafield mystery. First in a series. ISBN 0-930044-55-X   8.95

THE SOPHIE HOROWITZ STORY by Sarah Schulman. 176 pp. Engaging novel of madcap intrigue. ISBN 0-930044-54-1   7.95

THE BURNTON WIDOWS by Vickie P. McConnell. 272 pp. A Nyla Wade mystery, second in the series. ISBN 0-930044-52-5   7.95

OLD DYKE TALES by Lee Lynch. 224 pp. Extraordinary stories of our diverse Lesbian lives. ISBN 0-930044-51-7   8.95

DAUGHTERS OF A CORAL DAWN by Katherine V. Forrest. 240 pp. Novel set in a Lesbian new world. ISBN 0-930044-50-9   8.95

AGAINST THE SEASON by Jane Rule. 224 pp. Luminous, complex novel of interrelationships. ISBN 0-930044-48-7   8.95

LOVERS IN THE PRESENT AFTERNOON by Kathleen Fleming. 288 pp. A novel about recovery and growth. ISBN 0-930044-46-0   8.95

ODD GIRL OUT by Ann Bannon.   ISBN 0-930044-83-5   5.95
I AM A WOMAN 84-3; WOMEN IN THE SHADOWS 85-1;   each
JOURNEY TO A WOMAN 86-X; BEEBO BRINKER 87-8. Golden
oldies about life in Greenwich Village.
JOURNEY TO FULFILLMENT, A WORLD WITHOUT MEN, and   3.95
RETURN TO LESBOS. All by Valerie Taylor   each

These are just a few of the many Naiad Press titles — we are the oldest and
largest lesbian/feminist publishing company in the world. Please request a
complete catalog. We offer personal service; we encourage and welcome direct
mail orders from individuals who have limited access to bookstores carrying
our publications.